NO WORRIES

by

Lauren N. Sharman

WHISKEY CREEK PRESS
www.whiskeycreekpress.com

Published by
WHISKEY CREEK PRESS

Whiskey Creek Press
PO Box 51052
Casper, WY 82605-1052
www.whiskeycreekpress.com

ISBN 978-1-59374-563-X

Credits
Cover Artist: Jinger Heaston
Editor: Giovanna Lagana

Printed in the United States of America

WHAT THEY ARE SAYING ABOUT
NO WORRIES

Other Books by Author Available at Whiskey Creek Press:
www.whiskeycreekpress.com

Growing Up Little
"Her Shadow" in HATE: An Anthology of Murder and Mystery

Dedication

This book is dedicated to a good man in bad boy clothing; my husband, Joey. You are my hero, and I love you.

Julie, *No Worries* is for you, too. It's rare to find a friend dedicated enough to sit in a coffee shop at the mall with me and read a love scene out loud. But you did it! You helped me tweak everything in this book until it was just right.

Acknowledgements

First, I'd like to acknowledge my kids, Tanner and Chloe. You two have always been very patient, especially when sometimes the 'five more minutes' I needed to finish writing something turned into an hour and five minutes. I love you guys.

Special thanks goes out to my dad, Terry, for sharing his knowledge of firearms.

A BIG thank you also goes to my sister, Renae, for patiently answering all my questions regarding crime, punishment, and prison sentences.

Mom, you're always the first one in line to read my manuscripts. Thanks for the support.

Jeff G., you're my favorite proofreader (and you work fast, too!)

I want to say hi to all my friends and cousins who took the time to read bits and pieces of *No Worries* when it was still a work in progress. Some of you even got to read the entire first draft! You were all very helpful with your opinions and suggestions. Thanks to Joey, Renae, Mom, Dad, Jeff G., Bobbi, Julie, Sarah, Ronnie, Jessica, Shelley, Robyn, Caryn W., Susan (Sooze), Chari, Jinger, Erica, and Deanna.

Thanks to my critique partners Sarah and Ronnie, too. It takes a tough breed to belong to a critique group with a 'brutal honesty' policy. I'm so glad to have found the two of you.

And finally, I'd like to give a shout out to my faithful friends and fans who are a part of 'Lauren's Literary World' message board, my FM 'boarder' friends, and everyone at the Laurel, MD and Mt. Airy, MD Curves. I cannot thank you all enough for the amazing amount of support you've given me.

Prologue

April 1983

A fresh start.

A chance at happiness.

Was it really possible?

The heavy door squeaked shut and a thousand pair of eyes seemed to be watching as she made her way down the narrow aisle, clutching two knapsacks stuffed with everything she owned.

Gypsy Lance claimed the last remaining empty seat on the Greyhound bus, questioning her decision right up until the moment the driver released the air brakes and the bus began to inch forward. As they pulled away from the Baltimore Travel Plaza and merged into traffic on Interstate 95, Gypsy sank down into the worn, cloth seat and willed herself to relax.

Her mind racing, Gypsy reminded herself repeatedly that this was exactly what she'd planned to do. Did it really matter that she was doing it a few years ahead of schedule? And so what if she only had six hundred and fifty dollars to her name and no place to live? Wasn't her life worth sleeping in a shelter until she could get a job and get herself settled?

Gypsy knew the answers to the first two questions were no. She also knew that it didn't matter if she moved a hundred more times during her life; because wherever she was, she'd never be completely safe. She was, however, much safer today than yesterday, when an old friend called with the information that prompted Gypsy to immediately begin searching for bus schedules the minute she hung up the phone.

And she'd slept in worse places than a shelter.

As thunder rumbled and droplets of water began beating loudly against the metal roof of the bus, Gypsy turned to stare out the window at the gray storm clouds rolling toward them from the west.

Was this storm a sign?

Had the rain been sent to wash away her old life in order to make room for the new one?

A quick, bright flash of lightning seemed to spark a revelation in Gypsy's mind. Suddenly, the answers she'd been searching for were there.

Everything was crystal clear.

There was no reason she shouldn't embrace the opportunity to start a new life. After all, the one she left behind meant nothing to her. The past eleven years had been filled with feelings of loneliness, a desire to belong and be accepted, and her painful reputation as an outcast; all stemming from a tragic childhood.

But where Gypsy was going, no one knew her. And no one had heard the rumors or cruel gossip that had kept other children from being allowed to play with her. To everyone she met, she would just be Gypsy Lance, the new girl in town. Sure, she still had her problems and fears, but nobody knew about them, either. This was her chance to finally fit in and be normal.

Confident now that she'd made the right decision; Gypsy smiled to herself and closed her eyes. Even if she never was completely safe, she was bound and determined to experience some happiness.

She deserved it.

And she would succeed.

As long as her past stayed where it belonged.

Chapter 1

The man was poised for battle.

As Gypsy Lance stood frozen, staring wide-eyed and open-mouthed at not only his enormous size, but the length of the knife sheath on his belt, her first thought was that he was going to kill her.

Her second thought was to laugh at the irony.

She'd survived twenty-one years of living in the worst neighborhoods in Baltimore City without so much as a scratch. Now, after being a resident of the small western Maryland town of Hagerstown a mere eight hours, she was sure she was about to be raped, and God knew what else, by a man more than twice her size...in the middle of heavily wooded private property that she'd intentionally trespassed on...in a town where no one knew her, and no one would miss her if she disappeared.

The thought of turning around and running left her mind the instant the man noticed her. Chances were that those long legs of his would catch her in no time. And just where did she think she would go, anyway? They were in the woods...his woods, and she was hopelessly lost; which was why she was still wandering around at sunset as the early April air was rapidly turning chilly.

She'd have to face him; sooner rather than later because his long strides had already closed half the distance between them.

Pretend like he doesn't scare you to death, Gypsy, she thought to herself. *Take in everything you can about the man's appearance, just in case you survive whatever's about to happen and need to give the police a description of your attacker.*

As he stepped over fallen trees and trudged effortlessly through ankle-deep brush, Gypsy watched him closely, making mental notes of his approximate age, height and weight, which she guessed to be close to thirty, six-foot-four, and maybe two hundred and forty pounds. She noticed he was wearing what looked like old work boots, a pair of faded, grease-stained blue jeans with holes in both knees, and a jet black T-shirt, the exact same color of the straight hair that fell to his shoulders. When he reached her, he quickly scanned the area then turned to look directly at Gypsy.

The pair of intense royal blue eyes staring at her had Gypsy paralyzed with fear, the violent thud of her heart making her entire body to feel as though it was vibrating.

She'd always avoided men so that she never had to feel helpless and at the mercy of someone again.

Could he hear her heart beating?

Had he seen the fear she was trying desperately to hide?

He took a step back and raised his hands in the air. "I won't hurt you."

Oh great, he'd seen it.

Was he telling the truth? She supposed that if he'd been planning to harm her, he would've tried to do so by now. And the look in those magnificent eyes wasn't one that threatened violence, it was almost…was that concern she saw?

There was only one way to find out.

Keeping her eyes trained on him, she took a tentative step back, testing to see if he'd follow. When he didn't, she released the breath she hadn't realized she'd been holding and relaxed a little. Relieved he didn't seem to want to hurt her, at least for the moment, Gypsy dug deep and mustered all of her courage, offering a quiet, "Hi."

"Hi, yourself," he shot back in a voice laced with light sarcasm and just a hint of a southern accent. "Are you lost?"

Gypsy didn't miss the tone of his voice, but chose to ignore it. She nodded, hoping that being friendly would keep him from getting angry. "Actually, I am," she said, fighting desperately to keep the fear out of her voice. "Can you show me how to get out of these woods?"

He shrugged. "Yes, but what are you doing out here? You're not exactly dressed for a hike."

Gypsy could feel the heat of embarrassment creeping up her cheeks as she crossed her arms to cover numerous small stains on the bib of her overalls. She'd spent the morning cleaning her new apartment, which she'd been lucky to find on such short notice, and hadn't bothered to change before she left.

"I wasn't hiking," she told him, surprising herself by throwing back a bit of his sarcasm, "I was taking a walk and got lost."

What she left out of her explanation was that she'd been so preoccupied that she simply hadn't been paying attention. Walking through the town in a daze worrying about her financial situation, she'd looked up and had no idea where she was.

"Look, I've been going in circles for hours. If you could

just point me in the right direction, I'll gladly get out of your way."

When he didn't respond, she took a closer look at him and noticed the look of concern she'd seen in his eyes earlier had been replaced by a stoic, unreadable glare.

She took another step back.

Why had he turned on her so quickly?

Had he decided not to help?

Gypsy no longer thought he might hurt her, but if she made him angry, there was probably a good chance he'd refuse to show her the way out. Not wanting to spoil the chance of getting home sometime before dark, she willed her hand to remain steady as she extended it and forced a smile. "I'm Gypsy."

* * * *

Rebel McCassey had known by the loud, unmistakable sound of crunching leaves and snapping twigs that whoever was in the woods had no qualms about letting him know they were there. At first he'd thought it was one of his cousins; the land belonged to them, also, and one or two of them were always up there doing something. But he hadn't heard any voices. And the day any one of them went more than a minute or two without talking would be the day hell froze over.

It couldn't be one of the locals. Everyone knew this was McCassey property, and anyone who didn't want to get shot for trespassing stayed far away.

The sounds moved closer, and Rebel squinted against the fading sunlight, focusing on the person who'd invaded the woods. Surprised his uninvited guest was a young girl, he immediately stepped into plain view to avoid scaring her.

But it was too late. She'd stopped dead in her tracks the

instant she spotted him, forcing him to approach her.

Now that Rebel had seen her up close, he realized she wasn't as young as he'd first thought. He didn't know who she was, but her shaking hands and wary look told him she was terrified. He admired the bit of backbone she'd shown by mimicking his sarcasm, but it was obviously an act. No matter how brave she thought she looked, he wasn't buying it.

Rebel didn't blame her for being afraid, and was sure the way he was staring probably added to her discomfort. But he couldn't help it. He was more drawn to her than any other woman he'd ever seen. She may have been dressed·in ragged and dirty clothes, but she was beyond beautiful. The loose, fiery red curls that had escaped her ponytail had drawn his attention first. Rebel had never seen such a vibrant hair color. It accentuated her pale complexion and delicate features, reminding him of the treasured porcelain doll his great-grandmother had when he was little.

He wanted to talk to her, but hesitated. It had been a long day, and he wasn't in the mood to see the look of disgust women always gave him when they saw the dirt and grease embedded in his hands and under his fingernails. But she stood, hand out, until he gave in and shook it. When he did, he was surprised that the calluses on her hand rivaled his. "Rebel McCassey."

Rebel waited for the look; the one that usually followed someone finding out who he was. But it never came.

"McCassey?" she questioned. "Didn't I see that name in town somewhere?"

"You're not from anywhere around here, are you?" People for miles around knew the McCassey name; members of his family had been causing trouble in Washington County since before the Civil War. Rebel was no exception…though most of the trouble he wound up being involved in was usually started by someone else.

"No," she answered shyly.

Well, what she didn't know wouldn't hurt her. After all, she was in no danger from him. He'd never hurt anyone intentionally, at least anyone who didn't deserve it. So he took her innocence for what it was and answered her question.

"My uncles and I own a garage," he held up his battered, grease stained hands for her to see. "I'm a mechanic."

When Gypsy smiled this time, she seemed a bit more relaxed. "Do you live around here?"

"Yeah, you're standing on my family's land right now. It's private property, Gypsy. How the hell did you get all the way back here?"

"I didn't mean to trespass on your land," she apologized. "I mean, I knew it was private property because I saw the signs. But I was out walking trying to familiarize myself with the town and lost my bearings. I thought taking a shortcut through the woods would get me to my apartment on Franklin Street. I didn't think it'd be so easy to get lost in such a small town." She shrugged. "Guess I was wrong."

"Hagerstown is ten square miles in each direction, Gypsy, that isn't so small."

"It is where I come from."

His interest piqued, he asked, "Which is where?"

She seemed a little reluctant to answer, but eventually said, "Baltimore City."

Puzzled, Rebel wondered why this young girl had chosen to move all the way out to Hagerstown. It had the reputation of a backwoods, redneck town, and didn't offer any of the opportunities you could find in Baltimore. He wanted to ask more questions, but the look she was giving him suggested he change the subject. Now.

"Did you say Franklin Street?"

She immediately perked up. "Yes, are we far from there?"

"About three miles," he told her, taking a dark-colored baseball hat from his back pocket and placing it on his head backward. "I'll take you to the edge of the woods. Otherwise, you'll never find your way out."

The look of relief and thanks she gave him made Rebel feel good about himself; it made him want to do everything he could to help this innocent girl. He motioned for her to follow as he began walking, half-heartedly wondering if there was someone special waiting in the new apartment on Franklin Street for her to come home. Then he pushed the thought from his mind as quickly as it had entered.

As the two of them made their way through the woods, Gypsy seemed to gradually loosen up. She moved over to walk by Rebel's side instead of behind him, and every few minutes asked him a question or two about the town, what there was to do, and what some of the people were like, always pondering his answers before speaking again.

To his surprise, Rebel was enjoying Gypsy's company. It had been a long time since someone had been interested in him as an individual person. Usually, people were only interested in finding out if there was any truth to the bad reputation his infamous last name had earned him. He admitted to himself that he liked the feeling of not being automatically judged because of who he was related to. And although it was unlike him to open up to anyone, he found that he didn't mind sharing things with Gypsy, something he'd never felt comfortable enough to do with any other woman.

At ease with each other, they talked nonstop as they made their way through the thick woods. Once Rebel got the sense Gypsy was beginning to feel comfortable with him, he took a chance and asked about her life in the city and why she moved to Hagerstown.

Gypsy caught her lower lip between her teeth and remained silent, almost as if debating whether to reveal anything about herself. Several long seconds passed before she answered. "My mom died when I was ten, and because my father hadn't been around in years, I was put into the Child Welfare System and raised in a handful of different foster homes."

Rebel didn't know what he'd been expecting her to say, but it definitely wasn't that. Because he had a hard time hiding his surprise, the only response he could come up with was, "That must've been hard on you."

It made him sad to think about this beautiful, gentle girl not having a place to call home, so Rebel pretended not to hear the pain in her voice when she said, "I got used to it. I had to. There was no other choice."

He wondered why she'd lived in foster homes when she had a father, but didn't want to pry. Lord knew there were plenty of things in his past he didn't want anyone asking questions about.

"Are you still close with any of your foster parents?"

She shook her head. "I never was. Most of the families I stayed with only took in kids for the money given to them by the state."

"What about your friends?" he asked. "Aren't you going to miss them living way out here?"

Gypsy sighed. "To tell you the truth, as far as good-hearted, honest people I can call friends...there aren't any. It's hard to get close to people when you grow up in foster care because everyone's shuffled around so much." She raised her head and looked at him. "I guess that makes me sound pretty pathetic, huh?"

He smiled down at her, thinking of how close he and his brothers and cousins had always been. He knew he was lucky to be part of a big family, even if he sometimes felt they were more trouble then they were worth. Gypsy wasn't pathetic, but he could tell by the tone of her voice that she was lonely. "Not at all."

He was unsure of what to say next, but was interested and wanted to keep her talking. "Did you just get out of foster care?"

"No, my last foster family asked me to move out when I turned eighteen so they could make room for someone else. I packed my bags that night and slept in the bus station. The next day, I ran into a girl who'd stayed in the same foster home as me a few years earlier. She and two other girls were looking for another roommate. That's where I've been living for the past three years."

"You're twenty-one now?"

"I will be...at eleven sixteen tonight."

Rebel couldn't remember the last time he'd given a damn about a woman's feelings, especially those of one he didn't know. Taken aback by the protective emotions her story had stirred inside him, he suddenly wanted to gather her in his arms, tell her he was sorry for all she'd been through, and that everything was going to be okay. But a quick reality check forced him to keep his distance. He had a feeling that Gypsy's uneasiness when they first met was more than simply being afraid of a strange man. Her reaction had been one of terror, and he knew he'd have to walk on eggshells until she began to trust him.

Instead of offering comfort and reassurance, he settled for standing three feet away and wishing her a happy birthday.

The smile she tried to give him was the saddest he'd ever seen, so he changed the subject. "How'd you get all the calluses on your hands?"

Gypsy blushed again and jammed her hands into the front pockets of her overalls. "Working. Since I started living on my own, I've been cleaning houses during the day and waiting tables at night."

Rebel fell silent. He tried to imagine what life had been like for Gypsy the past eleven years. The people he knew who grew up without the love of a family had ended up bitter and hardened, but she seemed genuinely unaffected...at least on the outside.

She snuck a quick glance at Rebel. "I told you too much, didn't I?" He turned in her direction but didn't get the chance to answer. "It's just that no one's ever really been interested in me, and I got carried away," she continued. "Please say I haven't scared you off by telling my entire life story."

His voice was low and reassuring when he said, "I'm not going anywhere."

She nodded and they fell into step together, continuing their walk in companionable silence until they came to a stream. Rebel crossed first, pushing off with his right leg and effortlessly landing on the other side. Then he reached out to her. "Give me your hand."

* * * *

Gypsy shook her head slightly, staring at his hand as if she would break if he touched her. "No thanks, I can do it."

Even though her limited experience with men had proven that they only did nice things for women when they wanted something in return, Gypsy felt that Rebel was trustworthy, and his offer to help was genuine. She'd taken a giant step today by opening up to him, but wasn't ready to let him help her. Not yet.

Rebel withdrew his hand and backed off at Gypsy's reluctance. Relieved, Gypsy took a deep breath and crouched down, preparing to jump over the stream. Then the rock she was standing on shifted and she lost her balance. "Oh!" she shouted, and began flailing her arms to keep from falling.

Rebel sprang forward and caught her around the waist as she started to fall, pulling her safely across the water. As momentum propelled them backward, Rebel wrapped his arms tightly around Gypsy to keep her in front of him, using his body to break her fall. When they landed in a pile of brush beside the stream, Gypsy immediately pulled out of his grasp and got to her feet.

"Thanks," she said, brushing herself off, "I can't swim."

Rebel stood. "Well, I doubt you would've drowned in two feet of water, but you're welcome anyway."

"Oh." When she caught herself giggling, she paused at the pleasant sound, wondering how long it had been since she'd been happy enough to laugh. "Right."

When they were both brushed clean, Gypsy walked a few feet away and sat down on a large boulder. "Do you mind if I sit for a minute? I've got so much hair in my face I can hardly see."

"Take as long as you need."

She undid what was left of her ponytail, lowered her head upside down to shake her hair, then flipped it right side up. Watching her slow, graceful movements, Rebel sat down beside her.

As she turned to face him, the breeze caused a stray, red curl to fall in front of her face. "What about you, Rebel, have you lived in Hagerstown long?"

"All my life."

"How many years is that?"

"Thirty."

"Do you have a lot of family here?"

Rebel swallowed hard, giving Gypsy the feeling she'd hit on a touchy subject. "Almost everyone I'm related to lives here. The rest of the family's scattered around the county. But I have to warn you, Gypsy, we're not very popular. Your reputation could be ruined just for talking to me."

She shrugged. "You've heard my story. If that isn't something for people to gossip about, what is? How do you know *your* reputation won't be ruined by talking to me?"

He grinned and raised his hand, brushing at her stray curl. "People have always looked down on me because of the family I was born into. You won't be able to ruin the bad reputation I've been trying to outrun my entire life, Gypsy." Then he winked at her. "But thanks for your concern."

"You're welcome."

"Aw, what the hell," Rebel said. "If you're going to be living here, you'll hear about my family's history sooner or later. I might as well tell you the truth before you're subjected to whatever warped stories are floating around town."

Rebel scanned the ground and leaned over to pick a small tree limb. After inspecting it, he reached into his back pocket, took out a pocketknife, and opened it. Just as he began shaving off the bark, he turned to Gypsy and winked. "You want me to tell you a story?"

With a bright smile, Gypsy nodded. Just the way he'd asked her that question made her heart flutter. She'd never even been very interested in talking to a man before, but she just couldn't get enough of Rebel McCassey.

"My great-great-great grandfather, Patrick McCassey, won the very land we're sitting on in 1832 during a poker game at The Well, a saloon that used to be where the town hall now stands.

"There's ten acres in all, so that's what we call it, Ten Acres. This is good land, but it's never been used for anything but hunting. There's a one-room cabin in the middle of the property where my cousins and I stay in the fall during deer season."

She listened in awe as he told her of his family's troubled past, even forgetting to breathe occasionally when the tales became too intriguing.

"Wow," she said, wide-eyed, "horse thieves, army deserters, killers. That stuff is fascinating! But I have to admit, some of those recent stories made the hair on the back of my neck stand up. Does your family history have anything to do with how you got your name?"

The left corner of his mouth lifted into a lopsided grin. "Actually, it does. After so many years of giving birth to future criminals, the women in my family started naming some of their children after American outlaws. I have uncles and cousins named for Frank and Jesse James, Billy the Kid and Cole and Jim Younger.

"My eyes are blue now, but they were the color of Confederate gray when I was born. That's how I got the name Rebel."

"I love it," she told him. "Do you have a middle name?"

He cocked his left eyebrow. "Do you?"

"Amelia," she said shyly.

"Raider."

"Wow, what a great name!"

Rebel turned his attention back to the branch. "Yeah," he said sarcastically, "real great."

"You're lucky you can trace your heritage back so many years. My mom ran away from home at fifteen and never talked about her family. My father only came around a couple of times, and I don't know much more about him other than his name. If I was part of a big family like yours, I'd consider myself the luckiest person in the world."

"I've never considered myself lucky before. At least not in the way you're referring to. Being surrounded by my relatives while growing up definitely had its advantages, but it's not as great as it sounds. McCassey's are nothing but trouble. We have been for generations. Not many decent people want anything to do with us."

Rebel neither admitted nor denied his involvement in any of the trouble he said his family had caused, but Gypsy had a hard time believing he was as bad as he made himself out to be. "If people don't like you, how does your garage stay in business?"

He chuckled. "No McCassey's were ever good enough to step foot in anyone's house, but we are good enough to crawl under their cars and fix them. That just shows the high opinion everyone has of us."

Sad because Rebel really seemed to be bothered by who

he was, she gently laid a hand on his knee. "I didn't mean to upset you. I'd like to be your friend."

"My friend? I'd like that, Gypsy, but it's not a good idea. If you get mixed up with me, no one else will want anything to do with you. You should go home and forget you ever met me."

"Rebel, can I explain something to you?"

"Go ahead," he said, folding his knife and replacing it in his pocket.

"I'm new in town, don't have any family, and have been poor my entire life. Everything I own fits in two knapsacks and none of my clothes look any better than the ones I'm wearing. I've never had friends because nobody's bothered to look past those things and take the time to get to know me. You've been nicer to me in the past two hours than anyone has been since my mom died. In my opinion, that makes you a friend."

Gypsy knew it was probably hard for Rebel to tell her about his family, making her feel guilty for not being totally honest with him.

But she couldn't tell him everything.

Not yet.

Not until she was sure he would keep her secrets; the secrets that had almost…and would someday…destroy her.

* * * *

Rebel remained quiet as he seemed to be considering what she'd said.

"Reb," he said suddenly.

Confused, she looked at him. "Excuse me?"

"My friends call me Reb."

"If that's your way of telling me its okay for us to be

friends, then I accept." Gypsy was so happy, that before she realized what she was doing, she'd kissed him on the cheek, surprising them both. She had never initiated so much as a conversation with a member of the opposite sex, let alone a kiss. But Reb had a surprisingly powerful affect on her emotions.

He stood abruptly, tossed the limb to the ground, and adjusted his hat. "Come on," he motioned for her to get up, "it'll be dark soon and you need to get home."

Another half hour into their walk, while Gypsy was telling Rebel about the job she'd found at The Tea Cup Diner in town, a sudden movement fifty yards away caught Rebel's attention. Stopping in his tracks, he extended his forearm to stop Gypsy and put a finger to his lips. "Shhh."

They stood silently for a moment, then Rebel whispered, "My brother, Judd, is coming at us from that cluster of maples over there. Don't be afraid. His line of bull is all an act, he won't hurt you."

Gypsy looked up at Reb and held his gaze just long enough to let him know she believed him. She hoped he understood, because there was no time to explain. In the next second, Judd was upon them.

"Well, well, well, little brother. Where'd you find this cute little piece of ass?" Judd reached out to touch her hair, but Rebel smacked his hand away and stepped in front of Gypsy, putting himself between her and his brother.

"Lay off, Judd. What the hell are you doing out here?"

Judd looked at Rebel and laughed. "This is my land just as much as it is yours. So I could ask you the same thing."

"You could, but you won't get an answer. Beat it."

Amazed at how much the brothers looked alike, Gypsy

watched them closely as they stared each other down. They were exactly the same height, and both men were noticeably muscular in their torso and forearms. Even their amazing, royal blue eye color was the same. The only difference was that where Rebel's hair was straight and so dark it looked black, Judd's was a thick, rich brown mop of little-too-long untamed curls.

Judd glanced at Gypsy, smirked, and looked back to his brother. "I got me a date, and I'm headed to the cabin. So unless you two are planning to use it, I'll be on my way."

Rebel took what seemed like a protective step toward Gypsy. "Yeah, you do that."

"It was nice meeting you, honey," Judd said as he took a pack of Marlboro's from his jacket pocket. "What'd you say your name was?"

Rebel grabbed the cigarettes from his brother. "She didn't. And you know better than to smoke around all this dry brush. Get the hell out of here."

Judd gave Gypsy one last, long look and turned to Rebel. "This isn't over." Then he walked away cursing under his breath.

Rebel watched Judd until he was out of sight then focused his attention on Gypsy. "Are you okay?"

"Fine," she said, trying to understand what just happened. "Why is he so angry with you?"

"Because I was born. Judd and I are only ten months apart. He's older. The two of us have been beating on each other since we were strong enough to make fists, but it doesn't mean anything. Just a little sibling rivalry is all."

"That's all? It looked to me like you two were ready to kill each other."

"Trust me, Gypsy, that was nothing."

"But—"

"But nothing," he said curtly. "Shit like that happens all the time; if not with Judd, then someone else." Without warning, Rebel grabbed her shoulders and yelled, "Dammit, Gypsy, do you see what I mean now? Hanging around me will bring you nothing but trouble."

She looked at him, blinking in confusion at the sudden change in his demeanor. "Come on, Rebel, that was nothing more than a brotherly fight. I'll admit it was scary at first, since I didn't know what was going on. But everything's fine. It was no big deal."

He shook his head. "It was just a brotherly fight *this time*. And it was no big deal *this time*. But you won't be able to avoid trouble or danger by hanging around me, Gypsy. Just like I can't."

Unafraid, Gypsy stared at Rebel as he lectured her. The emotions on his face and in his voice may have been anger, but his eyes showed something different. The concern she'd seen in them earlier had returned.

Gypsy wished she knew why this man she'd only known a few hours cared about her so much. But it didn't really matter. She was tired of being alone and not having anyone to share things with. And it wasn't like she had so many friends in her life that there wasn't room for another.

Rebel let go of Gypsy's shoulders as quickly as he'd grabbed them. "I'm sorry," he said, offering an apology she wanted to tell him was unnecessary. "I don't know why I did that."

She reached out and brushed his large, rough hand with hers. "I do. It was because you're right. I understand now that being around you can definitely be dangerous. But I don't care about your family's reputation, Reb, or how much trouble you personally have gotten into. None of this changes my mind. I want to be your friend."

He shrugged and put his hands out at his side. "I still don't think it's a good idea. But you seem to know what it feels like to be judged for things you have no control over, just like I do. So if you're willing to accept me, bad blood and all, then who am I to turn down your friendship? Just don't say I didn't warn you."

She smiled again, her bright green eyes sparkling in the twilight.

They continued walking and reached the edge of the woods a few minutes after their run-in with Judd. Rebel stopped and pointed in the direction of the rising moon. "Franklin Street is just over that hill."

Gypsy frowned. "Aren't you coming?"

"I can't."

"Why not?"

"I have to get to the garage. I drive a tow truck when I'm not fixing cars, and I'm on duty tonight."

"Well," she said, still frowning, "thanks for walking me out of the woods. Will I see you soon?"

He shrugged, giving Gypsy the impression he was trying to avoid encouraging her. When he had been silent just a moment too long, she decided to speak up. "Did I do something wrong? Is there a reason you don't want to see me?"

"Not at all, Gypsy. But I'm pretty busy. Sunday's are my only day off."

She didn't believe for a second that was the only reason they couldn't see each other. Crossing her arms, she tilted her head and stared at him.

"You don't believe me, do you?"

Gypsy did nothing more than shake her head slightly.

Rebel nodded. "The truth is that I'd like very much to see you again. But honestly, the less time you spend around me, the better off you'll be."

Not caring that the disappointment in her heart was probably written all over her face, Gypsy continued to stare. When Rebel finally said, "You're going to be working at The Tea Cup, right?" Gypsy felt her sadness melt away.

"All breakfast and lunch shifts Monday through Friday," she said excitedly, "I'll be there from five-thirty in the morning until three in the afternoon."

"The garage is right across the street," he told her. "I go in for breakfast every now and then. Maybe I'll see you there."

It wasn't much, but it gave her hope that she might see him once in a while.

"I'll save you a table." She turned and left the woods without looking back.

.

Chapter 2

Rebel hadn't exactly lied.

He did have to work, but not until Jimmy's shift ended at eleven. In fact, he had every intention of going back to the garage and getting some sleep before his own shift started. But the more he thought about Gypsy walking home alone in the dark, the more uneasy he became. If she'd managed to get lost in the daylight, who knew what kind of trouble she could get herself into now that it was dark.

No more than twenty seconds after she'd left, Rebel decided to follow and make sure she got home safely. He walked hurriedly along the edge of the woods to catch up, watching until she was halfway up the hill. Then he crossed the road and tagged along at a safe distance until she made the right turn onto Franklin Street and entered the second, small, two-story, red brick apartment building on the right.

Rebel stood and watched the black shuttered windows, waiting for lights to go on in one of the four apartments. When he didn't see any, he walked around to the back of the building. Worried when he didn't see lights there either, he was about to go inside looking for her when someone raised a shade on the second floor and placed a lit candle in the window. Recognizing Gypsy's silhouette, he knew she was safe.

Rebel turned and left the yard.

He thought about stopping at a pay phone and calling Jimmy for a lift back to the garage, but it was only two miles away. The walk and a smoke would do him good.

After stopping at the convenience store on the corner of Franklin and Cannon Streets to buy a fresh pack of Marlboro's, Rebel started back to town. He walked slowly, drawing smoke deeply into his lungs and blowing rings as he exhaled into the cool, early April air. The walk was relaxing, but did nothing to keep his thoughts from drifting to Gypsy. Even if he never saw her again, those bright green eyes and the way she smiled at him would forever be etched in his memory.

But her looks weren't the only thing about Gypsy that Rebel found intriguing. There was definitely something special about her. What had really gotten to him was her bravery and fighting spirit. She'd shown it when they first met, and again after they ran into Judd. Most girls...hell, most people...would've been terrified if Rebel had grabbed them and started yelling. But Gypsy hadn't flinched. He could tell by the expression on her face that she'd seen through his act of anger. She'd looked into his soul and found the worry he felt for her safety and had been touched by it.

He knew how she felt because he'd seen it in her eyes.

She liked him, and he knew his heart was in trouble.

Thinking about his promise to be her friend, he snorted and tossed his cigarette butt into the street.

Some friend I am. Seeing the look on Gypsy's face when he said he wasn't going to walk her all the way home, made him feel like a dog. Oh, he'd wanted to go. But he knew the people in this town. If anyone had seen the two of them walk out of the woods together, her reputation would've been ruined before she even got home.

So he'd lied about having to work instead of trying to explain again why it wasn't a good idea for her to be seen with him. She was also damn convincing, and he wasn't sure he would've had the willpower to say no if she thought he didn't have anything to do and tried to talk him into walking her home. The quick kiss she'd given him in the woods was innocent, he was sure, but the flip his stomach did when her lips touched his skin proved that his body was no novice when it came to responding to a woman's touch.

But for all of her innocence, Rebel knew there were things Gypsy was hiding. Her reluctance to trust him with her safety at the stream revealed more than Rebel felt he had a right to know. But if she had issues with trust, why, after only a few hours, did she feel comfortable putting all of hers in him?

And what about Gypsy's parents? The sadness in her voice revealed that she'd loved her mother, but something didn't sit right with him about her father. Gypsy said she didn't know much more about him than his name, but there was something else to that story, he could feel it.

* * * *

Happy to find her building exactly where Reb said it would be, Gypsy entered through the front door and walked up one flight to the second floor. She loved her new apartment. It was small, unfurnished, and in a crummy part of town, but it was the first thing she'd ever had that was all hers.

Instead of turning on the lights, she lit a candle. After all the money she'd spent that day—twenty dollars on a bus ticket, five hundred for her first and last month's rent, plus another hundred on the bare essentials she needed to live—Gypsy had thirty dollars left to her name. The last thing she needed was an electric bill she couldn't afford to pay.

New, gray carpeting cushioned her steps as she walked past the small kitchen and into her bedroom, the flame casting one lonely shadow on the freshly painted white walls of the empty room. After raising the shade and placing the candle on her windowsill, she lay on her new bed, a sleeping bag from the sale rack at Ames. It was the first new thing she'd ever owned and it felt wonderful.

Lying back, she folded her arms behind her head and stared at the ceiling, thinking about her first day in Hagerstown. She liked what little she'd seen of the town. It was much smaller than Baltimore, but large enough that you'd need to drive or take a bus if you wanted to go across town.

The best part of the day, without a doubt, was meeting Rebel McCassey. Not only was she interested in the man, but the anticipation of seeing him again made her stomach feel like there were a thousand butterflies inside trying to get out. Besides being good looking, he seemed to genuinely care about her feelings. Most importantly, he was honest with her. Something she hadn't been with him, not completely, anyway. Knowing how good it would feel to share the fear she'd been harboring for eleven years with someone she trusted, she longed to tell him everything. But Gypsy wasn't sure she was ready to let anyone get that close. Her mother was the last person she'd completely trusted, and since then, Gypsy had kept everyone at an arm's length to protect herself. She wished she knew what it was about Rebel that made her throw caution to the wind and put all her trust in a man she just met.

What Gypsy knew for sure was that she was attracted to him. For that reason alone, she knew she should keep him at a distance. She'd never forgive herself if her past caught up with her, and he wound up getting hurt. Rebel may be accustomed to trouble, but it was nothing like what had been haunting her since the day her mother was murdered.

* * * *

Because she rarely slept well, Gypsy was already awake when the alarm buzzed loudly, telling her it was time to get up. Shivering, she crawled out of her sleeping bag, suddenly wishing she hadn't turned her heat down to fifty-eight degrees before going to bed. April nights still got pretty cold in the mountains, and although she was trying to save money, she didn't need to freeze to death doing it. Making a mental note to allow herself more heat at night, she dashed into the bathroom and got dressed.

Since she didn't own a heavy coat, Gypsy put two sweatshirts over her short pink and black waitress uniform to keep warm. She grabbed the navy blue knapsack with her change of clothes and left the apartment at five o'clock on the dot; figuring it would probably take a good thirty minutes to walk the two miles to work.

The streets were eerily quiet in the pre-dawn hour, and Gypsy found herself walking faster than normal. Part of the reason was because she was cold, but mostly...she was afraid. She knew it was silly for a twenty-one-year-old woman to be afraid of the dark. But darkness hadn't been kind to her, and she had a good reason not to like it.

Gypsy had been walking ten minutes when the sound of a loud truck came up behind her. She thought about running into the woods until it passed, but it was too late. The headlights were shining in her direction, meaning the driver had probably already seen her.

* * * *

Rebel was in his tow truck returning from a call when he spotted someone walking down the street. It couldn't have been much above thirty degrees, and whoever it was wasn't wearing a coat. He thought about offering the person a ride, but decided against it. He'd learned a long time ago that trying to do something nice for anyone in this town was a big mistake.

Then he noticed the walker was Gypsy and slammed on the brakes. "What the hell?"

Gypsy looked like she almost jumped out of her skin when the tow truck came to a stop next to her. She'd been forced to stop walking and was staring at the passenger door as he leaned over and rolled down the window. Rebel saw the relief on her face when she noticed it was him.

"Gypsy?"

Holding a hand in the air that looked red and numb from the cold, she waved. "Hi."

"What are you doing out here?"

"I'm on my way to work. Today's my first day."

"Is something wrong with your car?" he asked.

She shook her head. "I don't have a car."

He could see she was shivering. "Hop in; I'll give you a ride."

"Well…" she seemed to hesitate.

"I thought we decided to be friends," he reminded her. "What could one ride hurt?"

"Are you sure you don't mind?"

"I'm on my way back to the garage now. It's right across the street from The Tea Cup, remember?"

Rebel recalled how excited she'd gotten when he told her he occasionally went into the diner for breakfast. He was sure she hadn't forgotten and wondered if the possibility of seeing him sometime during the day crossed her mind a thousand times that morning the same way it had crossed his.

Rebel leaned over further and unlatched the door. Shivering, she climbed in and sat down on the black leather, bench seat.

"Where's your coat, Gypsy? It's below freezing out there." The second the words left his mouth, he wished he could've taken them back. Why the hell wasn't his brain working? The bulky sweatshirts should have clued him in to the fact that she probably didn't have one.

Gypsy turned away and stared at the floor.

Sorry for embarrassing her, Rebel ignored her actions and placed his heavy blue jacket in her lap. "It's too big for you, but that's okay. It'll keep you warm."

"Thanks," she said, shaking her head. "But I can't take your coat."

"I'm not using it." He touched her ice cold cheek with the back of his hand and frowned. It was so cold her face was probably numb. "Put it on," he ordered. But when she didn't move, he added, "Please."

* * * *

Because she felt frozen, Gypsy obeyed and was secretly glad he'd made her put on the polyester jacket that matched his blue mechanics coveralls.

She felt herself flush when she zipped it and saw the white oval patch where his name was written in red cursive. No boy had ever asked her to wear his letterman jacket in high school, but if he had, she imagined that this was exactly how it would've felt. The warmth of his jacket felt like two giant arms around her. And the scent on it was all male.

"Are you warmer now?"

"Yes," she said, smiling. "Much."

Rebel made sure she was settled in the seat before shifting the truck into first gear and slowly steering back onto the road. It took just a few minutes to drive the rest of the way to the diner. When they got there, it was still closed.

"It doesn't look like Sean's here yet."

He chuckled. "Yeah, ol' Sean has owned this place for the past fifteen years and not once has it ever opened on time."

"He didn't give me a key. What should I do?"

"Just hang out here with me. He'll be along soon."

"But—"

"Gypsy," he said, as he lit a cigarette, "the sign in the window may say the diner opens at five-thirty, but everyone in this town knows Sean. He never has any customers before seven because most of the time he isn't here to let them in."

"But don't you have to get back to work?"

"I am back," he said, pointing across the street.

She leaned forward and saw the large black and white McCASSEY'S GARAGE sign hanging under a light on the front of the red brick building.

"Oh, I forgot." She glanced at the small clock mounted on the dashboard...five-fifteen. "Are you sure I'm not taking you away from anything? I feel guilty making you sit here."

Rebel took a drag on his cigarette and set it in the ashtray. "I wouldn't have offered to stay with you if I didn't want to. And the only thing you're keeping me from doing is sitting in the garage with Outlaw."

"Outlaw?"

"My German Shepherd. He guards the place when no one's around."

She smiled. "I like the name. Did you give it to him?"

"Yeah. I think it makes him feel like part of the family."

They both laughed. Rebel reached over and touched Gypsy's cheek again. Finding it warm, he leaned forward and turned down the heat.

They remained quiet while he finished his cigarette. When he threw the butt out the window, she asked him how long he'd been smoking.

"Since I was twelve."

"My mom smoked, too," she told him.

"Tell me about her," he said softly, "what was she like?"

Gypsy wrapped her arms around herself and leaned her back against the passenger side door. She rested the left side of her head on the seat and closed her eyes. Seeing her mother's face exactly the way she remembered it, Gypsy began talking. "Her name was Ella and she was from somewhere in California. She ran away from home at fifteen and hitchhiked all the way across the country by herself. She met my father soon after coming to Maryland and had me when she was sixteen." She opened her eyes to find him staring at her. "It was just her and me, two kids sort of raising each other. She worked hard and we scraped by, but there was never money for anything extra. It didn't matter, though. We were happy together."

"What about your father?"

Gypsy suddenly felt all the blood drain from her face, and hoped it was dark enough in the truck so Reb wouldn't notice.

There was no way she could avoid such a direct question. She hadn't wanted to tell him yet, but was afraid of losing his friendship if he somehow found out the truth before she had a chance to tell him. He'd taken a chance and told her the embarrassing truth about his family after they'd known each other only a few hours, and she owed it to him to do the same.

She just hoped he could handle it.

Gypsy pulled the long sleeves of his jacket over her hands and squeezed the cuffs as hard as she could, almost as if they were giving her courage. She never imagined the first time she told the whole story to someone that it would be at five-thirty in the morning, in the front seat of a tow truck with a man she hadn't even known twenty-four hours. But he was the first person she'd trusted since her mother died, and this felt right.

She licked her lips and tightened the death grip she had on the jacket cuffs. Breathing deep in an effort to bring color back to her face, she began her story. "My mother was a dancer at one of the strip clubs on Baltimore Street when she first moved to Baltimore City. You know, the area down the street from the city police headquarters that they call The Block." Gypsy looked at Rebel to see if he needed a more detailed description of the city's red light district, but it was obvious that he didn't.

"I'm familiar with The Block, Gypsy."

She nodded. "My father was one of her favorite customers. He paid a lot of attention to her, made a bunch of promises she believed he'd keep. She was naïve and didn't know any better and eventually got pregnant. He lived with us in a run-down apartment in East Baltimore until I was about a year old; at least that's what my mom told me. They had a big fight one night, and he stormed out. He never came back...not even to get his clothes."

"That must've been hard on your mom," he said sympathetically, "seventeen years old with a baby to take care of by herself."

"When I was really little, she left me with a neighbor during the day and waited tables. The woman who owned the restaurant liked her and used to let her take food home sometimes. She didn't make much money, but we did okay.

"Just before I started kindergarten, the restaurant burned down. My mom needed to find a job fast. With a tenth grade education, dancing was the only thing she could do to make decent money. She'd put me in bed at eight o'clock, wait until I fell asleep, and leave for work. She was usually home by four the next morning. So she was always there when I woke up."

Gypsy paused and glanced at Reb, whose expression, from what she could see, revealed a mixture of anger and disbelief.

"I know what you're thinking. But people do the best they can with what they have. My mom took care of me the only way she knew how. But because she felt she didn't have much to offer me, she stressed everyday how important it was to stay in school. She made me speak correctly, too, because she said that no one would ever take me seriously if I sounded uneducated."

"I'm sorry, Gypsy," he apologized. "You shouldn't have to defend your mother. I'm sure she did everything she could to take care of you."

Then he changed the subject...slightly.

"What about your father? Did you ever see him again?"

"He came by the night of my tenth birthday. I was supposed to be getting in my pajamas, but was hiding behind the door eating the piece of cake my mother told me I couldn't have. The bedroom door was half open, but I was too busy eating and didn't hear him come in. At first, I thought she was yelling at me, but then I heard a man's voice. They were standing in the living room, and I had a perfect view of them through the crack behind the door.

"I stood quietly and listened to them fight. Most of it was about stuff I didn't understand; something about a key she took from him and refused to give back. But the rest was about me. That's how I found out he was my father. She wanted him to start giving her money.

"He suddenly shouted, 'you'd been with every guy in that club, Ella. I don't even know she's mine!'"

"Then my mother yelled, 'What are you talking about? Look at her red hair, Johnny! She looks just like you!'"

"Then he told her she was nothing but a whore and wasn't getting a penny for her bastard kid."

Gypsy drew in a ragged breath. "My mom stepped forward to slap him across the face, but he caught her wrist in mid-air and threw her back against the wall. Her head hit first then her body slumped to the floor. I thought she was hurt, so I ran out of the bedroom to try and help her. My father was shocked to see me and grabbed my arm before I could get to her. I was crying by then, begging him to do something for her. He didn't do anything but throw me in a chair and threaten to hurt me if I tried to get up.

"I sat and watched as he stared at her as if he'd been inconvenienced by her death. When he walked into the bedroom, I jumped up and took off out the front door. He hollered for me to come back, but I refused. Then he yelled that he'd kill me, too, if I told anyone what he'd done."

"How could such a thing happen in an apartment complex without anyone noticing?" Rebel asked. "Didn't any of your neighbors come outside to see what all the yelling was about?"

"People yelled and screamed at each other around there all the time. No one ever got involved in anybody else's business if they didn't have to."

Gypsy looked at Rebel's face but was unable to read his emotions. "Anyway, I was scared and didn't know what to do, so I sat down on someone's front stoop, buried my face in my hands, and cried. People kept asking me what was wrong and what my name was, but I refused to talk. Eventually, someone called the police and I was taken to Social Services.

"It took my caseworker hours to get me to tell her what happened, because I was afraid my father, Johnny Cooper, would really kill me. The police questioned me for what felt like half the night. My father was eventually arrested. He was convicted of murder back in 1973 and sentenced to fifteen years in a Baltimore City prison.

"It had always been my plan to move out of the city as soon as I turned eighteen, but I didn't have enough money then. Since I knew my father was going to be locked up until I was at least twenty-six, I thought there was plenty of time to save enough to move to the West Coast. I don't think he's ever been out of Baltimore City, so he wouldn't have found me out there.

"But a few days ago, the woman who'd been my caseworker called me. Her friend working at the prison told her that my father's up for parole in August. Apparently, he's been a model prisoner, so he'll probably be released.

"He swore he'd kill me if I went to the police, Rebel. He'll be looking for me when he gets out."

Rebel remained still and quiet for several long seconds after Gypsy had finished her story.

Unsure of how to read his silence, she responded with a hint of panic. "Oh no. I told you too much again, didn't I?"

He shook his head ever so slightly. "Tell me the rest."

It amazed Gypsy that Rebel had instinctively known there was more. She was in too deep to deny it, so she continued. "Foster families are always told what's wrong with the kids they take in, so everywhere I lived, people knew what I'd been through. Everyone always thought there was something wrong with me mentally because of witnessing my mother's murder. No one ever took the time to get to know me, including kids at the different schools I went to.

"I've spent my whole life wishing for a friend, Rebel, and feel that I've found one in you. Please tell me I haven't scared you away."

Rebel didn't answer. Instead, he opened his arms, inviting her into their circle of warmth and safety.

She went willingly, surprising them both.

Lying on her right side, Gypsy rested her head on Rebel's chest and relaxed. With her eyes closed, she concentrated on the beat of his heart and the faint, masculine smell of cologne mixed with cigarette smoke and a hint of perspiration. In his arms, Gypsy found a comfort that had been missing since she was a little girl.

"I'm sorry for everything you've been through, Gypsy," Reb whispered, lightly kissing the top of her head.

The show of affection brought tears to her eyes, and she knew right then that she'd found more than a friend in Rebel

McCassey.

But feeling the way she did about Rebel terrified her. She knew Johnny Cooper would come looking for her when he was released from prison, and although she wasn't sure he'd venture out of the city, there was always that chance. It wasn't fair to expose Reb to that kind of danger, so she would have to be very careful.

* * * *

Rebel felt Gypsy shiver and wondered if she was thinking the same thoughts he was…would her father ever come looking for her?

He kept his arms wrapped around the girl who had suddenly become so special to him, holding her tightly against his chest until her light, even breathing, told him she'd fallen asleep. Careful not to wake her, he loosened his hold and gently leaned forward to look at the clock on the dash. Almost six. Sean was thirty minutes late.

Rebel swore under his breath.

He was going to wait right there with Gypsy until her boss showed up, and planned on having a word with Sean about giving her a key. What the hell had that idiot been thinking? Any number of things could've happened to Gypsy if she'd been forced to sit alone in the dark waiting for him. It was a dangerous world, especially for unsuspecting, beautiful, young women.

Oh, God, what the hell was happening to him?

In less than twenty-four hours, Rebel's life had been turned upside down by a woman he hardly knew. Yesterday, he'd promised to be Gypsy's friend. But today, he knew that would never be enough. She'd done nothing except be herself, and had managed to work her way into his heart doing it.

He no longer wanted to keep his distance to save her reputation; he wanted to follow along behind her with his fists clenched ready to take on anyone who mistreated her.

Gypsy stirred briefly when Rebel reached onto the dash for his pack of cigarettes. He lit up, but since he couldn't reach the ashtray with her in his arms, simply flicked the ashes onto the floor. When Sean's truck pulled into the parking lot thirty minutes later, Reb woke her.

* * * *

"I'm sorry," she said, sitting up. "I didn't mean to fall asleep. It's just that…well, you were so comfortable." Sure that her face was turning ten shades of red, Gypsy was grateful for the darkness.

Rebel took one last long drag on his cigarette and flicked the butt out the window. "You obviously needed the rest," he told her. "Didn't you get any sleep last night?"

"A little. I don't like the dark and don't usually sleep well."

He squinted at her. "Why not?"

She might as well tell him. He already knew almost everything about her anyway. But what would he think of her when she told him the humiliating story?

There was only one way to find out.

"Let's just say that not all foster parents welcomed young girls into their homes because they wanted to help."

Rebel seemed to understand immediately. "Help themselves was more like it," he said angrily.

Gypsy couldn't believe she was about to say it out loud. She'd never told this story to anyone. She didn't even like to think about it.

Her voice was noticeably shaky as she began her story. "I

was sound asleep the night one of my foster fathers came into my bedroom. I didn't even know he was there until I felt his hand between my legs. When I opened my eyes, he put a finger to his lips telling me to be quiet. I wasn't about to obey him, but then caught sight of a butcher knife he'd laid on the pillow next to my head. There was no doubt in my mind he'd use it. He had nothing to lose, really. My bedroom was on the first floor, and I slept with my window open all the time. All he had to do was slit my throat and say someone had broken in and attacked me.

"He unbuckled his pants, tore away my nightgown, then grabbed my wrists and held them above my head with his left hand. I panicked and started to struggle. He reached for the knife lying beside me but hit the nightstand instead and knocked the lamp to the floor. It woke his wife, who slept in the bedroom across the hall from mine in the summer because it had a window air conditioner. She threw something heavy at her door and yelled that she'd come in and show me how to be quiet if I didn't shut up.

"Knowing his wife was awake was enough to change my foster father's mind about…about…"

Fighting to keep his anger at bay, Rebel finished her sentence. "Raping you."

Gypsy took a deep, quivering breath and stared past Rebel out the window. When she finally spoke, her words came out barely above a whisper. "Yes. He only bothered me that one time, but it scared me enough to stay awake and keep my door and window locked every night for the next month; until I was sent to a new home."

"How old were you?" he asked.

"Fourteen."

"Did you tell anyone?"

Gypsy's head gently shook. "It wouldn't have done any good. My foster father would've denied it, and I would have had to stay in the home until someone found the time to investigate my accusation. Things would have gotten worse for me then, if you know what I mean."

She tried to bend her head and stare at the floor, but he reached out and put his hand under her chin. She paused, looking him in the eye.

"I didn't trust or allow a man to come close to touching me until I met you," she tried very hard to manage a smile, but failed. "It's hard for me to believe I just told you my deepest, darkest secrets. But there's just something about you. I trust you, Reb. I believe you're a good person."

Rebel ignored the compliment, allowing her to finish.

"Nothing bothers me in the daytime. But I'm always afraid something's going to happen to me in the dark. Even living by myself, I still can't relax enough to sleep much. I don't sleep in nightgowns anymore, either, just in case."

* * * *

Rebel was quiet as he thought about how Gypsy had fallen into a deep, peaceful sleep as he'd held her. She obviously felt safe in his presence. What was it about him that made her feel that way?

"Every time I think about what happened, I feel dirty. I don't ever want you to think…" she began, as her eyes filled with unshed tears.

"What I think," he interrupted, "is that your father should be shot for what he did to you and your mother. You never would've been in that situation if it wasn't for him. Don't ever be ashamed of anything that happened to you, Gypsy.

None of it was your fault. You're here to start a new life. No one has to know anything about your past."

The tears finally broke free and spilled down her cheeks. She hurried to wipe them away. "Sorry," she apologized, "I can't even remember the last time I cried. I guess I just didn't realize what a relief it'd be to finally tell someone."

A loud knock on the window startled Gypsy, causing her to jump.

Rebel turned his head toward the sound. "It's Sean. Get yourself together. I'll go talk to him."

"Wait," she said, sniffing and brushing away the rest of her tears. "I'll go with you."

Rebel nodded his approval. There was that bravery he'd gotten a glimpse of the day before. She was tough. He liked that.

"Good girl." He gave her a wink, grabbed his cigarettes, and opened the door. When he was out, he turned to Gypsy, who was still wearing his jacket, and offered her his hand. She took it and jumped down, standing quietly next to him.

"Nice of you to show up, Sean," Rebel commented.

"Shut up, McCassey." Then to Gypsy, he said, "I'm sorry. I forgot you were starting today, or I would have tried to be on time. My mind just isn't what it used to be."

Rebel laughed out loud. Sean O'Grady wasn't more than fifty, hardly old enough to be suffering from memory loss.

Sean gave him a dirty look and pointed toward the garage. "Your parking lot is across the street. What are you doing here?"

Gypsy watched in amazement as Rebel's demeanor changed instantly. He had taken a defensive stance, and the soft expression he'd worn as he comforted her was gone, replaced by a stoic, unreadable glare.

"I was keeping your help company," he said in a voice that sounded like he was fighting to stay in control.

Ignoring Rebel's irritation, Sean turned to Gypsy again. "I'll give you a key to the diner. That way you won't have to wait outside for me anymore."

"Good idea," Rebel said.

Sean continued to ignore him. "I'll see you inside, Gypsy." He walked away, leaving them alone.

In the pink streaks of early sunrise, Rebel and Gypsy stood silently next to the tow truck until the lights went on inside the diner.

"What was that all about?"

"We don't get along," Rebel said, staring at the building.

"It's okay if you don't want to talk about it. It's none of my business. I should go inside and get to work anyway. Wouldn't want to get fired on my first day."

By the time Rebel turned back to her, his expression had softened. "Just make sure he remembers to give you a key. I don't want to wait outside again when I drop you off tomorrow."

"Drop me off?"

"Here," he said, pointing at the diner. "I'll be by to pick you up at five-fifteen tomorrow morning."

"You're going to pick me up and bring me to work?" Gypsy looked at him and blinked in bewilderment. "Why?"

"Because I have transportation," he said, patting the hood of his tow truck, "and you don't. Because you walking alone in the dark worries me…and because I want to."

* * * *

Gypsy was flattered by his offer, but afraid to accept it.

Never before had she been able to depend on anyone but herself. This man was definitely dependable, and she knew it would be very easy for her to come to rely on him.

"I appreciate the offer, Reb, but I can't ask you to do that."

"You didn't ask, Gypsy. I offered. And I don't offer to do things I don't want to do."

"But—"

"Keep my jacket, too. I don't wear it while I'm working."

Gypsy gave up on the idea of telling Rebel she could manage to get to work on her own. The truth was, she enjoyed being with him. And if all the time he had to spare for her was a five-minute ride in the morning, she'd take it.

"Okay. And thank you, Reb...for everything."

He nodded, climbed up into the truck and started the loud diesel engine. "No worries, Gypsy."

"See you tomorrow." She waved, turned away, and disappeared into the diner.

Chapter 3

Gypsy liked the short, middle-aged man with salt and pepper hair who was her new boss. They didn't have any customers the first half hour she was there, which gave them a chance to talk. One of his first questions was, "How'd you get involved with Rebel McCassey?"

She'd known that was coming and told him the story of how Reb found her lost in the woods the day before. In return, he repeated a lot of the things about the McCassey's that Rebel had already mentioned, including what people were going to say about her when they found out she was associating with them.

"I don't care what people think, Sean. I like him."

"Don't be fooled, Gypsy. He may make an honest living, but Rebel's no angel. And that family…they're a wild bunch. Tight-knit, too. Mess with one McCassey, you mess with them all."

She rolled her eyes and added a touch of sarcasm when she answered, "I'll keep that in mind," as their first customers trickled in.

Business was steady all the way through lunch, but that didn't stop Gypsy from thinking about her conversation with

Sean. The things he said intrigued her, and she was dying to find out more about Reb, who apparently had two very different sides. The gentle one he'd shown her, and the don't-mess-with-me-or-I'll-kill-you one he saved for everyone else.

She wanted to know more about his family, too. With all the talking they'd done, he'd mentioned only Judd and Jimmy by name, nothing about his parents or more siblings. And where did he live? She decided to ask him a few questions tomorrow morning when he picked her up for work.

When Gypsy left the storeroom after her lunch break, she was surprised to find the diner empty. A note on the counter from Sean said he went to the hardware store to have an extra key made.

Alone with her thoughts, Gypsy let her mind wander to Rebel, and what exactly it was about him that sent her running into his arms, instead of in the opposite direction.

* * * *

At two o'clock in the afternoon, there'd been no sign of Sean and not one single customer for almost an hour. Bored, Gypsy sat in a booth and glanced across the street at McCassey's Garage. The three, big bay doors were open and all the lifts had cars on them. Rebel's black GMC tow truck was parked on the left side of the building, with a huge German Shepherd asleep in the sun next to the front tire. Outlaw.

There were cars fixed or waiting to be worked on parked along the opposite side, and a handful of mechanics walking around with tools in their hands. It had turned out to be a beautiful spring day, and Gypsy envied them for being able to work in the fresh air.

Lost in thought, she jumped when the door opened. Standing up, Gypsy walked passed the customer wearing a blue jacket with McCASSEY'S GARAGE written in white script on the back and moved behind the counter. She recognized the man in faded grease-stained blue jeans as Rebel's older brother, Judd.

Gypsy wasn't sure whether or not he recognized her, but the way he was staring made her wish her waitress uniform wasn't so short. Pad and pencil in hand, she asked, "Can I take your order?"

* * * *

Judd McCassey was surprised to discover the girl working behind the counter was the same one he'd seen in the woods with his brother the day before. When he noticed how beautiful she looked in the light of day, Judd took a moment to study her. The red hair she'd pulled back into a ponytail really showed off the green eyes staring at him from behind long, wispy lashes. She wore just enough make-up to enhance her soft features, and her sweet smile was enough to make him forget, if only for a minute, who he was. This girl wasn't just beautiful, she was striking.

Still, after all that, he decided she wasn't his type—much too innocent looking. But he'd bet a whole month's pay that his baby brother was more than a little interested in her.

Judd stared intently another few seconds, knowing she was waiting for an answer to her question. While his reputation demanded it, he just didn't have the heart to harass her. "Sure, cutie pie," he said, "I need six ham and cheese sandwiches, three with a side of coleslaw, three with macaroni salad."

She scribbled down the order. "Anything to drink?"

"Yeah," he said, looking at his piece of paper. "Three Cokes, two iced teas, and a coffee. Black."

Gypsy rang up the order and Judd paid her. "It'll be just a few minutes," she told him and walked into the kitchen.

* * * *

Wondering dreamily which sandwich Reb would be eating, Gypsy got the food together as fast as she could, hoping to finish before Judd realized the two of them were in the diner alone. Just as she was putting tops on the drinks, the front door opened and Sean walked in.

"I thought I told you to stay out of here, Judd," her boss said as he walked behind the counter.

Gypsy packed the order in two large bags, but hung back in the kitchen and listened to their conversation.

"I'm here to get lunch."

"Don't come around here bothering my help," Sean said loudly, taking a step closer to Judd.

"I said...I'm here for lunch."

Gypsy didn't like what little she knew about Rebel's brother. But he hadn't been bothering her, and it wasn't fair to allow Sean to believe he had.

Before Sean had a chance to reply, Gypsy exited the kitchen. Wedging herself between the two men, she handed the bags to Judd and looked into his eyes. "He wasn't bothering me, Sean," she said with her back to her boss. "The man just came in for sandwiches."

Gypsy had no idea what kind of look was on Sean's face at that moment, but guessed it probably mirrored the utterly shocked one on Judd's.

Sean squinted and leaned in closer to Judd. "See that it stays that way." Then he turned and walked into the storeroom.

* * * *

No Worries

Judd turned and stared at Gypsy in surprise. He hadn't exactly endeared himself to her the day before by picking a fight with Rebel in front of her; and for that reason, couldn't figure out why she'd defended him. It probably hadn't taken more than her first five minutes in town to find out that taking the side of a McCassey wasn't something you did if you wanted to make friends with decent people. Yet, she'd spoken up for him anyway. Jobs were hard to come by in Hagerstown, and Gypsy could've lost hers by sticking her neck out for him the way she did.

When the door to the storeroom slammed shut, Judd tore his gaze from Gypsy and focused on the door as he spoke. "Just after he bought this place, Sean got robbed, and accused Rebel and me of being responsible for it. We were wild, out of control teenagers back then, destructive little bastards, too. But we drew the line at stealing. We told the sheriff a thousand times we had nothing to do with it, but he arrested us anyway. The charges were dropped two days later when the real thief came back for seconds while Reb and me were still in jail.

"I do my best to avoid this place. But Mondays are my day to buy lunch. There's five pissed off mechanics across the street because I'm two hours late with their food. You weren't busy, so I came in."

* * * *

Listening closely to Judd as he spoke, it was easy to hear the pure hatred in his voice. Why had he just told her that story? Was it because Judd, like Rebel the day before, wanted to set her straight about what happened before someone else filled her head with lies?

Gypsy was unsure of how he expected her to respond. "I

50

really don't know Sean that well," she told him. "We just met yesterday."

With the intention of heading back into the kitchen, Gypsy turned away.

Before she took one step, Judd's arm shot out and grabbed her. The instant they made eye contact, he let go. Nodding, he said, "No worries," then turned and left the diner.

Strange, Gypsy thought. That was the same thing Rebel had said to her that morning. She wondered what it meant.

"Now you've done it," Sean commented when he heard Judd leave.

She rolled her eyes. "Done what?"

"McCassey's say 'no worries' to each other all the time. It's how they let one another know their backs are being watched. By defending Judd, you earned his respect. He'll be keeping an eye on you now, watching out for you like you're one of his own. When people find out you're in with that family, they won't want anything to do with you."

"So you said." Gypsy had been through too much in her life to worry what anybody else thought of her now. All she knew was that Rebel said that same thing to her earlier. She hoped it meant he thought of her as more than a friend.

"Live your life the way you want, Gypsy. I'd just hate to see a nice girl like you get mixed up with the wrong people."

Gypsy sat down to roll silverware into napkins. "What's so bad about Rebel and Judd?"

"Most folks around here are afraid of Judd; he's a nasty son of a bitch. He causes a lot of trouble that Rebel usually has to bail him out of."

Gypsy wasn't sure she believed that.

"But he works at the garage, and they look pretty busy over there. People can't be that scared of him."

"Number one, Judd drives the tow truck during the day, so he's not even there half the time. And number two, none of those boys cause any trouble during the day. Like I said, they make an honest living. It's what they do when they get off work that's earned them their reputation.

"What about Reb?" she asked. "What's he done?"

Sean let out a long, low whistle. "Rebel McCassey doesn't start trouble, Gypsy, he finishes it. More often than not, it has something to do with Judd or one of their cousins."

"But he and his brother don't like each other."

Sean looked confused. "Says who? Those two are thick as thieves." Then he laughed. "No pun intended."

She ignored his joke. "Judd tried to pick a fight with Reb in the woods yesterday. I just assumed they didn't get along."

"I've only been in town since they were fifteen and sixteen, but from what I understand, those two boys have always beaten on each other. They're close," he assured her. "Trust me."

He walked to the front door and held it open. "Come on out here. I want to test the key I had made for you."

Just like that, their conversation was over.

Gypsy and Sean walked outside, and he made her lock and unlock the door ten times before he was convinced the key worked.

"I'm really sorry for being so late this morning. I would have felt terrible if you'd been sitting outside by yourself."

She touched his arm gently. "It's all right, Sean."

"Well, now you have a key. We don't usually get busy during the week until about seven, so you should be fine until

I get here. If you ever have any trouble, just dial 911; or if it's not an emergency, your friend Rebel is always right across the street."

"Always?"

"He lives above the garage. Didn't he tell you?"

"It never came up."

"His Uncle Jimmy owns the building. Rebel's lived there, I don't know, the past eight or ten years, I guess."

Burning with curiosity, Gypsy wanted to ask a dozen more questions, but decided Reb was the person she should talk to. Recalling the deeply personal information she'd revealed to him earlier, Gypsy wondered if Reb would be willing to do the same.

Did she even have the right to ask?

Just how much did their friendship entitle her to?

Chapter 4

With twenty-eight dollars in tips buried at the bottom of her knapsack, Gypsy left the diner after her first day of work happier than she'd ever felt.

Dressed comfortably in her old overalls, white T-shirt, and worn tennis shoes, she walked through the parking lot smiling as she thought of her good fortune; finally having a place of her own, a good job, a nice, although quirky boss, and a new friend. And just as she started thinking about her new friend, there he was, standing outside the garage.

The sight of Rebel McCassey was staggering. Wearing one-piece, blue mechanics coveralls with the sleeves cut off, he was leaning against the brick wall of the garage staring straight ahead and smoking a cigarette. His right leg was bent; foot flat against the wall, and his right hand came to a rest on his thigh every time he lowered his arm after taking a drag of the cigarette.

Gypsy recognized the backward baseball hat. It was the same black one with the word MARLBORO embroidered on the front in red that he'd been wearing yesterday. She also saw that there was a large tattoo on his left bicep, but was too far away to make out what it was.

* * * *

Rebel had just crushed the cigarette under the heel of his steel-toe work boot when he noticed Gypsy watching him. He waved her over, and she nervously made her way across the street.

"Hi," she said, staring at his softball-sized, black skull and crossbones tattoo.

"How was your first day?" he asked.

"Fine thanks. I met some nice people."

"Good. I heard there were a few living around here somewhere."

It wasn't until Gypsy smiled at Rebel's sarcastic comment that he noticed how incredibly beautiful she was. So far, he'd only seen her in the low light of dusk and the pre-dawn of early morning, neither doing justice to her beauty like the bright light.

Her hair was in a ponytail again; the color of the loose curls was twice as vivid under the glowing sun. Everything about Gypsy was mesmerizing, but most of all, he loved the way she was looking at him—adoringly, like she was happy to see him.

"Well," he said, "since you're here, you want to come in and meet the guys?"

Her face brightened. "Are you kidding? Big families fascinate me. I'd love to!"

Rebel took her bag and set it in the bed of his tow truck. As he started to escort her inside, the large German Shepherd rose from his spot in the sun and began barking ferociously.

Taken by surprise, Gypsy immediately grabbed onto Rebel's right arm and tried to move behind him.

"Its okay, Gypsy," he gently pried her hands from around

his arm, placed his right arm around her back and pulled her forward. "This is Outlaw," he said calmly. "Come here, boy."

Shaking, Gypsy pressed herself against Rebel's body as the dog came closer.

"Put your hand out so he can smell you."

Her eyes opened wide with fear. "What?"

"Dogs recognize you by your scent. Put your hand out."

Gypsy held her breath and did as Reb instructed. Outlaw spent a few seconds sniffing her hand, licked it with his soft tongue, then turned and retreated behind the tow truck.

Gypsy stood frozen.

"I'm sorry, I should have warned you. German Shepherds are very protective dogs. He wouldn't have acted that way if you weren't standing so close to me. But he knows you now so he won't do it again. Are you okay?"

She nodded. "Fine."

"Good, let's go inside."

Reb led her through one of the open bay doors, and the first person he introduced her to was a tall, thin man with light brown hair, who didn't appear to be much older than Reb.

The man looking at her with a pair of beautiful, McCassey, royal blue eyes said, "James Younger McCassey, at your service. But you can call me Jimmy." He offered her his grease-stained hand, and Gypsy giggled as she shook it.

He grinned in return. "Heard about our family history, did you?"

"Mmm-hmm."

Rebel saw the smirk appear on his young uncle's face and jumped in before he had a chance to say anything. "Don't you go feeding her any bullshit, Jimmy," Rebel told him, "I don't want you scaring her away."

"Aw come on, Rebel, it's all in good fun."

"Excuse me, Gypsy," Reb said. Quicker than lightening, he took off his baseball hat and threw it at Jimmy, who was already halfway across the garage. An older man wearing the same coveralls as Reb, with the sleeves still attached, picked it up and handed it back to him.

Breathing heavily, Rebel introduced them. "Gypsy, this is my uncle, Frank. He's the peacekeeper around here, does his best to keep us all from beating on each other, and patches us up when he can't."

"It's nice to meet you," she said.

Frank nodded. "You, too, little lady."

"And over there," he said, gesturing toward two, blonde-haired men about the same age as Rebel and Jimmy but several inches shorter, "are my cousins Brady and Kane. They're two of the best body men in the business," he said, just before they started arguing over whose turn it was to use the new welder, "when they get their work done."

When Rebel yelled at his cousins to quit fooling around, one of them let loose with a string of curses that would've made any ordinary woman blush.

Pretending to ignore their rudeness, Rebel took Gypsy's hand in his and gave her a tour of the rest of the garage. After introducing her to Frank's wife, Rose, their bookkeeper and receptionist, he walked her up a set of metal steps that led to the second floor.

Halfway up, they ran into another one of Rebel's cousins; a tall, dark-haired boy barely out of his teens.

"Gypsy, this is Flynn."

"Hi," she said shyly.

He nodded. "Hey."

"He doesn't say much," Reb told her when they started climbing the stairs again, "but he's smart. Slick, too. Has this way about him that just makes people want to talk. If there's ever any information we need, Flynn's our man."

Once at the top, a short walk down a dark hallway took them past the fire escape to the door of a small studio apartment.

When Reb opened the door and turned on the light, Gypsy saw they were standing in a tiny kitchen.

"What's this?" she asked.

The floor was nothing but wooden planks. Thick, room-darkening shades covered each of the three windows and all four walls were painted beige. The apartment was sparsely decorated; just two framed pictures hung on the wall. A king-sized bed in the far corner left just enough space for the pine chest of drawers where a twelve-inch TV sat.

"This is where I live."

"By yourself?"

He laughed. "Flynn crashes here every now and then; but other than that, I'm all alone. There isn't much room for anyone else. The only thing you can't see from where we're standing is the bathroom...and that's because it's down the hall."

"I'm impressed by how neat your place is. Are you always this clean or did you straighten up just for me?"

"I spend most of my time in the garage," Reb told her. "If I am here, I'm usually sleeping."

"Wow, you really work that much?"

"Yes and no. I fix cars six days a week. Judd drives my tow truck during the day, and Jimmy and I split the eleven to seven shifts during the week."

"The tow truck belongs to you? I thought you and your uncles are in business together."

"Jimmy, Frank, and I own equal parts of the garage, but the towing business is mine. I pay Jimmy and Judd by the hour."

"Oh," Gypsy said somberly. "It sounds like you don't have much time for anything else."

The disappointment in her voice took Rebel by surprise.

When he smirked and said, "I'm the boss, Gypsy. I have time for anything I want," her shy smile gave him hope that she was as interested in spending time with him as he was with her.

Rebel suddenly thought about how different Gypsy was from all the girls who'd been chasing after him since he was a teenager. In his wilder days, the girls he knew were only interested in what kind of good time he could show them. And truthfully, he'd never disappointed a single one of them. All night parties on the bank of Antietam Creek and bonfires with his brothers and cousins behind their grandfather's barn were weekly occurrences. There were drag races in fast cars down dirt roads, free pizza at Pizza Hut, courtesy of one of his uncles, and always plenty of beer and moonshine.

But no matter how much fun he had with those girls, none of them were good for anything more than a quick fuck at the end of the night. Rebel had never met a girl as special as Gypsy. She was someone he really cared about and wanted to get to know. And if they ever did wind up in bed together, he already knew that being with her would mean a hell of a lot more to him than anything he'd shared with those other girls.

* * * *

Gypsy's heart began to race when Rebel said that he had time for anything he wanted. Did that mean he was going to make time for her? The way she felt inside excited her, making her want to find out even more about him. She decided to start with the framed photographs.

"Is it okay if I look at the pictures?"

Rebel stepped in front of her, turned on another light, and opened all three shades. "Help yourself."

She walked across the room to where two framed pictures hung on the wall. One was of Reb, Judd, and an older boy leaning against the trunk of a large tree. They were wearing camouflage jackets and holding rifles.

"That's our older brother, Blackie," Reb said when he saw her studying the picture. "We were hunting up at Ten Acres that day. I was fifteen, Judd sixteen, and Blackie was twenty."

Feeling as though she was looking through a window into the past, Gypsy gazed intently at the photograph. Rebel and Judd looked much as they did now; big and intimidating. Blackie's appearance was terrifying. Much bigger than his younger brothers, his eyes exuded recklessness and violence. They invited trouble. Trouble she had a feeling he enjoyed.

Their stance was one of unity, defiance, and power. The brothers stood shoulder to shoulder, ready to take on anything.

The next picture was of a man and woman sitting in the bed of an old blue pickup truck. But what Gypsy saw there was something completely different.

The woman's tightly pulled back hair accentuated the look on her gaunt face; worry and fatigue etched into every line. Her hazel eyes looked as if they'd forgotten how to laugh, making Gypsy wonder what could've gone so wrong for her to be that sad.

Though his build wasn't as large, the man beside her was the spitting image of Blackie, right down to the cold madness in his eyes. Generously stuffed with chewing tobacco, his left cheek bulged, while his right one bore the remnants of a fading bruise.

"Who are they?"

"Those are my parents, Dolan and Mary McCassey. My mother died when I was twelve. She was only thirty-two. My father went a few years later."

"Oh, Reb, I'm sorry."

Rebel sat down on his bed and lit a cigarette. "Don't be. We all knew his abuse was going to kill her. It just wound up happening sooner than later." He pointed to his father. "He got himself shot trying to cheat his partner out of money they made selling moonshine."

Rebel paused and gave his head a slight shake. "My father was a brutal man. He beat me and my brothers senseless when we were kids for doing nothing more than looking at him the wrong way. I've done a lot of things I'm not proud of, but I never once hurt someone who didn't deserve it." He gestured toward the picture again. "I look at that every day and promise myself I'll never turn out like either one of them."

Gypsy suddenly understood why Reb had gotten so upset when she told him the story of her father threatening to kill her. His compassion made him that much more attractive, and before she could think about what she was doing, she stood in front of him, bent down, and kissed his lips.

* * * *

Giving him a kiss was the last thing Rebel expected her to

do when she heard that story. He thought maybe she'd cry, or be so scared she didn't want anything to do with him and his family. But he definitely hadn't expected to be kissed.

He had a hard time controlling himself when he felt the touch of her soft, wet lips on his. Still holding a cigarette low between the index and middle fingers of his right hand, Rebel put his arm around the back of her neck and drew her closer. Opening his mouth, he deepened their kiss as Gypsy wrapped her arms around his waist and pressed her body against his. She returned the kiss with more passion than Rebel was ready to handle, and he found himself needing to pull away before things went too far.

"Did I do something wrong?" she asked.

He cleared his throat and took a long drag on his Marlboro. "No, Gypsy, darlin', you did everything right. That's why I stopped."

When she turned her back to him, he was afraid he'd made her self conscious. Rebel stood up and turned her around, pulling her over to the bed. They both sat down. "There's nothing wrong with what you did, Gypsy. And I like you. I like you way too much for only knowing you a couple of days. You make me feel things I've never felt for a woman. Protective mostly. I feel like I want to lock you away up here so nothing bad ever happens to you. That's why I said 'no worries' to you this morning. My family members say that to each other when we want someone to know they're being watched out for."

She nodded. "I know. Sean explained that to me this afternoon."

"Sean?" he questioned suspiciously. "Why?"

"Because he heard Judd say the same thing to me a couple

of hours ago."

Rebel's expression turned dark. "Judd didn't mention he'd seen you. What happened at the diner?" he demanded.

When she finished telling him the story about defending Judd, Rebel asked why she'd stuck up for his brother.

"Because he didn't do anything wrong."

"Sean hates Judd, Gypsy. And me too, for that matter. You could've lost your job for what you did."

She shrugged it off like it was no big deal. "I know."

"My brother's a lot like my father," he explained. "Most people would have jumped at the chance to blame him for something. He respects you for speaking up for him. That's why he said what he did to you."

"What about you?" she asked. "Are you angry?"

"Why would I be angry? Family looks out for each other. And like it or not, girl, you're in."

She smiled. "I like it. Besides my mother, I've never had family before."

"Well, you do now." Reb leaned over and gave her a quick peck on the lips. "I have to get back to work. You want me to take you home?"

"No thanks, I've been stuck inside all day. I'm looking forward to the walk."

Rebel took her hand and led her downstairs, half expecting the boys who'd known they were alone in his apartment to throw out a sarcastic comment or two. But with the exception of Brady and Kane, who were now cussing each other out over something else, everyone was too busy to even spare them a glance.

On their way out to retrieve Gypsy's bag from the bed of the tow truck, Jimmy stopped them. "You come over and see us any time, Gypsy."

"Thanks, I will."

"Judd told me what you did for him at the diner this afternoon. Not too many people are going to like you when they find out."

"I just did what was right, Jimmy. I don't care what people think of me."

He nodded his approval. "Well, in any case, you just holler if you ever need anything over at the diner. There's always four or five of us hanging around here."

"That means a lot," she said, "it really does. Thanks."

Watching the friendly exchange between Gypsy and Jimmy made Rebel happy. He was glad to see that his family had so readily accepted her, because if he had any say in it, they were going to be seeing a lot more of her.

"I should go," she told him. "The twenty-eight dollars I made in tips today is my grocery money for the week. I need to stop at Safeway on my way home."

Rebel frowned. Twenty-eight dollars wasn't going to buy much food. He wanted to offer her more money but didn't want to embarrass her. Instead, he offered to drive her to the store.

She turned him down. "But I'll see you in the morning, right?"

He nodded. "Five-fifteen."

As she turned to go, Rebel reached out and stopped her. "Be careful, Gypsy."

She smiled. "For a bad boy, Rebel McCassey, you're pretty soft inside."

He gave her a wink and grinned. "Don't tell anyone."

* * * *

Every time Rebel saw, talked to, or even thought about Gypsy, his feelings for her grew stronger. Yesterday, he was wondering what the hell was wrong with him for feeling the way he did about her. Today he didn't give a damn. He'd spent the rest of the afternoon thinking about their kiss, the damn twenty-eight dollars worth of groceries she planned to buy, and worrying so much that he didn't get any work done.

She had no car, no warm coat, and no telephone; something he found out after calling information to get her number, and wondered if she'd spent everything she had on rent.

Not having any money would explain the reason everything she owned fit in two knapsacks, as well as why she didn't turn on any lights in her apartment the night before, despite being afraid of the dark.

He admired Gypsy for working hard and trying to make it on her own. What else could she do? She had no family, no friends, and no one to go to for help if she needed it. Knowing the reason she lived in a run down part of town was because that was all she could afford made him worry even more. It made him want to run over to her apartment and stand guard outside her door.

Chapter 5

Twenty-eight dollars bought Gypsy just enough food to fit into one very heavy, double-paper grocery bag. She was sure her arms were going to give out by the time she got home, and if it wasn't such a beautiful day, she would've been sorry she'd turned down Rebel's offer to give her a ride.

Gypsy shifted the bag from hip to hip every few minutes as she made her way down Franklin Street, thinking about the time she'd spent with Reb at the garage. The members of his family she met had been nice. Although she wasn't sure she could tell one from the other. That made it hard for her to understand why nobody liked them. She hadn't actually talked to Brady and Kane, but the way they were playing around made them seem like good-natured people.

What really stuck in Gypsy's mind was the kiss she and Reb had shared. It had felt so right. She hadn't expected it to turn into something hot and heavy either, but was glad it did. He was interested in her, she could tell, and she was just as interested in him. Gypsy wasn't sure if she believed in fate, but if there was such a thing, then meeting Rebel McCassey in the woods was it.

It was seven o'clock by the time Gypsy put away her few

groceries, showered, and sat down on the floor with her dinner; a peanut butter and jelly sandwich and glass of ice water. The meal wasn't her first choice, but she couldn't afford to be extravagant.

Without a TV or anything to read, the only thing to keep her company while she ate was the radio. By eight o'clock, she was bored stiff and decided to go to bed.

After setting her alarm for four-fifteen, Gypsy climbed into her sleeping bag. She was grateful for its warmth, because even though the heat had been turned up to sixty-three, her hair was still wet and the extra five degrees didn't make much of a difference.

Then she remembered Rebel's jacket.

She'd felt guilty when he practically forced her to keep it, but now was glad he did. Crawling out of the sleeping bag, she took the blue polyester jacket out of her knapsack and put it on. It was big enough to keep her plenty warm, but what she liked best was that it smelled like him.

"Reb," she whispered, pulling the cuffs over her hands and touching her face. She got back into bed, and her heart began to beat faster as she inhaled his scent. Feeling like he was right there with her, she relaxed and fell asleep.

* * * *

It took Gypsy a few minutes to realize that the faint pinging noise she heard was not part of a dream, but something hitting her bedroom window. Hoping it was just a tree branch blowing in the wind, she laid quietly for another minute waiting for the noise to go away. But then there was another ping, and another, and she realized it was pebbles hitting the glass.

Rising, she walked to the window and peeked out the shade. There, standing in the shadows cast by a streetlight outside her window, was Rebel. Gypsy's heart fluttered at the sight of the man who'd been in her thoughts as she'd fallen asleep.

She unlocked and opened the window. "Rebel?" It was hard to tell, but it looked like he was still wearing the same sleeveless mechanics overalls he had on earlier that afternoon.

"Yeah," he said in a loud whisper. "Can I come up?"

She didn't know why he didn't just do that in the first place. "Of course."

She closed the window, walked to the living room, and unlocked the front door.

"Hi," she said and invited him in.

* * * *

The first thing Rebel noticed when he entered the apartment was how cold and empty it was. The second was that Gypsy was wearing his jacket, which, he admitted to himself, made him feel good. He remembered her saying she never slept in nightgowns anymore. Were those threadbare sweatpants her pajamas? As much as he wanted to say something, he just couldn't. She wasn't stupid and probably knew exactly what he was thinking. There was no point in humiliating her.

"Hey," he said, taking a close look at her disheveled hair. "It took you a long time to come to the window, were you sleeping?"

"Yeah. I'm sorry," she said, trying to fix her hair with her hand. "My hair gets really curly and wild when it air dries. What time is it?"

"Nine-thirty." He touched Gypsy's hand to stop her from messing with her hair. "Don't, it looks beautiful."

It really did look great. And so did she. He never thought he'd find anything attractive about a woman who'd just rolled out of bed. But at that moment, Gypsy was more beautiful than anyone he'd ever seen.

When she stopped fussing with her hair and turned her attention to his bare arms, she immediately blushed. "Oh, you must be freezing. Here," she started removing the jacket, but he stopped her.

"I'm fine, Gypsy," he took hold of both sides of the coat and wrapped her back up. "I told you to keep it."

"Then I'll turn up the heat." She made a move toward the thermostat, but he stopped her again.

"I said I'm fine."

Gypsy shrugged, giving Rebel the impression she was uncomfortable. And why wouldn't she be? She was standing in front of him in her pajamas with her unruly hair sticking out in every direction. It was so cold in her apartment that she'd obviously been sleeping in his jacket, and she hadn't asked him to have a seat because there was no place to sit but the floor.

"I'm sorry I woke you. I didn't think you'd be in bed so early."

"Normally, I wouldn't have been, but I didn't have anything else to do. I'm surprised, actually. I don't usually sleep so well. I think it had something to do with your jacket," she said quietly. "It made me feel like you were here."

Rebel smiled. By the look on Gypsy's face, the words must've left her mouth before she had a chance to stop them. To save her from further embarrassment, he bent down and lightly kissed her lips, then turned toward the door. "I should probably let you get back to sleep."

"No!" she grabbed for his arm. "Don't go."

He looked at her and raised his eyebrows.

She let go of him and took a step back. "I mean, you could

at least tell me why you came over."

"I don't go on duty until eleven and thought you might want to go out for a beer or something. I would've called, but…"

"I know," she said, "no phone. But we're friends, Reb. You don't need to call first. And you could have come to the front door."

"I didn't want to scare you."

It was Gypsy's turn to raise her eyebrows. "And you thought throwing rocks at my bedroom window wouldn't scare me?"

He did his best to look ashamed without laughing. "Sorry."

"Oh, I don't care about that," she said, touching his hand. "I'm just glad you're here."

He gave her an extra squeeze before releasing her. "Me too."

Nothing in all the experience Rebel had with women prepared him for the way the tenderness of Gypsy's admission pierced his heart. He hadn't been looking for someone to love when she practically fell into his lap, but that's exactly what he'd found. After knowing Gypsy just two days, Rebel was falling in love with her.

He took hold of Gypsy's hand and pulled her into his arms. But there was no kissing this time. Just a firm, comforting hug, and she clung to him as tightly as she had in his truck that morning. He stroked her hair and planted tiny kisses on top of her head.

"There's no way to describe this," Gypsy said just above a whisper.

"Describe what?"

"The feeling of being held in your arms. I never want to

lose it."

Rebel knew exactly what she meant, because he felt the same way. So much so that he could feel his body starting to respond to their closeness. He would've loved to stand there and hold her longer, but needed to let go before the situation became embarrassing for both of them. Reluctantly, he took a step back.

Gypsy cleared her throat. "Do you want me to get dressed?"

Oh, God, had his physical attraction been that obvious? "Dressed?"

"To go out for a beer."

"Oh." That was a relief. "Nah, you're ready for bed. We can hang out here instead. That is…if you don't mind the company."

"Mind?" she put a hand over her heart. "No, I don't mind. But I'm afraid there isn't much to do."

"You don't have to entertain me, Gypsy. We can just hang out."

She smiled. "That sounds great. But I have to go lock my window first."

"Lead the way," he said and followed her into the bedroom.

Rebel couldn't believe what he saw when he entered the room. Her clothes, what little there was of them, were folded neatly in the corner against the wall. The only other things in the room were a sleeping bag, pillow, and small clock radio. She didn't even have a blanket.

Was Gypsy really so broke that this was all she owned? He should've been subtle, beat around the bush a little to find out the answers to his questions. But he just couldn't hold it in any longer.

"What's going on, Gypsy?" he asked as calmly as he could. "Why the hell are you living like this?"

Gypsy took a deep breath and extended her arm, inviting Rebel to sit down. "I'm sorry for not explaining things to you earlier. You've been so nice to me, and it's the least I should've done, so you wouldn't have been so surprised when you walked in here."

She took another deep breath. "Like I told you this morning, I left Baltimore City in kind of a hurry. With all of the other expenses I knew I was going to have, I only budgeted twenty dollars for a bus ticket. I ended up in Hagerstown because it was an additional twenty-three dollars to go to Pittsburgh. I would've loved to leave Maryland, but just couldn't afford it."

Then she explained where every penny of her money had gone and that all she had left was thirty dollars.

"My apartment's empty because I don't own anything, not even a coat. I used to have one, but it was stolen a few months ago."

"What about clothes?" He gestured toward the small pile. "It doesn't look like you have more than a few days worth over there."

She glanced at the corner of her bedroom. "I don't. No matter how hard I worked, I never seemed to have extra money for anything after paying rent, buying food, and putting something in the bank. It didn't matter though. The waitress jobs provided uniforms, and I didn't need to wear anything nice to clean houses."

Rebel had been in and out of trouble his whole life, and most everybody in town, except his family, hated him. But no matter what, he'd always had clothes to wear and there'd always been people in his family who cared about him. He had some good memories of being a kid, a bed to sleep in, and could afford to heat his apartment. Gypsy never had any of those things, and it pained him knowing that she'd worked her fingers to the bone for years and still had nothing.

Her voice broke into his thoughts. "You shouldn't worry about me, Reb."

He looked at her sitting with her arms wrapped around her knees, which were pulled to her chest. "Who said I was worried?"

"The look on your face."

Goddamn right he was worried. She'd be lucky to make rent every month only pulling in twenty-eight dollars a day. "Will you make me a promise?"

She rested her chin on top of her knee and looked at him suspiciously. "If I can."

"Promise you'll come to me if you ever need anything."

"I appreciate the offer, Reb. But asking you for help would be relying on someone else to solve my problems, and I can't do that. I know it'll be hard to survive earning such a small amount of money, but I can do it. I've survived on much less."

"Hard? Gypsy, it'll be nearly impossible!"

She shook her head. "I have to find a way to survive on my own."

Rebel didn't know whether to strangle Gypsy or hug her. He admired her strong work ethic, but why the hell was she being so goddamn stubborn? Didn't she know that friends helped each other out when they were in trouble?

And then it hit him.

Of course she didn't know. She'd never had any close

friends. The only person she'd ever been able to count on was herself. He felt like an ass for not understanding sooner.

Well, he'd be damned if he was going to stand back and watch her live in poverty. She was going to accept his help whether she liked it or not...she just didn't know it yet.

"Fine. But I'm going to say just one more thing before I let the subject drop." His features softened as he reached out to caress her cheek. "You're not alone anymore, Gypsy, McCassey's take care of their own. Ask any one of the boys. They'll tell you the same thing."

Before Gypsy had a chance to respond, he stood and pulled a pack of Marlboro's from the side pocket of his coveralls. "I'm going outside for a smoke. I'll be right back."

On his way out, Rebel noticed something that had slipped by him before; the only lock on the front door was the one on the knob. Making a mental note to bring over and install one of the extra deadbolts he had at the garage, he quietly closed the door behind him.

* * * *

Gypsy was so surprised by Rebel's comment that she sat on the floor a full minute after he was gone trying to figure out what he meant. McCassey's take care of their own? Did that mean she was his girl? Or maybe he just considered them good friends. Whatever it meant, Gypsy had a feeling he was going to give her help whether she asked for it or not.

When Rebel returned, Gypsy was in the kitchen making hot chocolate. She met him in the living room and handed him a cup. "I forgot I had this. It's not beer, but it's the best I could do."

He smiled. "My brothers and cousins and I used to drink this in my grandparent's kitchen when we were little," he explained as he blew on the hot liquid. "It's perfect. Thanks."

They went into the bedroom where Gypsy had raised the shade and re-lit a candle. She put the radio on low and they sat on the floor again. This time, Rebel leaned back against the wall, his legs stretched out long in front of him, left foot crossed over the right.

Gypsy sat next to him.

When he extended his left arm inviting her to come closer, she leaned back against him and rested her head on his chest.

"Tell me about your mother," she said.

Rebel sighed. "She got pregnant with Blackie when she was fifteen and married my father, who was seventeen, because her father forced her to. My father thought she trapped him into marriage and hated her for it."

"Did she?"

"Did she what?"

"Trap him into marriage."

"At fifteen?" Rebel snorted. "I doubt it. My mother's father, who I had the unfortunate pleasure of meeting for the first time at her funeral, was the meanest person around these parts back then. She was afraid of him, but not enough to go running into the arms of Bad Dolan McCassey. It was probably something more like my father met her, got her drunk on moonshine, and forced himself on her.

"Once her father found out she was pregnant, he probably threatened to beat the hell out of her until she told him who did it. The way the story goes, he hunted around for my father until he found him harvesting corn in my granddaddy's fields. He dragged my parents to the courthouse, and they had a shotgun wedding, literally, on a Thursday afternoon."

Gypsy couldn't say anything but, "Wow."

Rebel took a deep breath. "I always wondered if her father would've done things differently if he'd known he was signing his daughter's death warrant by forcing her to marry my father."

"I'm sorry she had such a rough life."

"Me too. Anyway," he continued, "she suffered two miscarriages after she had Blackie. Probably from being beaten every time she turned around. I was born ten months after Judd, and my father never touched her again after that...at least sexually. She was a good woman, but the years of being browbeaten and abused by my father took their toll. All that was left of my mother by the time she died was a shell of the woman she once was."

Not quite sure what to say, Gypsy was suddenly sorry she'd brought up the subject. She covered by asking if he and his brothers were close growing up.

"Judd and I were at each other's throats more often than not. Blackie didn't have much use for his two, warring younger brothers until we were teenagers. The two of us had calmed down a bit by then." With a smirk, he added, "But not much."

"You're close now?"

"Yeah, we're close," he told her. "But we still beat the hell out of each other every once and a while...just to keep in practice."

Gypsy could imagine being close to a brother or sister. It was something she'd longed for her entire life.

"I would have given anything to be close to someone growing up. You guys are lucky."

"Judd's the lucky one. He would've been dead a hundred times already if I wasn't around to save his ass. He's got a short fuse and tends to react to things before he has a chance to think about what he's doing. That's usually what gets him in so much trouble."

Gypsy was afraid she'd made him angry by prying into his personal life. But then he reached up with his right hand and started playing with her hair, winding the tight curls around his fingers.

Letting herself relax, she put down her cup, snuggled against him, and closed her eyes. For such a wild and supposedly dangerous man, Rebel McCassey had an amazingly soft touch.

In the silence, he continued to play with her long, curly locks. When she snuggled closer, he wrapped his left arm around her body, resting his hand on her stomach. She entwined her fingers with his and held on tight.

"What about Blackie?" she asked.

"What about him?"

"How come I didn't meet him? Does he work with you at the garage?"

"He used to. He's been in prison in Baltimore City the past few years for armed robbery."

She swallowed the lump in her throat. Gypsy didn't want to tell Reb again that she was sorry, so she remained quiet, hoping he would say something else.

"Blackie thrives on the rush he gets by causing trouble. The more severe the consequences, the more exciting it is for him. He didn't even need the money he got from robbing the liquor store. He just did it for fun. The fact that he got caught a few hours later didn't even bother him.

"He and Judd are a lot alike, only Judd doesn't carry things as far. At least he hasn't yet."

"Wow," she said. "You're family sure is interesting."

Rebel gave his head a slight shake. "Don't make us out to be more than we are, Gypsy. We may have interesting stories, but all the fun we have and trouble we get into comes at a price. I just hope to hell I don't wind up dragging you down."

Gypsy was almost asleep, but she could hear the worry in his voice. "I don't care what happens to me, Rebel," she whispered sleepily. "As long as I'm with you, I'll never be afraid."

* * * *

Rebel wished she knew what it did to him to hear her talk like that. And he would love to know what he did to deserve so much trust and admiration from a sweet girl like Gypsy.

When he was sure she was asleep, he re-positioned himself so he was lying on his back, wrapped his arms around Gypsy, and rested her head on his right shoulder. After covering both of them with the sleeping bag, Rebel focused on the ceiling and let his mind wander.

If someone had told him a week ago that he was going to meet a girl like her, one who would like him for who he was, and trust him unconditionally, he would have told them they were crazy. But here she was, lying in his arms sound asleep. He knew she was a girl he could love the minute she flashed him that first trusting smile.

Eleven o'clock came and went and Rebel decided to forget about going to work. After all, he owned the tow truck and had the right to take a night off.

He closed his eyes but didn't sleep. Instead, he thought about Gypsy, convincing her to accept his help, and how he was going to take care of her if she refused it. Telling her he loved her also crossed his mind, and how the hell he was going to do that without scaring her off. He knew that if a girl said she loved him after they'd only known each other a few days, he'd automatically think she was after something. The only thing Rebel wanted from Gypsy, other than the respect and trust he already had, was her love.

When the alarm clock rang at four-fifteen, Rebel reached over and turned it off. "Gypsy," he whispered, not wanting her to be scared when she woke up and realized he was still there.

"Hmmm," she moaned, slowly opening her eyes.

Rebel was pleasantly surprised when the only reaction she had to him lying next to her was to snuggle closer. "Your alarm went off, darlin', it's time to get up."

Still half asleep, she closed her eyes again. "Five more minutes."

It wasn't until he said, "If you don't get up you'll be late for work," that Gypsy seemed to become aware of the situation. After a brief glance at the clock, she gave Rebel a wide-eyed look. "Oh, no! You missed work. Why didn't you leave?"

She tried to get up, but Rebel pulled her close, and she rested her head on his chest. "I'm the boss, remember? I don't have to work if I don't want to."

Rebel went outside for a smoke while Gypsy took a quick shower and got dressed. Uniform on and hair in a ponytail, she handed him a toothbrush when he came back inside.

"It's extra," she told him shyly. "In case you want to use it."

Rebel gave her a suspicious glance. She barely had enough money to buy food, but had bought an extra toothbrush? It was too much to hope she'd gotten it with him in mind, so he thanked her and walked into the bathroom.

She was wrapped in his jacket and standing by the front door when he asked if she was ready to go.

"Ready." She picked up the knapsack that held her change of clothes. Before she could drape it over her left shoulder, Rebel took it and slung it over his.

He opened the door, and she walked out. When it was closed, he twisted the knob several times to make sure it was locked. "I'll be by tonight to install a deadbolt. A five-year-old could pick this worthless lock in seconds."

She started to protest, but he stopped her. "No arguments. I want you safe."

"Okay," she gave in, "thank you."

Rebel pulled Gypsy close for a minute, then loosened his hold and bent down to give her a kiss. Not just a peck on the lips, but a slow, deep, sensual kiss that she eagerly returned.

When they parted, Reb planted one extra kiss on her forehead and chuckled. "You're sweet as honey, darlin', but that's a lot more than I can say for the way that jacket smells," he waved his hand back and forth. "It could use a good washing. Probably two."

She held her forearm up and sniffed. "I like it. The scent reminds me of you."

He laughed. "Do I really smell that bad?"

"No…that good."

And that was the moment Rebel McCassey knew Gypsy Lance was his, heart and soul. No woman thought the combination of grease, cigarette smoke, and perspiration on a man smelled good unless she felt more for him than just friendship.

Chapter 6

Rebel and Gypsy spent a lot of time over the next four weeks getting to know each other. Since she had more free time than he did, she spent a lot of her afternoons hanging around the garage after her shift at The Tea Cup.

"I feel a little awkward," she said at first. "I'm afraid your family will think they have to walk on eggshells around me because I'm a woman."

"You've got nothing to worry about, darlin'," Reb reassured her, "With the exception of Frank, not one of those guys would know how to act properly around a woman if they took lessons."

Gypsy was pleasantly surprised to find that Reb had been right; none of them went out of their way to be extra nice. Instead, they talked to and teased her the same way they did each other, making her feel more than welcome.

Rebel was happy Gypsy and the boys had taken to each other so well. But much to his chagrin, they occasionally treated Gypsy too much like one of the guys.

There was an incident where she, Brady, and Kane wasted two hours telling each other the most disgusting jokes they knew, and one with a loose oil plug on a car that had

Gypsy scrubbing 10W40 out of her hair all afternoon; Rebel still wasn't quite sure what happened there. But when he caught a glimpse of Gypsy sticking her middle finger up at Kane, he kicked himself for not putting a stop to his cousin's lewd behavior when Gypsy first started hanging around the garage. She'd picked up one too many of their bad habits.

"That's it!" he yelled one day, "from now on, I forbid anything other than work to take place in this garage between the hours of seven in the morning and four in the afternoon!"

Most of the time, Gypsy did everything she could to help around the garage. She answered the phone when Rose was busy, ran errands, and was learning a little about cars from Rebel, too. He even taught her how to hotwire his pickup truck by crossing the battery and ignition wires.

"You shouldn't be teaching that sweet, innocent girl to do a thing like that, Rebel," his uncle, Frank, lectured.

"Easy, old man," he teased. "I'm just teaching her some basic survival skills."

Frank shrugged and walked away, muttering something under his breath about what kind of thing Gypsy could possibly have to survive that would require her to hotwire a vehicle.

Rebel gave Jimmy all the early shifts with the tow truck so he could spend more time with Gypsy in the evenings. Even though her apartment was empty, it was slightly bigger than the one Reb had over the garage, so they spent most of their time there.

Sometimes they played cards or watched the old twelve-inch black and white TV Reb brought over. Other times they just sat and talked. But no matter what they wound up doing, one thing was always the same. Every night, Rebel stayed with her until she fell asleep.

By the middle of May it was much too warm for extra covers, but Gypsy always insisted that he drape his jacket over her each night before he left for work at eleven.

Rebel would never forget how he felt the first night he found her sleeping with it. She'd given him a key the day he installed her deadbolt and told him he could come over whenever he wanted, even if she was sleeping.

That particular night, Jimmy was out sick and Reb was supposed to work a double shift driving the tow truck. Instead, he quit at ten o'clock, stopped at the liquor store on North Locust Street for a six-pack of Budweiser, and went to Gypsy's.

Knowing she'd be asleep, he entered the apartment quietly and put the beer in the fridge. When he went in the bedroom to check on her, she was curled into a ball on top of her sleeping bag, his jacket tucked under her arm. Reb smiled at the sight, his love for her growing stronger as he realized she took comfort from something that belonged to him.

Squatting beside her, he started to take the jacket away. But she stirred, and stopped him. "Don't take it," she pleaded, half asleep. "It makes me feel like Rebel's here."

He brushed the hair away from her face and kissed her forehead. "I am here, Gypsy." Taking the jacket, he laid it in the corner with the rest of her clothes. His six-pack forgotten, Rebel stretched out on the floor and gathered her into his arms. Gypsy settled herself against him with ease and immediately fell back to sleep.

Chapter 7

Thunder rumbled low in the distance at the same time on a slow, sultry, Friday afternoon at the end of July that Rebel and his cousins were in the garage playing Seven Card Stud. The noise was upsetting Outlaw, causing the German Shepherd to bark incessantly.

"I give up." Kane slammed his cards down on the table. "Not only is it hotter than hell in here, but that damn dog is making me crazy. What's with him today?"

"Lay off, Kane." Rebel whistled and Outlaw trotted over.

The dog nudged his master's arm, whined, then loped outside through the open bay door. Rebel knew exactly what was wrong with his faithful friend.

By the time Judd pulled the tow truck into the parking lot twenty minutes later, everything outside had become eerily still. There were no cars on the road and no breeze; not even a single bird chirping.

Judd walked into the garage and came to a stop behind Brady. After looking at his cousin's cards, he grinned, seeing the perfect opportunity to have a little fun at Brady's expense. "Wow!" he said, with exaggerated excitement. "Three aces."

Brady threw his cards on the table and jumped out of the chair. He tackled Judd, and the two men fell to the oil-stained cement floor laughing like kids. As the rest of the guys watched from the safety of the card table, Brady and Judd rolled around for a good minute or two, each trying to get the better of each other. But when Brady accidentally pushed Judd too hard and he slammed against one of the tool cabinets, the fun ended with a stream of curses from Rebel.

"If you two shit heads want to kill each other, do it outside! Quit wrecking my damn garage!"

Judd stood and straightened the cabinet. "Can't," he said, offering Brady a hand up. Brady accepted, and the two men brushed themselves off and made their way back to the table. "Bad weather's coming this way. I was just at the campground in Clear Spring picking up a tow. The sky over there is black, man. Black. There's a tornado watch from Cumberland to Baltimore."

Judd's announcement ended any thoughts the cousins had of continuing the poker game.

Irritated by his brother, Rebel, who'd been balancing his chair on its two back legs, set all four on the ground and leaned across the table. "Quit being so dramatic."

"Who's being dramatic?" Judd extended his arm toward the door. "Go look for yourself."

Rebel didn't need to look outside to know what was coming. Approaching storms were the only thing that made his dog uneasy, and Outlaw hadn't sat still all day.

After the next boom of thunder and quick flash of lightening caused the garage lights flicker, Rebel backed his chair away from the table. "Let's call it a day."

Following their cousin's lead, Brady and Kane rose and

began returning the chairs to Rose's office while Flynn lowered the big bay door and turned out the lights.

Reb pulled his brother aside. "Will you stay here and keep an eye on things for me? Gypsy's shift at The Tea Cup is due to end in an hour. She'll be heading over when she's through, and I don't want her here alone."

Judd scratched his head and shrugged. "Sure, bro. Where you going?"

"To get my guns from the hunting cabin on Ten Acres. I'm not sure that old building can survive a tornado."

"Your guns? You should stay here in case Gypsy needs you, man. I'll go."

Rebel shook his head. "You can't. I was cleaning them and the pieces are scattered all over the place," he told his brother, wishing for the millionth time that Judd had taken the time to learn to assemble a firearm. Everyone else in his family could put one together in the dark with two hands tied behind their backs. And although Judd could shoot any type of gun with amazing accuracy, he couldn't put one together in broad daylight with an instruction book.

"You better get moving, then," Judd shouted over a loud clap of thunder. "It doesn't look too good out there."

Rebel glanced out the window. "That's an understatement." Since Judd had come in, the sky had turned pitch black and the wind had picked up. It was blowing fiercely, scattering debris everywhere.

The diner appeared to be busy, which was good. If Gypsy had to work late, he wouldn't have to worry about her refusing Judd's company and trying to walk home in the storm.

Reaching into the pants pocket of his sleeveless coveralls, Rebel pulled out his keys. Adjusting his baseball hat backwards, he lit a cigarette and turned to his brother. "I'll be back as soon as I can."

When a strong gust of wind nearly ripped the door from its hinges as Reb opened it, he whistled for Outlaw, who came running.

"The guns can wait," Reb announced when he walked back into the garage. "I'm going to the diner."

It wasn't often that Rebel worried about anything, so when Brady and Kane apparently noticed how concerned he was about Gypsy, they offered to go with him.

"Hell," Judd said. "We'll all go. Sean will never confront all of us. Come on, Flynn."

As the five McCassey's made their way to the door, they were stopped short by the sound of a rain barrel crashing against the metal bay door. Rushing to the window, they watched as the wind bent the trees so far over they looked as if they'd snap in half. Large hailstones began pounding the roof, and the sky let loose its torrential rains. Then high winds gave way to a deafening roar sounding remarkably like an on-coming freight train.

They all saw the funnel cloud at the same time.

Rebel started to run out the door. To get him to stop, Judd, Brady, and Kane had to tackle him from behind. "You can't go out there!" Judd yelled.

Rebel shrugged them off. "I have to get to Gypsy!"

"Well, you won't do her any good by getting yourself killed, goddammit!" Judd hollered. "Let's go!"

As Rebel struggled against them, his brother and cousins dragged him toward the steps leading down into the pit at the back of the garage. It was ten feet under ground and fifteen yards long, mainly used for storing tires, old tools, and car parts. But there was plenty of room for all of them, including Outlaw, to ride out the storm.

One by one they descended into the dark pit to take seats on the concrete floor. Other than objects being blown into the heavy metal bay doors and a couple of loud crashes of glass, they couldn't hear anything over the roaring wind.

"I'll go with you to check on Gypsy when this blows over," Judd yelled to Reb. "We all will."

Rebel only grunted in response, soothing his anger by thinking of ways to make his brother pay if anything happened to Gypsy. Deep down he knew there was no way he would've made it across the street before the tornado struck, but sitting here doing nothing to make sure Gypsy was safe made him feel useless.

The chaos outside lasted no more than a minute. The instant it ended, Rebel flew up the metal stairs followed by the other four. Outlaw brought up the rear.

Other than some broken windows and scattered papers, there wasn't much damage to the inside of the garage. Rebel glanced out the window, sighing in relief when he saw the diner hadn't suffered much damage, either. He tried to lift one of the bay doors, but it wouldn't budge. Neither would the other two.

"Power's out," Flynn announced, after trying to turn on the lights.

"Forget about the damn lights and get your ass over here," Rebel snapped. "There must be a thousand pounds of debris piled against these doors."

It took the strength of all five men to finally get one of the doors open. Jumping over downed tree limbs and scattered debris, Rebel and his cousins ran toward the diner, slowing to a walk as they reached the parking lot.

Then suddenly, without warning, the roof of the diner caved in, causing two of the walls to collapse.

"Oh, shit!" someone yelled. But Rebel never heard it. He was already up to where the front door of the diner used to be.

"Gypsy! Gypsy!" he shouted. And without hesitation, began throwing broken pieces of wood and brick out of his way looking for a hole to crawl through. He had to get inside. He had to get to Gypsy.

Judd ran up behind his brother, followed by Brady and Kane. "The phones are out so Flynn ran down to the sheriff's office," he said, then put a hand on Rebel's shoulder. "Help will be here soon."

Rebel nodded then spoke as if he hadn't heard a word his brother had said. "We'll never be able to move all this by hand. Brady, Kane, run over to the garage. Get flashlights, ropes, chains, shovels, and whatever else we've got. Hook up the snowplow to my pickup truck, too. We'll push this stuff out of the way if we have to."

The boys took off running just as the first faint screams from terrified customers started coming from inside the diner. Desperate to get in and find Gypsy, Rebel and Judd tore frantically at the debris.

The police and fire departments showed up at the same time Brady and Kane drove into the parking lot in Rebel's 1978 one-ton, black pickup truck, clearing away debris with the plow. After parking the truck, they quickly made their way to the front of the building with tools in hand.

The McCassey cousins worked side by side with the firemen, police, and volunteers from town for thirty minutes before they were able to clear a safe path. When the firemen began going into the building, the volunteers were asked to step aside and let the professionals do their job.

Rebel watched anxiously for an hour as they pulled victims, most unconscious but alive, one by one, from the collapsed building. "Twenty people have come out of there already. Where the hell is she?"

"They'll find her," Judd told him. "They'll find her."

When dusk faded into darkness, a local paving company showed up and donated the use of portable lights they had for working on the roads at night. Around nine o'clock, the two remaining walls of the building gave way, trapping the remaining victims inside.

"We can't get to them from the front of the building anymore!" the fire chief shouted. "We'll have to go through the top!"

Rebel stood alone and watched from the side of the building as the fire department positioned a hook and ladder over what was left of the diner's roof.

The chief shouted final instructions as the ladder was double checked. "Lower men in, have them search for victims, then lift them out with a stretcher attached to the ladder."

The first person they brought out was Sean. When Rebel spotted him, he ran to the stretcher. "Where's Gypsy?"

Dazed, Sean answered. "Basement. She was...in the basement."

"In the basement?" Rebel questioned. He took off his baseball hat, ran a hand through his hair, and began to pace. "What the hell was she doing down there?"

Sean never got the chance to answer, and Rebel watched helplessly as he was loaded into an ambulance and taken away.

Wasting no time, he ran to tell the fireman that someone was trapped in the basement.

"Sorry," the fire chief shook his head. "We've suspended the search for now."

"What?" Rebel yelled. "Why?"

"There's a gas leak in there. As much as I want to get the rest of those people out, I can't risk the lives of my men."

Anger and an overwhelming feeling of helplessness overcame Rebel. Deep down, he knew the chief was right. Those men had families and they were already in a dangerous situation. A single spark around a gas leak would mean certain death for everyone. But it also meant that Gypsy was now in even more danger. He had to get her out.

"Then I'll go in and get her myself," Rebel said and took off toward the pile of rubble.

"Wait!" the chief ran after Rebel and caught him by the arms. "I can't let you do that, McCassey. We have to wait for the gas company to get here."

"Screw the goddamn gas company! They could take all fucking night to get here! Now, either have me arrested or get the hell out of my way."

The two men stared at each other until the chief bent his head and held out his arm, giving Rebel permission to do what he wanted.

"Judd!" Reb called to his brother. "Get me one of those flashlights the boys brought over. I'm going after Gypsy."

Judd stared openmouthed at his brother.

"Go goddammit! This place could blow at any minute, and I'd like to have Gypsy out of there before it does!"

Judd ran off as Rebel climbed to the top of the building. Thirty seconds later, his brother and cousins were standing next to him with flashlights and rope.

"I'm going in with you," Judd told him. "Brady, Kane, and Flynn will stand by in case we need help."

Knowing that every second counted, Rebel nodded, tossed his hat to Flynn and headed down into the hole.

Armed with flashlights, the brothers sidestepped bricks and crept over broken furniture as they made their way through the diner. When they reached the area where the basement door was located, Rebel began calling Gypsy's name.

No answer.

Rebel's heart almost stopped beating when he noticed the door was blocked by pieces of the collapsed roof. Was there even the slightest chance anyone in the basement hadn't been crushed to death? Thinking only of Gypsy's safety, Rebel ignored the pain as sharp objects sliced into his hands and arms as he and Judd quickly cleared away debris. When they finally reached what was left of the door, Rebel ripped it off the hinges and threw it aside. "Gypsy?"

"Reb?" she called weakly.

Thank God! She was still alive!

Rebel turned to Judd, who was standing ten feet behind him and gave a thumb's up. "It's me, darlin'. Is there anyone else down there with you?"

"No. I'm...I'm the only one."

"It's all right, Gypsy. Hold tight, I'm coming down."

Rebel tied the rope around his waist and handed the slack to Judd. "I'm going down," he told his brother. "If it feels like this floor's going to go, get the hell out of here."

Judd shrugged and tied the other end of the rope around himself. "Just go get your lady, so we can all get out of here. I need a smoke."

Making jokes was Judd's way of dealing with things that made him nervous. It didn't happen often, though, because he wasn't usually on the receiving end of something intimidating.

Shining his light through the doorway, Rebel called out to Gypsy again as he headed down the rickety stairs.

* * * *

Relieved to hear Reb's voice, Gypsy started to cry. The tornado had struck so fast that it was a miracle everyone in the diner was able to get into the building's basement. When the noise stopped, they started climbing the stairs to go back into the restaurant. Sean had gone up first to make sure his customers got out all right, and she'd stayed behind to help the people still downstairs.

Gypsy was walking around the basement one last time to make sure no one had been left behind when she heard a low rumble, followed by screaming, a loud crash, and finally, silence. Another small crash came a minute later, causing heavy pieces of the building to rain down on her. She dove for cover, but not before she was struck on the side of her head by a brick.

When the rumbling stopped, Gypsy was grateful to see that the steps leading upstairs were intact. When she climbed them and tried to open the door, it wouldn't budge. She worked for hours trying to alert the rescuers to her presence, but nothing had worked. She was buried under too much wreckage for anyone to hear her.

When the rest of the building collapsed a couple of hours later, Gypsy was taken by surprise as everything from bricks, metal chairs and tables, to roof shingles and shattered glass fell on top of her. Unable to take cover, she was buried under thousands of pounds of the building's remains.

When Gypsy came to, she found herself pinned painfully under the bulk of a large beam. The end of it was resting on what was left of the basement wall, taking some of the weight off of her body. Had it not been for the wall, she was sure she would've been crushed to death.

Unable to move the beam and barely able to breathe, Gypsy closed her eyes and convinced herself that she was going to die. Her last thoughts had been of Reb as she drifted back into unconsciousness.

* * * *

Gypsy thought she was dreaming, but as she slowly regained consciousness, she realized it really was Reb calling her name. He told her to hang on; he said he was coming to get her.

"Gypsy?"

"It's dark down here, Reb," she cried.

"I know. It's all right. I'll be there in a minute. Just keep talking to me, so I can follow your voice."

She sniffed. "Okay."

"Can you move?"

"No. There's a...a beam on top of me."

"Jesus," he muttered. "Does anything hurt?"

"My left side," she paused, "and my head."

Rebel reached the bottom and shined his flashlight across the floor, searching for Gypsy. "Talk to me, Gypsy, honey. Where are you?"

"Over here."

Rebel turned the light to his right, and there she was. Her face was filthy; the only clean spots were two white streaks down the sides where tears had washed away the dirt. She was lying on the floor in a small pool of blood from the cut on her head; the support beam was halfway across her body.

Gypsy burst into tears again the second she spotted Rebel. He was on the floor kneeling by her side before she had the chance to utter a single word. "It's okay," he said, brushing the hair away from her face. "I'll get you out of here."

Still crying, she nodded.

Rebel crawled over to inspect the part of Gypsy's body the beam was lying on and grimaced when he noticed it was directly against her ribcage. He stood up to examine the beam then knelt beside her again. "Do you think you can move?"

Gypsy could tell by the slow monotone sound of Reb's voice that he was trying to hide his worry. The situation had to be much worse than she thought for him to be so worried. That scared her even more. "I...I don't know," she said and began sobbing.

"Listen, Gypsy," he said harshly. "I know you're scared. Hell, when this whole thing's over I'll sit down and cry right along with you. But I know you. You're tough and you're brave. And right now, I need you to be both. Turn off the waterworks. You can cry later."

Suddenly, Sean's words, "Rebel McCassey doesn't start trouble, he finishes it," echoed in her mind. Reb had come here to save her. He'd risked his life to climb down into the basement of a collapsed building because he wanted her to be safe. At the very least, she should do as he asked. With one final sniff, she wiped at her tears and managed a slight smile. "Okay."

"Good girl." Rebel flashed a quick grin and tucked his flashlight into the side pocket of his coveralls. "Now...I'm going to lift this beam. As soon as it's in the air, I want you to scoot out from under it. Can you do that?" He was talking to her like she was a child, but she knew he was only trying to keep her calm.

"I can do it."

"All right, here we go." Rebel braced his shoulder against the beam to get leverage, grunting as he lifted it into the air.

With his left leg bent in front and his right one behind him to keep from sliding, he raised his arms all the way above his head to give Gypsy enough room to free herself. When the beam was as high as he could get it, Gypsy choked back her cries of pain and moved as far away as she could.

Gasping for air, she let Reb know she was free.

"Good," he said. "I'm going to count to three and let this thing go. It's probably going to stir up some dust and cause a few things to fall, so I want you to bend your head toward the floor as much as you can without hurting your ribs and cover it with your arms. Are you ready?"

"Wait!"

"Gypsy, I'm strong enough to lift this beam over my head with no trouble, but I ain't Superman," he said, his voice laced with strain. "This thing is getting pretty damn heavy, honey. What is it?"

Gypsy swallowed the lump in her throat. "Just in case the whole upstairs caves in and crushes us when you let go of the beam, I don't want to die without letting you know that I love you," she whispered. "And thank you for saving me."

"Damn," he cursed with an obvious hint of humor. "I wanted to be the first one to say it. I love you, too, darlin'," he said with a softness Gypsy had never heard. "But don't thank me yet. The whole building could come crashing down when I let go of this thing. Are you ready?"

"I'm ready."

And with that, Rebel counted to three and let go. The building started to rumble and shake as he dove toward Gypsy. Shielding her body with his, she heard him whisper a prayer to a dozen saints she'd never even heard of to keep them from being crushed to death.

Judd raced to the basement door and started calling his brother's name when the floor began to move. "Rebel! Where the hell are you?"

"I'm here!" Rebel shouted when everything stopped moving. "I've got Gypsy. We're coming up."

Judd shined his light into the basement. "The steps are still standing," he called to his brother, "but you'd better hurry, they don't look too steady."

"Did you hear that, Gypsy? We have to go now."

It was getting hotter by the minute down there, and Gypsy watched Rebel run a hand through his sweat-soaked hair before helping her stand. The pain caused her to be unsteady on her feet, but she managed to follow slowly behind Reb as he picked up debris and tossed it aside, clearing a path for her to walk. They were no more than a few yards from the stairs, but it took them nearly ten minutes to get there.

"Judd! Start clearing some kind of a path to that hole we crawled through to get in here. Gypsy's hurt pretty bad. I'm going to have to carry her out."

Judd did the best he could clearing a walkway as Rebel and Gypsy made their way up the steps, but it didn't do much good. There was just too much rubble and nowhere to put it. When he heard them at the top of the stairs, he moved toward the doorway as fast as the piles of wreckage would allow.

"Light the way!" Rebel shouted, tossing his flashlight to

Judd. He untied the rope from around his waist and scooped Gypsy into his arms.

She wrapped her arms around Reb's neck and held on tight as he followed Judd, carefully stepping over whatever was in his way. When they finally made it out, waiting paramedics tore Gypsy from Rebel's arms and rushed her to an ambulance.

"Reb!" she called desperately.

"I'm here, Gypsy. I'm right behind you." Rebel stood just outside the ambulance doors as the EMT's worked on her, the look on his face daring anyone to tell him to move. Moments later, he was joined by Judd and their three cousins.

"You want to ride with her?" someone from inside the ambulance asked him.

Without hesitation, Rebel climbed in.

"We'll meet you at the hospital," Judd shouted just before the back doors of the vehicle closed.

Lying on the stretcher covered by a blanket, Gypsy opened her eyes long enough to see Reb smile. "You have a nasty gash on the back of your head, and the paramedics think you might have a couple of broken ribs," he told her. "But you're going to be fine."

"Thanks to you," she whispered. "You saved me."

He took hold of her hand and gave it a gentle squeeze. "I'll always be here to save you, Gypsy. I love you."

Those were the last words Gypsy heard before she gave in to fatigue and passed out.

Chapter 8

When Gypsy opened her eyes, she was lying in a hospital bed. The clock on the wall read two in the morning.

Reb was dozing in the chair next to her and Judd, Brady, Kane, and Flynn were sound asleep, slumped in chairs lining the wall on the opposite side of the room. The instant she stirred, Reb opened his eyes.

"Hey," he said.

She attempted a smile. "What's everyone doing in here?"

"Waiting for you to wake up."

Gypsy took a look around the room. "I don't want to stay here, Reb. I want to go home."

He sat up straight and ran a hand through his hair. "Gypsy, you have two broken ribs and a mild concussion. You also have thirty-two stitches holding the gash on the side of your head closed—"

Panicked, Gypsy's hand suddenly flew to the side of her head. She'd seen how doctors shaved patient's heads when they needed stitches. Afraid she'd lost half of her curls, she tried feeling around the wound, but Reb reached out and stopped her.

"Don't mess with it," he warned, "you don't want to re-open that cut."

"But—"

"Don't worry, darlin', they only shaved a small area. With all that hair you have, no one will be able to see a thing."

Relieved she wasn't bald, Gypsy sighed deeply, but still couldn't relax. "I want to go home," she repeated.

"No way. You belong in the hospital…at least for tonight."

"Please, Reb." Her voice rose as she started to panic again, waking the four sleeping men on the other side of the room. "Get me out of here."

"All right, all right," he gave in, after a few moments of silence. "Judd, go see if you can find a doctor, Gypsy wants to go home."

Judd jumped out of his chair and raced from the room. He was only gone a minute, during which time Rebel threatened to make her stay in the hospital if she didn't calm down.

"The doctor said he'd be by in a minute," he said, reclaiming his chair. "You're one famous woman, Gypsy. There must be fifty reporters in the hall waiting to talk to you."

All five men watched in apparent dismay as the color drained from Gypsy's face.

"No." She shook her head. "No reporters." She turned to Rebel and made a desperate plea. "Please," she begged, "make them go away."

Why, Gypsy wondered, hadn't it occurred to him that the reason she didn't want to talk to reporters was because they might use her name in a story, or worse, her picture? If any information about her wound up in the paper, there was a chance her father would see it. Then he would know where to come looking for her.

"No worries, Gypsy," Rebel said as if suddenly understanding. "I'll take care of it."

When he left the room, Gypsy turned to the four curious faces staring at her. It was Judd that finally spoke. "Um, Gypsy..."

"I don't want to talk about it!" She cut him off.

It probably hadn't taken much for Judd and the others to figure out that Gypsy was hiding something. But from everything she'd heard about them, she knew there was a pretty good chance each one of them had a thing or two they didn't want anyone else to know. Praying they wouldn't start playing Twenty Questions, Gypsy continued to stare at Judd without blinking.

"We just wanted you to know that we're glad you're okay."

She had a feeling that wasn't exactly what he'd been planning to say and was grateful to him for respecting her privacy.

When Rebel returned, he looked curiously from his family to Gypsy. "What's going on?"

"Nothing, bro. We just told Gypsy that we're glad she's okay."

Rebel glanced at Gypsy. She knew he was looking for conformation that nothing had happened, so she nodded. He seemed satisfied, at least for the moment, and she was grateful when he let it go.

"I ran into your doctor in the hall," Reb told her. "He said he'd discharge you if I promised to watch over you for the next few days. The reporters are gone, but I don't know for how long. So let's get you dressed and out of here before they come back."

The look of gratitude on Gypsy's face said it all, but she

thanked him anyway. "I don't know what I would've done if I'd had to stay here."

"Just seeing you relax is thanks enough for me, darlin'. It even makes up for having to deal with that arrogant doctor of yours. I had to threaten the man with physical harm before he agreed to let you go home."

Gypsy's eyes widened, but she didn't say anything. She knew Rebel's days of getting what he wanted by threatening people were long gone, and that he normally wouldn't have done such a thing. But he knew how desperate she was to leave. And she was grateful he'd fixed it so she wouldn't have to spend one more minute in the hospital.

Rebel tossed her a large pair of white nurse's scrubs and flashed the boys a dirty look. "A little privacy, please."

Judd, Brady, Kane, and Flynn practically tripped over each other trying to get out the door.

When just the two of them were left, Rebel sat down on the edge of Gypsy's bed as she tried to figure out how to put on the scrubs. "Sorry about the size. It was all they had. You need some help?"

She nodded. "Please."

Reaching behind her, Rebel untied the hospital gown then turned his back so she could put the top on.

As she gingerly worked her way into the shirt, Gypsy wondered—if the situation hadn't been serious and she wasn't so desperate to leave the hospital—whether or not Reb would've turned away. She hadn't forgotten that they'd declared their love for each other in the basement of the diner. And even being as scared as she was right now, Gypsy couldn't shake her nervous excitement; Reb standing beside her while she was only half-dressed was making her insides tingle.

After helping her step into the pants, Reb opened the door and brought in a wheelchair.

Gypsy took one look at the chair, placed her hands on her hips, and shook her head. "No way, Rebel. I am *not* riding in that thing."

He smiled at her defiance. "Sorry, darlin', hospital rules. If you don't ride, you don't leave."

Gypsy reluctantly gave in and walked slowly across the floor, carefully planting herself in the chair. When she was seated comfortably, Rebel walked around and knelt beside her. "You didn't want to talk to the reporters because you're afraid that if your name gets in the paper, your father might see it. Am I right?"

She bent her head and looked down at the floor. "He's going to know where to find me now."

He put a finger under her chin and tilted it back up until she was looking into his eyes. "Gypsy, I love you. And I'll always do everything in my power to make sure no one hurts you. Do you understand?"

She nodded. "I understand. I love you, too."

He took her hand in his. "No matter how hard you try, it's going to be almost impossible to keep your name out of the papers. You know that, don't you?"

"I know."

"Whatever happens, Gypsy, we'll deal with it together. Okay?"

Gypsy wished she had a little more fight left in her, but right now she just wanted to get out of the hospital, go home, and lose herself in the safety and comfort of Rebel's strong arms. "Okay."

"Good. Now, first thing's first. The power's out at the garage, but I'm going to take you there to stay with me anyway."

"How come?"

"Because it may not be safe for you to stay in your apartment alone. I have to work and help the guys put the garage back together, but I want you close enough where I can keep an eye on you."

"Do you really think my father will come after me?"

"You can answer that question better than I can. But if what you've told me about him is true, I'd say it's a very real possibility."

Gypsy closed her eyes and bent forward. Rebel moved closer so she could lean on him. "Why, Reb? Why is this happening? My worst nightmare is coming true and there's nothing I can do about it. I'd hoped that by leaving Baltimore I might be free of my father. Now he's going to be led right to me."

"It'll be okay, Gypsy," he promised, "in the end, everything will be okay."

She nodded. "I hope you're right."

"I don't like to make promises without knowing exactly what I'm up against, but you've got my word, Gypsy. I'll do whatever it takes to keep you safe."

"I know you will, and I love you for it. But what about my stuff?" she asked. "There are a few things I'm going to need."

"You can make a list when we get to the garage. After I get you settled, I'll send Judd and one of the boys over to pick up your things."

Warning bells went off in her head. "But what will your

brother and cousins think when they see my empty apartment? I know they've already figured out that I'm hiding something. Am I going to have to tell them everything now?" she asked, her voice just as panic stricken as when she first awoke. "This is all happening so fast that I can't even think straight."

Rebel tilted his head to the side and placed a light kiss on her cheek. "I know you didn't want anyone to know your secrets, darlin', but we need to let everyone know what's going on."

"Everyone?"

"Not *everyone*, just the guys who work at the garage, including Jimmy and Frank. They need to know...just in case."

Gypsy's head snapped up. "Just in case what?"

"In case of trouble, Gypsy. They can't help you if they don't know something's wrong."

"Why?" She didn't understand. "Why would they want to help me?"

"I told you months ago, you're family now. And family takes care of each other. Why the hell do you think the boys were asleep in those chairs over there instead of outside getting drunk in the bed of my pickup truck?"

He gave his head a slight shake when she shrugged. "It breaks my heart that you've never experienced what it's like to be part of a family, to have people care and worry about you. And they do care about you, Gypsy. Each one of them refused to leave when the doctor tried to throw us out of here. I know you've got issues with trust. But my family and I won't betray you. Accepting help from people isn't a sign of weakness."

Gypsy actually smiled. "I can only imagine what a hard

time you all must have given the doctor when he tried to get you to leave. You're all such good men. And that's exactly why I don't want anyone putting themselves in danger for me. I'll handle this problem alone, just like I've always done."

Looking puzzled, he stared at her.

"They don't even really know me," she explained. "And it isn't fair to make them feel obligated to help me."

"They've known you for months, Gypsy." Seemingly angered by her resistance, he yelled. "They like you; and they're going to watch out for you whether you want them to or not! So it would be a good idea to let them know what kind of trouble might be coming. Don't you think?"

Gypsy was silent for a long moment. "I guess I can't argue with that," she gave in. "But you have to understand something, Reb." She looked up into those McCassey royal blue eyes. "This is all new to me. You've always had people to watch your back, but in the past twenty-four hours, I've gone from not wanting to rely on anyone else to being completely dependant on an entire family. I hate knowing I might not be able to take care of myself if something happens. But you're right. I know the boys won't betray me, so let's tell them."

Rebel nodded his approval and turned the wheelchair toward the door. "We'll do it once we get back to the garage. I don't want you anywhere near here when those reporters start sniffing around again."

* * * *

Judd and the rest of the boys rode in the bed of the pickup truck on the way to the garage, so Gypsy and Rebel could have some time to themselves.

In order to be able to drive through the part of town that hadn't been cleaned up yet, Rebel was forced to slow the

truck to a crawl and lower the snowplow. He pushed debris
to the side of the road, clearing a narrow path for the truck.
He saw Gypsy close her eyes as they approached the diner,
and was thankful when they finally pulled into the dark parking lot of the garage.

Outlaw ran out to meet them, and Judd showered the
dog with attention as Rebel helped Gypsy out of the truck.
One by one, Brady, Kane, and Flynn jumped from the back.
They were met by Frank and Jimmy, each holding a flashlight.

"It's three o'clock in the morning," Frank said, shining his
light on the truck. "We didn't expect to see you boys until
sometime tomorrow."

"We came to clean up," Brady told him.

"In the middle of the night? There's no power, and it's
too damn dark in there to see anything. You all might as well
go on home."

"Aw, shit," Kane complained. "I don't feel like walking
all the way home, I was counting on crashing here tonight."

Gypsy turned to Reb. "We could all stay at my place."

He looked at her in surprise.

"I know it's small, but if the guys don't mind sleeping on
the floor…"

"Hell, I'm all for that," Kane yelled and jumped back into
the truck's bed. "Let's go to Gypsy's."

"Shut the hell up," Reb scolded, and Kane immediately
stopped talking. Reb turned to Gypsy. "Are you sure this is
what you want?" he asked, knowing that once the others saw
her empty apartment, there'd be no turning back; she would
be forced to explain everything.

"I'm sure. I want to tell them what they need to know
before I lose my nerve."

"All right, all of you back in the truck. We'll spend the rest of the night at Gypsy's apartment and come back here at first light."

"No hurry," Frank told them. "We're heading out, too. Let's meet back here around noon. Outlaw can take care of things until then."

At the sound of his name, the dog let loose with a loud bark as if to assure them that the garage and its contents would be fine.

Since Gypsy was almost asleep by the time they arrived at her apartment, Rebel eased her out of the truck and carried her upstairs. He tucked her into the sleeping bag and whispered, "We're all going out for a smoke," even though he knew she didn't hear him. He brushed the hair away from her face and softly kissed her lips. "I'll be back in a few minutes."

The electricity was out at the apartment, too, so before he left, Rebel lit one of Gypsy's candles and placed it on the bedroom windowsill. He didn't want her to be scared if she woke up before he came back inside.

On his way out to the living room, Rebel decided he was going to have to be the one to tell his family what was going on with Gypsy. The guys had been nice enough not to say anything about the empty apartment when they first walked in, but he knew they were curious.

Shining his flashlight on the four men sitting in the dark on the living room floor, he motioned toward the door. "Let's go outside for a smoke."

They walked single file out of the building and stopped outside at the bottom of the concrete steps. Four of them stood in a line leaning on the brick half-wall. Rebel stood in front.

Brady dug a pack of Marlboro's out from the front pocket of his jeans and passed it down the line, each cousin taking a cigarette, striking a match, and inhaling deeply as he lit up.

When the pack got to Judd, he lit an extra one, handed it to Rebel, and asked the question that was on everyone's mind. "Why's her place so empty?"

"It's a long story."

"In your whole life, bro, you've never worried about anything until it's been absolutely necessary. What's eatin' you?"

Rebel raised his head and looked over at his family. They were a motley crew; that was for sure. There was Flynn, the quiet, skinny nineteen-year-old who puzzled them all, and Brady and Kane, who spent as much time bickering and goofing off as they did working.

Then there was Judd.

Rebel and Judd had always had a unique relationship. As kids, they'd nearly killed each other a dozen times; the ten months that separated them being the fuel that fed their raging sibling rivalry. They found common ground as teenagers, partying and stirring up trouble with the rest of their cousins, but then they'd gone down different roads.

By age twenty, Rebel had grown tired of loose women throwing themselves at him, messing around with the law, and the alcohol induced hazes he was always trapped in the mornings after hard nights of partying.

Now, even at thirty-one, Judd still hadn't outgrown the wild life. He worked as hard as anyone else at the garage during the day, but as soon as it was quitting time, he took off and caused trouble with the rest of the McCassey's who'd yet to calm down. They'd all gotten into a lot of trouble over the years, and the task of rescuing them usually fell to Rebel.

Somehow, he'd become their unofficial leader. His cousins all looked up to him, even the older ones. He hadn't asked for the job, even occasionally resented it. But when push came to shove, he was always there when they needed him. That's how he knew they'd be there for Gypsy now.

Cigarette in hand, Rebel sat down on the steps and brought his knees to his chest. In a weary voice, he launched into Gypsy's story. He included everything; her mother's murder, her father's threat to kill her, and all the different foster homes. He even threw in the fact that she'd never had any friends and why. To save her from further embarrassment—if that was possible—Rebel left out the part about her almost being raped.

"I'm sorry, bro," Judd said sincerely. "Gypsy always seems so happy. It's hard to believe she's been through all that. She doesn't deserve to have it so rough."

"No, she doesn't." Rebel took a long drag on his cigarette. "And I have a feeling the worst isn't over. Gypsy's father's probably pretty close to being released from prison, if he hasn't been already." Rebel took another long drag. "And my gut tells me that if Gypsy's name winds up in tomorrow morning's paper, which it probably will, he'll come here looking for her. But as sure as I'm sitting here, I'll kill that bastard before I let him lay a hand on her."

"He'd have to get through all of us to hurt her," Judd said. "And that'll never happen."

"That's right, Rebel," Kane added, his voice void of its usual humor. "No one gets past the McCassey boys. We'll keep Gypsy safe."

Brady and Flynn ended the conversation by echoing their cousin's statement.

Judd sat down on the step next to his brother, made a fist, and held it out in front of him. The gesture was something Rebel and his two brothers had done since they were kids. It was their silent way of saying all for one, and one for all. "No worries."

Rebel didn't want to thank Judd for offering his help because he hoped to hell he wouldn't need it. Instead, he touched his brother's fist with his own, saying nothing.

* * * *

Saturday morning dawned as dreary as Friday night had ended. It was hot and humid again, the skies dark with another approaching storm. Although it wasn't raining yet, thunder rumbled loudly.

Gypsy stirred awake early, the pain from her broken ribs making it almost impossible to get comfortable. To her right, Rebel was sound asleep in his filthy coveralls.

Still wearing the nurse's scrubs, she was desperate to get washed, dressed, and into some of her own clothes. Having lost one of her knapsacks and a complete change of clothing when the diner collapsed, the only clothes she had left were two pair of cut-off jean shorts, one pair of long pants, her overalls, and a few T-shirts.

"Where are you going?" Rebel asked when she stood up.

"Sorry," she whispered. "I didn't mean to wake you."

He sat up and reached for his boots. "Don't worry about it. I'm surprised I was asleep with all the rumbling going on outside."

Her face blanched. "Are you worried about the weather? Do you think we'll have another tornado?"

Rebel pulled on one boot, then the other. He tied the long laces in double knots, stood, and held out his arms.

Gypsy walked into them and received a gentle hug.

"The weather's the least of our problems," he told her. "Right now, I'm more interested in what's in the morning paper."

Gypsy's knees weakened, and she had to hold onto Reb for support. She'd almost forgotten about the reporters. What was she going to do if her name was plastered all over the front page? And what if her father saw it?

"Mrs. Gibson across the hall gets The Record Herald on the weekends, and she's never up before noon," Gypsy explained. "I'm sure she wouldn't mind if we read her paper as long as we put it back before she gets up."

Rebel nodded. "I'll go get it. You need a hand getting dressed?"

She managed a half-smile. This wasn't exactly how she'd planned on having Reb see her bare body for the first time, but she didn't have a choice. Her sore ribs made it hard to move.

"Just with my shirt, if you don't mind. And maybe you could check the bandage on my ribs, it feels loose."

As if undressing injured women was something he did everyday, Rebel carefully removed Gypsy's shirt and gently ran his hands along the bandage to make sure it was securely fastened. She was grateful he pretended not to notice the uncomfortable look on her face and the tear that slipped down her cheek as she stared at the wall on the opposite side of the room. The pain in her side, mixed with the embarrassment of having to turn to someone else for help was almost too much for Gypsy to handle. She was relieved when Reb finally pulled the T-shirt over her head. After helping to guide her arms into the sleeves, he excused himself and left the room so she could change her shorts.

After waking the guys asleep in the living room, Rebel retrieved the newspaper from across the hall. Just as he'd feared, the tornado was front page news. Even worse, the reporter had written all about how he and Judd had risked their lives to pull Gypsy from the wreckage of the diner.

"Damn!"

"They mentioned my name, didn't they?" Gypsy asked as she walked into the room.

"I didn't mean for you to find out this way, but yeah, your name's in here. Mine, too. And Judd's. There's a story about the three of us on page two."

He held the paper in the air for Gypsy to see, just as she lowered her head and buried her face in her hands. "Why? Why couldn't the reporters just leave us alone?"

Rebel tossed the paper to his brother and walked to Gypsy. He put his right arm around her shoulders and carefully drew her close. "Freedom of the press, darlin'. They have the right to print anything they want."

"It's not fair," she cried.

"No, it isn't. But there's not a damn thing we can do about it."

Scared of what could possibly happen to her, Gypsy looked to Rebel for reassurance. His hands cupped her face, and he looked into her eyes. "Nothing's going to happen to you. I promise."

Judd cleared his throat, interrupting their tender exchange. "We're all going to back to town so you two can settle everything here."

Without taking his gaze off Gypsy, Rebel waved to his brother and cousins as they quietly slipped out the door.

After regaining her composure, Gypsy spent the next half hour gathering her meager belongings so Reb could load them into the bed of his pickup truck. When everything was secure, he went back inside to help close the blinds and tend to a few last minute details...including returning Mrs. Gibson's newspaper.

Despite the circumstances, Gypsy decided she was excited about moving in with Rebel, even if she was a little sad at the way it had come about. They loved each other and probably would've moved in together eventually. Still, part of her couldn't help but wonder if he was going to resent having to look over his shoulder all the time. He was a busy man, yet bound and determined to protect her from anyone and anything that could possibly harm her.

She'd never had such unconditional love, and cherished the feelings Reb had for her. That's exactly why, at the first sign of trouble, she'd be gone.

Chapter 9

McCassey's Garage was up and running two days after the tornado had devastated parts of downtown Hagerstown. Refusing to live with Reb without doing something to earn her keep, Gypsy insisted that he accept her help at the garage. Although Reb thought that was ridiculous, he told Gypsy he understood her need to feel useful and gave her a job helping Frank's wife, Rose, answer phones and book appointments. As it turned out, Rose couldn't have gotten by without the younger woman's help. In addition to their regular customers, the garage was swamped with calls from people whose cars had been damaged by the tornado's flying debris.

Gypsy and Rebel both enjoyed the living arrangements, and found that no matter how much time they spent together, it never seemed to be enough. They shared his king-sized bed at night, platonically for the moment, because of her broken ribs. But with each passing night, Rebel found it harder and harder to keep his hands off her.

Gypsy knew he wanted to make love to her. And although she wanted the same thing, she was nervous because she'd never been with a man before. Reb was definitely the right man for her, and she promised herself that by the time the doctor gave her the okay to participate in physical activity, she'd be ready.

During the three weeks it took Gypsy's ribs to heal, she was content sitting behind a desk and answering phones. The days passed quickly, and she felt like she was contributing something to Reb and his family in exchange for all they were doing for her. However, even after the doctor had given Gypsy a clean bill of health, Rebel was still refusing to let her do anything or go anywhere by herself.

"Rebel, please," she pleaded as he bent over the engine of a car. "I just want to go pick up lunch."

"Today's Monday," he shouted from underneath the hood. "It's Judd's turn."

"Then can I at least go with him? It's been weeks since I've been out of the garage for more than five minutes. I'm going stir crazy in here!"

Covered in grease, Rebel put the torque wrench he was holding into the back pocket of his coveralls and wiped his hands on a rag.

Gypsy could tell by the look on his face that his answer was going to be no. Frustrated because she felt he didn't understand her needs, she sighed, put her hands on her hips and glared at him.

Then she noticed he was still holding the oily rag.

Seething with anger, Gypsy reached out, grabbed it from his hand, and shook it at him. "I do not need a babysitter, Rebel McCassey!" Turning on her heel, she stormed toward the open bay door, almost colliding with Frank, who was walking inside.

"What's up, Gypsy? Where are you going?" Frank asked, innocently.

"Out!" she called without looking back. But the hysterical laughter coming from Brady and Kane stopped her. She'd picked up some highly colorful language hanging around the garage, and would've used it on them if she hadn't still been holding the oily rag. Crumpling it into a ball, she turned toward the two cousins and hurled it at them. Kane stepped to the side as the rag sailed by and landed on the floor between him and Brady. "Oh, get back to work!" Gypsy yelled, then to Reb's older brother, said. "Let's go, Judd."

* * * *

Rebel had known the moment he saw Gypsy's expression that he should let her go. He had no real claim to her and no right to tell her what to do. Yet, ever since she'd gotten hurt, she'd listened and followed his orders about not going anywhere alone. He admitted that she did need to get out, but she wasn't safe out in the open, especially with Judd. He was too impulsive in dangerous situations to be able to protect her.

Rebel didn't want Gypsy leaving, but he knew by the intensity of her outburst that there was no stopping her. So he decided to let her go, hoping the time away would help her cool off.

Had the situation not been so serious, he would have admired her spirit and the fearless way she'd stood up to him. But every minute she was in public, Gypsy was in danger of being spotted by her father, or anyone he'd sent looking for her. When she returned from picking up lunch, Rebel was going to remind her just exactly how much danger she was in.

Looking from Judd to Gypsy's retreating figure and back again, Rebel stared at Judd, who had yet to follow Gypsy, silently instructing his brother to keep a close eye on her.

Judd nodded and walked outside.

Although Brady was still laughing after Judd and Gypsy were gone, he was half-heartedly trying to work. Kane, however, was more interested in ragging on his cousin. "Man, I heard them red heads have fiery tempers," he teased. "She sure told you, Rebel!"

She sure had. But Rebel wasn't about to admit it to those two fools. Instead, he reached into his back pocket, pulled out the wrench he'd placed there earlier, and threw it across the garage where it landed with a loud clank against Kane's tool cabinet. "Shut the fuck up, or you're both fired!" he yelled, which successfully put an end to Kane's smartass comments.

* * * *

Gypsy climbed up into the tow truck next to Rebel's brother, and he pulled out of the parking lot headed for Pizza Hut.

"That sure was something, Gypsy," Judd said, grinning. "Remind me never to make you mad."

At the sound of Judd's voice, Gypsy turned to look at him, suddenly realizing that with the exception of that day in the diner, this was the first time the two of them had ever been alone. Unsure of what to say, she guessed offering an apology for her outburst was a good start. "I'm sorry, Judd. I shouldn't have yelled like that."

Still grinning, Judd shook his head. "You don't need to apologize to me, girl. Other than Blackie, you're the only person I know who's ever yelled at Rebel and lived to tell about it. Watching that was more fun than I've had in a long time."

Gypsy smiled at him. After observing Judd for the past few months, she'd learned two things about him. The first was that Judd knew people were afraid of him and seemed to enjoy doing his best to live up to his bad reputation.

But that was only around people other than his family.

Because the second thing was that Judd, along with every other McCassey she'd met, was extremely loyal to his family. They put each other first before anything else, including business. When he was at the garage, Judd was one of the guys. He laughed and joked around with everyone, including her, yet she still got the feeling he was more sensitive than he let on.

"Rebel loves you, Gypsy," Judd said, breaking into her thoughts. "He just wants to make sure you stay safe."

"I love him, too. But it's been almost a month since the tornado and no one's come looking for me."

"Yet."

Her heart fell into the pit of her stomach. "What's that supposed to mean?"

"Aw shit, Gypsy, I shouldn't have said anything. It's not my place to get into this with you."

"Well, it's too late now," she huffed, "spit it out."

He gave her a sideways glance. "Fine. Rebel's gonna kick my ass for upsetting you, but here it is. You shouldn't be under the impression you're safe. Just because there hasn't been any trouble from your father so far doesn't mean there won't be. He might just be biding his time, waiting to come after you when you least expect it."

"Oh God, I hadn't thought of that! No wonder Reb doesn't want me going anywhere alone. And I yelled at him for it! How could I have been so stupid? For all we know, someone was watching the garage, just waiting to catch me by myself."

Judd reached across the bench seat and gently squeezed her hand, causing her to flinch. "I didn't mean to scare you, Gypsy. But you need to understand that Rebel's a smart man. He never does anything unless it's for a good reason. If he wants you to stick close by, you should listen to him. It's for your own good."

Gypsy was quiet the rest of the way to Pizza Hut as she mulled over Judd's words. Were he and Reb right? Was her father hanging back, waiting for just the right moment to sneak into town and kill her?

No longer concerned for her own safety, Gypsy's thoughts turned to Reb. She knew he'd stop at nothing to protect her, and she suddenly felt sick to her stomach as she realized what needed to be done.

If she wasn't in town when her father came looking for her, Reb wouldn't have to protect her. He wouldn't be in danger. He was the only person to ever show genuine love and concern for her, and she loved him too much to let him get hurt.

"...to get the pizza. Gypsy?"

Gypsy whipped her head around when she realized Judd had been talking to her. "What?"

"I said...I'm gonna run inside and pick up the pizza." He gave her a questioning look. "Are you okay?"

She nodded slightly and forced a smile. "Fine."

Judd squinted and looked at her with an accusing stare. "I don't believe you." When she didn't respond, he added, "I'll be right back," then opened the door and climbed out of the tow truck. Gypsy watched as he lit a cigarette and tossed the pack onto the seat. "Don't move," he ordered, then slammed the door and walked inside the restaurant.

As soon as he was out of sight, Gypsy pulled the handle of the passenger-side door and opened it just enough to slip out. She took a deep breath and told herself, "It's now or never," knowing this would probably be her only opportunity to slip away unnoticed. Back at the garage, there would be a dozen pair of eyes watching her and escape would be impossible.

She had no idea where she was going or what she would do when she got there, but that could all be worked out later. Right now, the most important thing was keeping Rebel and his family safe, which meant she had to get out of town. Sneaking around to the side of the building, she walked up the small incline to the main road and stuck out her thumb.

As the minutes passed, she couldn't figure out why so many cars were passing her by. Then she heard a familiar voice behind her. "Just what the hell do you think you're doing?"

Gypsy whirled around and saw Rebel standing five feet away, arms crossed, looking madder than she'd ever seen him. "How long have you been standing there?"

"Long enough to know you're trying to hitch a ride," he said angrily. "Where's Judd?"

It was then that Gypsy spotted Judd walking toward them wearing the same angry look as his brother. Knowing all hell was probably about to break loose, she pointed in his direction. "Right behind you."

The two waited quietly as Judd approached. When he reached them, Judd surprised his brother by lighting into him. "You could have at least come inside and let me know you were taking her!"

Rebel looked puzzled. "What?"

"It scared the shit out of me when I walked outside and

she was gone. Why didn't you tell me you were leaving?"

Rebel turned his head slowly and glared at Gypsy. "Well, the man asked you a question. Why didn't you tell him you were leaving?"

"You mean she didn't leave with you?"

"No!" Rebel hissed. "I found her out here hitchhiking."

"Hitchhiking?" Scowling, Judd turned to Gypsy. "I told you to stay in the truck! For Christ's sake, Gypsy, I thought somebody grabbed you!"

"That's exactly why I left!" she yelled, startling both men. "It isn't your job to watch out for me, Judd. Or yours." She pointed to Reb. "Don't you understand? If my father comes looking for me and I'm not here, he'll just leave. But if I'm staying at the garage, he'll come after all of you, too. I couldn't stand it if anything happened to any one in your family because of me." Directing her attention to Reb, she said, "Especially you."

When Rebel reached out and pulled her close, Gypsy knew his anger had faded. She wrapped her arms around his waist, not caring that traffic on the main road had slowed to watch them.

"Come on." Judd pushed them toward the parking lot. "We've given these people enough of a show."

When they reached the tow truck, Gypsy explained more about why she thought leaving town would keep everyone safe.

"But it won't keep you safe," Rebel reminded her. "I don't want you to be alone."

"I've been alone all my life, Reb. No one has ever really cared about me, except those who were paid to by Social Services. But then you came into my life and loved me for real. I can't fool myself into believing I'll be able to hide from my father forever. He'll find me eventually, and probably kill me like he promised to all those years ago."

Rebel took a step toward her, placed one finger under her chin and tilted her head until her gaze met his. "Don't give up that easily. I know you must be tired of running, Gypsy, so stay. Stay here with me and fight. I'll protect you."

Gypsy wanted to stay with all her heart. She hadn't known it was possible to be as happy as she was with Reb. He loved her, and she suddenly realized that not only did he want her to stay so she would be safe, but for his own happiness as well. Gypsy knew she had no right to deny him that happiness, so she decided to stay. There was only one thing still bothering her.

As if he was reading her mind, Rebel shook his head. "I'll be fine, too. I promise."

She nodded. "Then I'll stay."

Rebel sighed and pulled her to him again. She buried her face in his chest and closed her eyes.

"But you have to trust me, okay? No going anywhere alone and no more running away. Got it?"

"I got it," she said, then remembered she owed him an apology. "Reb?"

"Hmm?"

"About before...at the garage..."

Rebel chuckled. "Forget it, darlin'. I'm just sorry it took you standing in the middle of the garage shaking an oily rag in my face for me to realize you were right. You needed to get out. And from now on, when you want to go somewhere, I'll take you."

Rebel kissed the top of her head as he scanned the parking

lot for Judd, who had silently retreated and was sitting on a bench by the Pizza Hut smoking a cigarette. Rebel gave Gypsy a final squeeze before releasing her and motioned for his brother to join them.

Judd walked over and leaned against the back of the tow truck. Gypsy cautiously approached him, praying he wasn't going to start yelling at her again. "I shouldn't have run away," she admitted. "I'm sorry for scaring you."

"You should be sorry, girl. My damn life flashed before my eyes when I thought I was going to have to tell Rebel I lost you."

Gypsy didn't know what to say until she saw the corners of Judd's mouth curve up into a smile. "So I'm forgiven?" she asked shyly.

"Yeah, but my chaperoning days are over. Next time you want to go out, tag along with someone else." Then he surprised her by leaning down and kissing her cheek. "No, worries," he whispered and looked at Reb. "I'll see you two later. I've got pizzas to deliver."

Rebel took Gypsy to Margie's Deli for lunch and they wandered back into the garage an hour after Judd had returned with the pizzas. No one bothered to give them a second glance when they came in, which Gypsy assumed meant that Rebel had probably threatened Brady and Kane with something after she left earlier. It also meant that, to his credit, Judd hadn't told anyone what happened at Pizza Hut. If he had, Gypsy had no doubt she would've had a thousand questions thrown at her, no matter what Reb had threatened to do to his cousins if they didn't get any work done.

* * * *

After Rose had gone home for the day, Gypsy sat behind

her desk moping, questioning the decision she'd made to stay in town. Kane wasn't the only one to notice how unhappy she looked, but he was the only one with enough nerve to approach Rebel, who was under the hood of a car again with his head buried in the engine.

"Something happen at lunch today?" Kane asked his cousin.

"Whatever's on your mind, Kane, just spit it out. I'm in no mood to play games with you."

When Judd, Brady, and Flynn heard the exchange between the two cousins, they slowly made their way over until all four of them were standing just a few feet behind the car.

Kane winked at them and grinned. "Well, if you insist."

Annoyed, Rebel backed away from the car and stood upright. When he saw everyone staring at him, he knew he was about to be ambushed. He threw out a sarcastic, "What?" and waited to hear what they had to say.

Kane suggested a campout up on the hill behind their grandfather's barn. "Come on, man," he said, excitedly. "We'll take the girls up, a few cases of beer, a little Zeppelin…"

"A few joints," Rebel broke in. "Maybe a little drunken target practice…no thanks, Kane. I'm done messing around with that shit."

"Aw, ain't none of us mess around with it anymore either, Rebel. It'll be good clean fun. I promise."

Rebel's gaze flew to Kane, who was grinning like a fox. Kane was only right about one thing. Everything the McCassey cousins did together was good fun, but nothing about any of it was clean. Rebel had gotten into more trouble than he cared to remember during their campouts, and had stopped taking chances with the law years ago.

"If you want to go camping, Kane, go ahead. You don't need my permission."

But Rebel knew he wanted it.

Still trying to convince his cousin, Kane added, "I'll even make sure Sheriff Johnson doesn't bother us."

Bile rose in the back of Rebel's throat at the mention of Sheriff Ben Johnson. He had grown up with Dolan McCassey, Rebel and Judd's father. Johnson hated every last one of the McCassey's for something that had gone on between him and Dolan decades earlier, and had spent the better part of his career trying to catch them in the act of doing something illegal. The big bust had always eluded him, but he'd gotten Rebel and a handful his cousins on a number of misdemeanors over the years.

Rebel reached into the back pocket of his sleeveless coveralls and pulled out a pack of cigarettes. Staring back at the anxious faces of his brother and cousins, he lit one and sat down to think.

Camping out with his family had been one of his favorite things to do as a kid. They'd all spread sleeping bags in the woods behind his grandfather's barn, light a campfire, and spend hours trying to scare each other in the dark. When they got older, their innocent fun gave way to dangerous games when they discovered alcohol and firearms. Still, those were some of the best times Rebel ever had.

He missed the fun that had come to an abrupt end when the boys were in their late teens and their grandfather's nearest neighbors started calling the police every time they heard gunfire.

Thinking about how much fun a campout would be, Rebel smiled to himself. It had been a long while since he and all his cousins were together. Gypsy would probably enjoy it too, since she'd never been part of a real family. But even though it probably would be just good, clean, fun, he wasn't taking any chances.

Rebel put out his cigarette. "I'll take care of Sheriff Johnson," he told them. "Brady, Kane, spread the word. Flynn...get beer." Suddenly remembering the gruesome experiences they'd had with moonshine as teenagers, he pointed at his cousin, saying adamantly, "And only beer. We'll meet behind Granddaddy's barn at ten. Not a minute before."

* * * *

By eight o'clock, Gypsy had showered, dressed in her only pair of jeans and old white T-shirt, and was hanging her head of thick curls upside down over the side of the bed waiting for it to dry.

Rebel entered the room wrapped in a towel from the waist down, his shoulder length hair still dripping. He took one look at Gypsy lying on her back and laughed. "What are you doing?"

She rolled over and sat up slowly. "My hair takes forever to dry. Sometimes hanging upside down speeds up the process."

"I see," Rebel said, still smiling as he walked to the dresser and opened the bottom drawer. He pulled out a hair dryer and threw it to her. "Try this next time."

"Thanks." She raised her arms and caught it in mid-air. "Don't tell me this is yours."

Rebel shook his head. "You won't find any beauty secrets here, darlin'. That contraption belongs to Flynn." He winked at her. "But you didn't hear it from me."

She thanked him again and walked down the hall to the bathroom. When her hair was dry, she returned to the apartment. Rebel was standing in front of the bed waiting for her, dressed and ready.

"I'm not used to seeing you wear anything other than mechanics coveralls," Gypsy commented, "you look really good."

Reb chuckled. "Thanks for the compliment. You don't look so bad yourself, darlin'."

"Maybe, but I'm sure those faded blue jeans clinging to your muscular legs wouldn't look nearly as good on me."

"Oh," he said with a sly grin as he touched his black sleeveless shirt—which revealed to Gypsy what she was used to seeing everyday; his tattoo, and large biceps and forearms. "But this would."

Rebel wrapped his arms around Gypsy and pulled her close, but she stopped him suddenly. "Hey, I didn't know you wore jewelry," she said when she noticed a thin silver chain around his neck.

His hand moved to the necklace. "My mom gave me this when I was ten. It used to be a lot bigger…I've grown since then."

"It's nice. Do you wear it a lot?"

"All the time. The damn thing's soldered on."

"Why?" she asked.

"Because when Blackie was fifteen, he discovered our grandfather's soldering gun and decided to have a little fun. He stole a spool of solder from the hardware store and told me he could fix my necklace so it'd never fall off. Like an idiot, I let him do it."

"Well…" she said, defending him. "You were only ten."

"True. But you know what I got for my trouble?"

"I'm afraid to ask."

"You should be. Blackie dropped the gun on the back of my neck and I wound up with a second degree burn." Rebel sat on the edge of the bed and swept his hair, which was almost dry, away from his neck. "See?"

Gypsy climbed onto the bed behind Reb and propped herself up on her knees. She lightly ran her finger over the two-inch scar. "That must've hurt."

"Not more than your broken ribs, but enough to scare me away from playing with anything hot, or trusting my brother, for a long, long time."

He tried to turn around, but Gypsy leaned into him, forcing him to stay put. Her hair spilled over his shoulders as she lowered her head, softly kissing the back of his neck. A low groan escaped his lips as her hands roamed down his arms and across his chest.

With an overwhelming need to touch her, Rebel suddenly stood and turned around. "Do you have any idea what you do to me?" His question went unanswered as he kneeled on the bed and put his hands behind her head, drawing her to him.

His mouth claimed hers in a kiss that was slow and easy at first, deepening with every thrust of his tongue. When Rebel felt her body press against his, he nearly lost control.

Easing her onto the bed, time stood still as they touched and fondled each other. It wasn't until Outlaw started barking that Rebel remembered his brother was supposed to meet them at the garage.

He pulled away reluctantly, ending the kiss. "We have to stop, Gypsy. Judd's downstairs."

"He can wait," she whispered, trying to pull him close

again.

"Of course he can…for about two minutes. If we don't get down there, he'll find his way up here."

Frowning, she followed him when he climbed off the bed. They stopped in the doorway and shared one last kiss. "You ready to go?"

"I was," she said, "but I think I'd better look in the mirror first. I don't want to meet the rest of your family looking like I've been rolling around in bed."

"Take your time," he told her. "I need to talk to Judd anyway."

When Gypsy headed into the bathroom, Rebel went downstairs to meet his brother.

"Hey, bro. Where's Gypsy?"

"Getting dressed."

"We got time for a smoke?"

Rebel yelled to Gypsy that they needed a cigarette, and the brothers walked outside.

"How are you going to make sure Sheriff Johnson doesn't bother us?"

Reb laughed. "I'm going to make a little house call in about twenty minutes, insure that there's no possible way his squad car will be leaving the station tonight."

Judd smiled. "Need some help?"

"Nope, I got it covered. Just stay here and keep an eye on Gypsy for me, will you? I'll be back when I'm done, then we'll head up to the barn together."

"Sure thing, bro."

Judd and Gypsy only had to wait ten minutes for Rebel to return. He walked inside holding the spark plugs from Sheriff Johnson's car, causing Judd to break into a fit of laughter.

"The car won't start without these," Rebel explained to Gypsy, "and since Johnson doesn't know anything about cars, he won't know how to fix the problem."

"How do you know he doesn't know anything about cars?"

"Because he brings in his personal car—the one he drives when he's off duty—to be fixed every time it makes a strange noise. The problem last time was that one of the fan belts needed to be tightened. If he had half a brain, he could've fixed it himself; all he had to do was open the hood and pick up a wrench. Instead, he dropped off the car—swearing the entire time he was here that the engine sounded as if it was going to seize any minute—and thought nothing of paying the two hundred dollars I charged him when he came to pick it up."

Gypsy's eyes widened. "You charged him two hundred dollars to tighten a fan belt?"

"I would've charged him four if my conscious would've let me get away with it. He's done nothing since I was a kid but harass my family and cause us trouble. He's damn lucky I even agree to fix his car. And if he's too stupid and lazy to learn the basic mechanics of a car, then he deserves to be ripped off."

After clearing her throat, Gypsy took a deep breath. "I guess we're safe, then."

"Yup. Johnson won't be bothering us—or anyone else—tonight."

Chapter 10

Gypsy stared straight ahead as Rebel drove his tow truck slowly along the one lane dirt road leading up the mountain. It was surrounded by trees, their full branches hanging low over the road, making the area so dark it was hard to see, even with headlights.

Near the top, he turned right and followed a long gravel driveway. When it ended directly in front of a large, white farmhouse, he made a quick left, which led to the backside of the barn where several pickup trucks were parked. Rebel pulled up next to the edge of the woods and shut down the engine. Judd jumped out of the passenger door and Gypsy climbed out behind him.

"Doesn't your grandfather mind you all having parties out here?" Gypsy asked.

Rebel unloaded two oversized sleeping bags from the bed of his tow truck and set them on the ground. "Not now that we're responsible enough not to set the whole mountain on fire," he told her. "But he used to run us off with a shotgun when we were younger...if he knew we were here."

"Either that or a fire extinguisher," Judd explained. "Sometimes he'd come outside with one of those big ones you see in buildings, squirt us down, and chase us away."

Judd paused the story when he and Rebel were laughing too hard to talk, making Gypsy think how nice it would be to have just one memory she could laugh about.

"He was still farming back then," Rebel explained, after catching his breath, "and was scared to death we were going to burn down his whole crop. He doesn't care what we do now, but someone should go up to the house and let him know we're here. It's been a while since our last get together and I don't want him calling 911 thinking this is a brush fire."

Judd lit a cigarette. "I'll go. You take Gypsy out back and introduce her. Leave the bags. I'll get them."

When Judd took off running, Rebel grabbed onto Gypsy's hand and led her into the night. The walk was short, and when they reached the woods, someone shined a flashlight at them. It was Flynn.

"It's about time you two showed up," he teased. "Where's Judd?"

"He went up to tell Granddaddy we're here. I don't want any uninvited guests showing up. Where's the beer?"

"There's seven cases of Bud in the back of my truck," Flynn said and threw Rebel his keys.

"Christ, Flynn, why didn't you just get a keg?"

"It was too late. Cut Rate Liquors didn't have any left."

Rebel threw the keys back. "Then you should've tried another store."

He shrugged and tried unsuccessfully not to laugh. "Yeah, I guess I should've."

"Shut up and give me the damn lighter fluid," Rebel told him. "Let's get this party started."

Cheers went up from the large group of people sitting on

the ground, and Gypsy backed away as Rebel caught the can Flynn tossed him. He opened it and drenched the small pile of wood. Using a lighter to ignite the matchbook he'd taken from his back pocket, he tossed the flaming pack into the pile. The logs caught immediately, and just like that, they had their bonfire.

On his way back to Gypsy, Rebel was swarmed by a crowd of people. She watched as someone handed him a beer, and envied the way that they were all happy to see him. Watching the scene intently, she gasped when someone touched her arm.

"Easy, Gypsy," Judd said, raising his hands in the air. "It's just me." He offered her a can of beer. "Here, this'll settle you down."

Her eyes never leaving Rebel, she accepted it. "Thanks."

As she sipped the beer, Judd began pointing to each of his cousins, helping Gypsy put names with faces. "That's our cousin, Billy. Everyone calls him Tank because he's so big. And over there," he pointed to a slightly overweight woman with feathered blonde hair, "is his wife, Ann. She's big too, but nobody calls her anything because she'd kick our asses."

Gypsy laughed. The more time she spent with Judd, the more she liked him. She'd heard every horror story there was about the things he'd done, but they no longer bothered her. Deep down, Judd was a good man, and he'd treated her with nothing but respect since the day she defended him in the diner. He was a good brother to Rebel, too; they hadn't even had an argument since the day the three of them ran into each other in the woods. In fact, Gypsy realized, a brother was exactly how she'd come to think of him. Without even realizing it, she'd become part of a family.

Rebel joined them just as someone put Led Zeppelin in a portable cassette player. After giving Gypsy a quick kiss on the lips, he put his arm around her shoulders and pulled her close. "Sorry I was gone so long," he apologized.

Gypsy didn't mind standing to the side waiting for him. She enjoyed watching him joke with and embrace the cousins he didn't see regularly. He made sure to stop and talk to each one of them, making it obvious how important family was to him. "It's okay. Judd kept me company."

"Thanks," Rebel told his brother. "That reminds me, what'd Granddaddy have to say?"

Judd grinned and took a long drink from his beer can before answering. "He said don't burn down the mountain, and bring Gypsy up to the house before you leave. He's curious about the woman whose tender love was able to tame his wild grandson."

Rebel gave his brother a playful punch in the arm. "Bullshit."

"Hey! Don't shoot the messenger, bro. You wanted to know what he said, and that's what he said."

"Fine. Since you opened your big mouth about her being here, you can join the two of us in the morning when we go up to say hello."

"No problem," he said, grinning again. "I didn't see any food in the back of your precious tow truck, and I'm getting too old to have beer for breakfast. We should go up around nine. Granddaddy's griddle ought to be hot and full of flapjacks by then." Judd winked at Gypsy and walked away.

"That boy should've been a lawyer," Rebel remarked. "He's got an answer for everything."

During the next few hours, Gypsy was introduced to so

many people she didn't know how she'd remember all their names. Most of the men were McCassey cousins who'd brought along their wives or girlfriends.

"Don't you have any female relatives?" Gypsy asked when she and Rebel walked to Flynn's truck for another case of beer.

"A few," he told her. "But campouts were always a guy thing. None of the girls wanted to sleep outside with the bugs and wild animals."

"I'm guessing the wild animals we're talking about here were two legged and not four."

"You got it," he said, laughing as he dropped the tailgate of Flynn's pickup truck. "We were all hellions back then; each one of us wilder and more destructive then the next. The girls weren't really into that." Rebel hopped up into the bed and lifted two cases of beer from the large ice chest. Gypsy picked them up and set them on the ground. Rebel jumped down, closed the tailgate, and gave her a quick kiss. "Let's get this beer back before the natives get restless."

A case of beer in each hand, Rebel led the way back to the fire as Gypsy followed. By the time they returned, the large crowd had separated; couples were huddled together sitting close to the fire, and the handful of men who'd come alone—Judd, Flynn, and Brady included—were standing off to the side talking. Rebel sat down, ripped into the case and took cans for himself and Gypsy. Then he passed it to Kane, who was sitting to his left.

After the beer was passed around, most of the couples got up and walked off into the darkness with their sleeping bags. "Are they going to sleep?" Gypsy asked.

"They're just going to find some privacy," Reb explained.

"How about it?" He stood up and offered her his hand. "I got a spot all picked out for us."

Gypsy smiled and took his hand. He picked up their sleeping bags and led her away. Slowly, they walked hand in hand through the knee-high grass of the uncut field.

Having spent her life smothered by the overpowering lights of Baltimore City, Gypsy marveled at the bright stars sprinkling the dark sky. Fascinated by the flickering yellow light from a thousand lightening bugs, she suddenly realized she wasn't the least bit afraid of the darkness. Rebel's strong, reassuring presence made her feel safe and very much at home with the night and its numerous sounds.

Chirping crickets and croaking bullfrogs from the nearby pond were a far cry from screaming sirens and noisy traffic, but Gypsy didn't miss the city. Her place was here now, in the country, standing by Reb; the oversized, overprotective man who loved her and vowed to protect her with his life.

As they neared the edge of the woods, Rebel veered to the right and guided Gypsy toward a large rock. Hidden behind it was a small clearing where he set down their two sleeping bags, untied and zipped them together, then laid them on the ground.

"What do you think of this spot?" he asked as he unlaced and removed his boots.

"It's nice," she said mockingly, "but I bet you bring all your girlfriends here."

Rebel grinned, crossed his arms, and removed his shirt. Bare-chested, he stepped in front of Gypsy and cupped her face in his hands. The look he gave her was so intense, she barely heard him whisper, "Only the beautiful ones with sparkling, bright green eyes."

Gypsy's lips parted automatically under Reb's sensual stare, and when his head tilted and began to lower, she closed her eyes and leaned into him. The first time their lips met was quick; each of them pulled back as though they'd been shocked by a bolt of electricity. When they touched again, Rebel's tongue gently began teasing; first her lips, then the inside of her mouth.

As the kiss deepened, Gypsy was unsure of what to do with her hands. Following her instincts, she allowed them to roam. Starting on his washboard stomach, Gypsy let her hands move slowly up Reb's chest, brushing against his shoulder-length hair as they traveled over his broad shoulders. On the way down, they stroked his biceps, finally coming to rest on the small of his back.

Rebel's hands began roaming, too. Only not in the same curious, exploratory way Gypsy's were. His touch was slow and sensual, more tender than one would expect from such large, powerful hands. The feeling of his hands on her body, combined with the slight chill in the air, sent a tingling sensation through Gypsy causing her to shiver.

He broke their kiss, licking her moisture from his lips, and backed away. "Are you cold?"

"Just a little," she told him. "But I'm okay. Maybe you should just kiss me again."

"I've got a better idea." He unzipped the sleeping bag. "Why don't you take off your shoes and join me in here?"

Feeling wicked and excited, she slipped off her shoes and socks and stepped onto the makeshift bed. She and Reb had been sleeping in the same bed for weeks, but because of the injury to her ribs, the only time he touched her at night was when he wrapped her in his arms, holding her until she fell asleep. But tonight was different. She was healed and they were alone, both wanting what they knew was about to happen.

"This is pretty soft," she commented, inching her way into the sleeping bag next to him.

"So are you," he said, his voice rough.

Rebel rolled over on his side and lowered his head to kiss her. She raised her arms and wrapped them around his neck, kissing him back hungrily, as if she couldn't get enough. The sensual movement of his tongue, combined with his breath, warm and sweet from the alcohol, was threatening to drive Gypsy over the edge.

Again, Rebel was the one who broke their kiss. But this time he didn't back away. He simply gazed at her. "I love you, Gypsy. I think I fell in love with you the first day we met. Never in a million years did I think someone as amazing as you would love me in return."

She suddenly moved away and sat up next to him, then removed her shirt and unhooked her bra, baring round breasts, perfectly proportioned to her petite body. Gypsy could see the passion swimming in Rebel's eyes as he watched the slow, graceful movements she made slipping out of her jeans and panties. She set them in the grass next to her other clothes and looked down at him.

Gypsy didn't feel the least bit vulnerable standing in front of him with nothing on. She knew he loved her and felt that him seeing her this way somehow made her his forever, heart and soul. "Make love to me, Rebel."

* * * *

Light from the Hunter's Moon spilled over Gypsy's bare body creating shadows that only enhanced her beauty.

The sight was more than Rebel could handle.

He stood and removed his jeans, never taking his eyes off her. "Are you sure?" he asked.

Before answering, she tugged on his neck, forcing him to come closer and lower his head. Then she kissed him gently on the mouth, her sweetness filling his senses. "I'm sure. I love you more than anything. I want to be with you."

Rebel reached out and removed the band holding Gypsy's ponytail in place, causing tight, fiery red ringlets to spill over her shoulders. Carefully taking two handfuls of her hair, he caressed the back of her head as he leaned and began to tenderly kiss her neck. Then he moved his head up until his lips were nearly touching hers. "Please make sure this is what you want, darlin'. Because once we start, I might not be able to stop."

Breathless, she whispered, "I want to know what it's like to feel the man I love inside me."

Rebel's last ounce of restraint gave way. With her hands in his, he sat down on the sleeping bag and pulled her down beside him. After dragging the covers over them, Rebel rolled onto his left side and moved Gypsy onto her back.

Distracted by his kiss, she gasped when she felt his hand slide between her thighs.

He removed it immediately. "What's wrong?"

Gypsy looked up into the royal blue eyes she loved so much. "I've never...I mean, I haven't..." She sighed. "I'm just a little nervous."

"I won't hurt you," he whispered. "I'll never let anything hurt you."

"I know. Touch me, Reb, touch me."

Slowly, he replaced his hand. The wetness he felt told

him she was ready, but he didn't want to rush her. Continuing their kiss, he ran his hands along her slender body, caressing her silken breasts, wanting desperately to explore every inch of her, taste her sweetness. But she'd never been with a man before, and he didn't want to frighten her by doing too much. So he took it easy, kissing her, teasing her hard nipples with the tip of his tongue trying desperately to control himself. Not until he heard her whisper, "Now," which told him she was ready to take the next step, did Rebel move on top of her.

When his erection brushed against Gypsy's thigh, Rebel watched as she threw her head back and let out a quiet moan. With the need to be inside her growing, he waited until Gypsy opened her legs wide, inviting him to make her his.

"I'm sorry," he whispered, "but there's no way to keep this from being uncomfortable." Rebel lowered his head and kissed her, catching her sharp intake of breath with his mouth when he entered her, taking her virginity. He remained completely still until the tension in her body gave way to him. Then, thrusting forward, he buried himself within her. He moved slowly, trying not to hurt her.

After just a few moments, Gypsy began to move. She wiggled and bucked her hips, wrapping her arms around Rebel's back trying to get closer, trying to push him deeper inside her.

Sensing she was close, he reached down and touched her clitoris, rubbing it ever-so-gently with his index and middle fingers. Gypsy's response was instant, and she was suddenly meeting his every thrust, writhing beneath his body as if she couldn't get enough. Moments later, panting and breathless, she murmured, "Reb," and climaxed.

Hearing his name accompanied by Gypsy's soft moans

pushed Rebel over the edge. Placing his hands on the ground for support, he raised himself over her and his slow, steady rhythm became more rapid. Knowing Gypsy was watching his every move as he claimed her body was what finally drove him over the edge. With one final thrust, he spilled his life deep inside her quivering body.

His energy spent, he bent down and rested his forehead on hers. "That was amazing, Gypsy," he said, trying to catch his breath. "Are you okay? I didn't hurt you, did I?"

"Hurt me? We just experienced the most intimate thing two people can share. I can't even describe how good you made me feel. I'm more than okay, Reb. I'm wonderful."

Relieved she was all right, Rebel whispered, "I love you," then turned and collapsed onto his back, pulling her with him.

Once again covered, she rested her head on his chest and draped her arm across his stomach. "I love you, too. I hope I was...okay. Did I do everything right?"

He turned to the left and softly kissed her forehead. "You did fine, darlin'. Just fine."

As they lay together in silence, Rebel's mind was racing, reliving what had just happened. Being with Gypsy had been an incredible experience. Their lovemaking hadn't been anything wild or out of the ordinary, but it was the first time he'd had sex with a woman he loved, and it'd had an unexplainable effect on him. The overwhelming feelings he had before of wanting to protect Gypsy were suddenly twice as strong. She was his now, completely. And he'd do everything in his power to make her happy and keep her safe.

* * * *

Gypsy had no idea how good it would feel to be intimate with a man; never thought she'd trust or love someone enough to want to share something intimate with him. But nothing had ever felt better than having the man she loved moving within her. What she'd told Reb was true. She loved him completely, and that would never change.

Her contented state, combined with the slow rise and fall of Reb's chest, eventually lulled Gypsy to sleep. When she awoke, she was enveloped in darkness. Clouds had rolled in, hiding the light from the moon, and she found herself alone in the sleeping bag.

"Reb!" she sat up and yelled, panicking.

He was at her side in an instant. "I'm here, Gypsy."

She grabbed for him in the dark, finding his leg first, and realized he was wearing his jeans.

"Where were you?"

"I needed a smoke and didn't want to wake you. I was sitting on the rock."

She sighed in relief.

"I know what you were thinking, Gypsy. But I wouldn't have left you here alone." He pulled her into his arms. "I wouldn't have walked five feet away if I thought you'd wake up while I was gone."

"It's so dark," she said, her voice noticeably shaky. "I thought something happened to you."

"It's okay." He slowly rocked her in his arms. "You never have anything to worry about when you're with me. As long as I'm around, everything will always be okay."

"I love you," she said quietly.

"And I love you." He rocked her until her erratic breathing returned to normal, then asked her if she wanted to wash up. "There's a stream about fifty yards south of here. The water should be fairly warm this time of year."

She smiled into the darkness, touched by his sensitivity. "I'd love to."

He gathered her clothes and handed her his T-shirt. She slipped it over her head and was relieved it was long enough to cover her all the way to her knees.

When they reached the stream, Rebel removed his jeans while Gypsy took off the shirt he'd given her and added it to their pile of clothes on the bank. He took her hand and led her into the rippling, chest high water. With an ironclad grip on his hand, she followed. "Remember, I can't swim."

"I'm here," he reminded her. "Everything's fine."

She nodded, even though she knew he couldn't see it.

"Let's go under, okay? On the count of three. Don't worry, darlin', I won't let go." When she stiffened, he added, "I promise."

She didn't want to do it, but the stream was as warm as bath water, and she knew it would feel good. "Okay."

"One, two, three," he counted, then grabbed both her hands and pulled her under the water before she had a chance to change her mind.

"Are you okay?" he asked when they surfaced.

"I'm fine." She squeezed excess water from her hair. "This actually feels pretty good."

"Come on over here," Rebel said. He shifted onto his knees, bringing the water up to his chin.

Gypsy turned her body and backed into him. He wrapped his arms around her, tightly securing her back against his chest. "We used to play out here all the time as kids," he told her. "I reluctantly learned to swim the day Blackie threw me in the pond behind my granddaddy's house."

She stiffened. "Is that your way of telling me you're going

to throw me in the water, because I don't know how to swim?"

He chuckled. "No. If you want to learn how to swim, I'll teach you. In fact, I think that's a pretty good idea. But not in the middle of the night, and definitely not when you aren't wearing any clothes; I have a feeling not much teaching or learning would get done."

"Thanks for the warning. I guess I should learn to swim. How old were you when Blackie threw you in?"

"Five."

"Five?"

"Uh-huh. He did the same thing to Judd."

"Wow, he must have really not liked you guys."

"He didn't do it to be mean, Gypsy. He did it because all Judd and I did when we were that age was play out here. There are streams and little water holes all over these woods, and if one of us had fallen in and not been able to swim, we would've drowned."

"But I thought you said you two fought so much that he didn't want anything to do with you until you were older."

"He didn't. But hanging out with your younger brothers and teaching them survival skills are two different things. He was just looking out for us."

"I can't imagine what it would be like to have someone care about me that much. You're so lucky."

Rebel turned her around, brought his hands up out of the water and caressed her face. "I care about you a hundred times more than that, Gypsy. I want to marry you."

"Marry me? Why?"

"What do you mean, why? I love you. That's why."

"But what if my father comes after me?"

"I can handle your father."

"But there's no telling what kind of trouble he'll bring if he shows up here."

"Trouble is my family's middle name. We can handle it."

"But—"

"Gypsy!" he interrupted loudly, his sudden, angry tone causing her to jump. "My family loves you, goddammit! So your last name doesn't have to be McCassey for them to help you if you get in trouble."

"What are you saying?"

"I'm saying they're going to give you help whether you want them to or not, so get over it."

Gypsy was a little surprised by his outburst. "Why are you angry with me?"

Rebel sighed and leaned his forehead against hers. "I'm worried, not angry. You mean a lot to me."

"You mean a lot to me, too. So does your family. That's why I'm so afraid."

"What, Gypsy? What are you afraid of?"

"Losing you; being responsible for something happening to your brother or one of your uncles or cousins."

"Nothing's going to happen to me. Or any of the boys, either. You're part of a family now, and at the risk of sounding sexist, let us take care of you. Let *me* take care of you."

"You don't have to—"

"I want to, Gypsy. And as far as marriage goes, I don't need a piece of paper to tell me you're my girl." With a hint of humor in his voice, he added, "But it might be easier on our kids if their parents have the same last name."

At the mention of kids, Gypsy's hand went to her abdomen. They hadn't used any protection when they made love earlier, and she wondered if Rebel's seed had taken root; his child already growing inside her.

Gypsy sighed and gave in. "I don't have anymore arguments, Reb. You love me and want to take care of me, and to be honest; my heart skips a beat every time I think about it. I admit that it feels good to be part of a family, too. The only thing still bothering me is that my father is a violent criminal. I just don't feel right about putting my new family in danger."

Rebel only laughed. "It takes one to know one, Gypsy. Chances are...me and the boys will smell him long before he gets to town."

"This isn't funny."

"Who's laughing?"

"You are."

"I'm sorry, darlin'. Please don't put your life, our life, on hold just because something might or might not happen. For all we know, your father may not want to go to the trouble of tracking you down. But if he does show up, we'll deal with it when the time comes."

She sighed. "Okay, but I'm still worried about you."

"Why?" he questioned.

"Because I know what you'd do if someone tried to hurt me, and you can't be a good husband from behind bars."

He put his hands on both her shoulders and squeezed them gently. "Does that mean you'll marry me?"

"Only if you promise to be careful."

"I'll make you a deal. You put your trust in me to take care of and protect you, and I promise only to do what's necessary to keep you safe. No extra acts of revenge. Deal?"

"Deal."

"Good. Now come on." He guided her to the edge of the

water. "The sun will be up in a few hours, and I think we should get some sleep."

They dressed quickly in the chilly, night air and walked hand-in-hand back to their sleeping bag.

"When do you want to get married?" she asked, as they climbed back into their makeshift bed.

"You pick the date, darlin'. We can do it at the court-house first thing Monday morning if you want."

"So soon?" she asked. "Don't you want your family there?"

"We can invite them," he told her, "but for obvious reasons, none of them are too fond of being in the courthouse."

"Should we have it somewhere else then?"

"Well, to tell you the truth, they don't get too excited about weddings, either."

Gypsy could understand that. She wasn't crazy about formal occasions herself. A quick ceremony at the courthouse sounded perfect.

"How about next Friday?"

"Okay," he agreed, "but why Friday?"

"I don't know. I think I'd feel weird getting married during the week."

"Friday it is. Now close your eyes and get some sleep."

Gypsy nodded off almost immediately, but even in the safe confines of Rebel's arms, it was an unsettled, fitful sleep.

* * * *

The only time Rebel remembered Gypsy having a hard time sleeping was when they first met. And even though she was asleep now, she was restless, tossing and turning, clutching his hand with a death grip she refused to loosen. There was no mistaking the fact that something was on her mind;

probably the conversation they had about her father. She was obviously scared that someone was going to get hurt, and it pained him to know that his numerous attempts to reassure her hadn't done any good.

Rebel also knew that no matter how hard he tried, he'd never be able to look at the situation through her eyes. His whole life, no matter what kind of problems he had, there was always an army of McCassey's there to back him. For the past eleven years, Gypsy had no one.

But that was over.

She had him now. And he'd kill anyone who tried to hurt her.

Anyone.

Chapter 11

Word of Rebel and Gypsy's upcoming marriage spread fast through the McCassey clan. During the entire week leading up to the wedding, relatives from all over Washington County filtered into the garage to get a look at the girl who'd finally captured Rebel's heart. Overwhelmed by all the attention and marital advice, Gypsy was ready to run away and hide by Thursday afternoon.

Gypsy was sitting on a tree stump behind the garage when Judd came up to her. She had her knees up, arms folded across them, head down. "Mind if I sit?"

She looked up. "Only if you promise to talk about something other than weddings, Rebel's unholy promiscuity as a teenager, or the hundreds of different ways to cook and store venison."

He sat in the grass across from her and apparently tried to hide his smile. "The family finally got to you, huh?"

Gypsy rolled her eyes and put her head back down.

"It'll be over soon, girl. Right now, you're a novelty. No one ever thought ol' Reb would settle down, and here he is getting married."

"No kidding," she said without bothering to look up, "one

of your great aunts even offered me money to tell her the trick I used to trap your brother. It seems her granddaughter is...how did she put it...looking to nab an unsuspecting man just like I did, and could use all the help she can get."

Judd winced. "Having to deal with stuff like that kind of makes hanging out with us guys at the garage all the time not seem so bad, huh?"

When Gypsy gave no response, he continued in a serious tone. "You're good for him, you know."

That brought her head up, but she remained quiet.

"For both of us actually. He and I haven't had a fight since we met you."

She'd noticed. It piqued her interest that it seemed to be important to Judd. "How come?"

He shrugged. "I can't speak for Rebel, but when I found out about everything you'd been through, it seemed pretty silly to me for two brothers in their thirties to be fighting like kids. I started most, if not all the problems we had. Rebel's been bailing my ass out of trouble ever since I can remember, and sometimes it just gets to me that he's a better person than I am."

It saddened Gypsy to hear Judd put himself down. He was every bit as good as Reb. He just hadn't realized it yet. "That's not true, Judd."

"Yeah, Gypsy, it is. My brother's a born leader. People are drawn to him. They look to him for approval. The camp-out we had last weekend wouldn't have happened if Rebel hadn't given the okay."

"Why?"

Judd shrugged again. "That's the way it's always been. Growing up, Rebel was as wild and reckless as the rest of us.

But being smart and sure of himself was what made him different. He was never much for starting trouble, but was always there to finish it if me and the boys got into something we couldn't handle. My brother deserves the best, and he found that in you."

Embarrassed by the compliment, she smiled shyly. "I don't know what to say."

"You don't need to say anything, just listen. Being around you these past few months has really affected me. You've been to hell and back, yet still find something to smile about everyday. Besides Rose, you're the only woman who's ever gotten my respect, and you've earned every ounce of it. You make me want to be a better person, Gypsy. I'm proud to be getting you as a sister."

"A sister, really?"

"Really."

"Even though my father—"

"Don't even go there, girl. My brother loves you, I love you, and the rest of the family loves you. There's no way the McCassey boys are going to let anything happen to you. And no one's going to get hurt, either."

"Reb told you?"

"He's concerned that you're so worried about us, so I'm going to set you straight once and for all. Our family's been fighting one battle or another for well over a hundred years. Most of us have been shot at, arrested, and in and out of trouble our whole lives. We're used to it. Some of us even thrive on it. And not much of anything scares us. So do yourself a favor and stop worrying. Everything will be all right."

"How can you be so sure?"

"Look, you may be Rebel's wife, but you're going to be

my sister. And no self respecting man ever lets anything bad happen to his sister."

"But—"

Judd stood up and pointed at her. "That's enough, Gypsy. Forget about your father and enjoy the fact that you're about to marry a man who loves you."

He was right. If by chance The Baltimore Sun had picked up the article about her being rescued, and her father had seen it and decided to come to Hagerstown, there was nothing she could do. They'd deal with it when the time came, just like Reb said.

Judd offered her a hand up and she took it. "You're coming tomorrow, right?"

"I wouldn't miss it," he told her. "I'm wearing my good jeans and everything."

She smiled. Judd wouldn't be Judd in anything else. "Perfect."

He put his arm around her shoulders and started to lead her around to the front of the garage, but she stopped him. "Judd?"

"Hmm?" he murmured, trying to light a cigarette.

"Thanks."

"For what?"

"Being such a good brother to Reb. And to me. When I was a kid, I thought I'd be safer if I had a big brother to look out for me. And now I do." She stood on her tiptoes and kissed his cheek. For once, it seemed Judd McCassey was almost speechless.

"No worries, Gypsy. Remember that."

* * * *

Aside from his duties at work, no one had ever, could

ever, count on him for anything important. Now, suddenly, the girl who had once jumped into an argument between two men she didn't know, just to defend him, was asking him to watch out for her. Judd had no idea that being needed could feel so good, and he had his brother to thank for that.

Rebel was tough and smart, much smarter than he was, and he didn't think his brother was going to have any trouble protecting Gypsy. But Judd was going to be there for them…just in case.

* * * *

Rebel and Gypsy exchanged their vows in the judge's chambers of the Hagerstown Municipal Courthouse, at eleven-thirty Friday morning. Judd, Frank, Rose, and Jimmy were their witnesses.

The first thing Gypsy did when the ceremony was over and they left the courthouse, was pull out the dozens of pins holding her hair up. Since she'd refused to wear a wedding dress, Rose had insisted Gypsy at least do something elegant with her long thick hair. So Gypsy had allowed the older woman to fuss over her, and wound up with most of her curls pinned on top of her head and a few spilling down over her shoulders.

Judd shook hands with his brother and kissed his new sister-in-law's cheek. "You made a beautiful bride, Gypsy."

"Uh-huh," she said, returning his kiss. "I'm sure *Modern Bride Magazine* will be here any minute to take my picture for their cover, jeans and all."

"Hey, I like your jeans," he told her. "They're as old and ugly as mine."

"Thanks, Judd, you really know how to make a girl feel special."

He winked and lit a cigarette. "So I've been told."

Gypsy looked at her new family and stifled a giggle.

Rebel punched his brother in the arm. "Shut the hell up. No one wants to hear that shit. Especially me."

"What's wrong, little brother? Afraid you won't measure up to my talent?"

"No, asshole, I'm afraid I'll throw up."

That time Gypsy giggled out loud. Then she squeezed between the two brothers, looped one arm around each of them and began leading them toward the parking lot.

When the wedding party got back to the garage, it was deserted.

"Where the hell is everybody?" Rebel asked.

"Frank and I made an executive decision to close up at noon," Jimmy told him. "We figured you and Gypsy deserved a little privacy on your wedding day."

Gypsy blushed and stepped forward to hug Frank and Jimmy. "Thank you," she said. "And thanks for being there today."

"We wouldn't have missed it," Rose told her. "Welcome to the family, Gypsy."

"Hey, where's mine?"

Gypsy turned to see Judd standing behind her grinning. She smiled and walked into the arms of the man she now called 'brother'. He gave her a gentle squeeze. "You take good care of my baby brother," Judd said. "But if he gives you any trouble, I want to hear about it. No man messes with my sister and gets away with it."

Rebel laughed and threw out a sarcastic, "I'll be sure to remember that."

Judd winked at Gypsy. "You'd better."

"Go on upstairs, darlin'," Rebel told his new wife. "I'll be up in a minute."

She nodded and headed for the metal stairs. "Bye, Judd."

"See ya, girl."

Once Gypsy was gone, Rebel dug into his tool cabinet and pulled out a pack of Marlboro's. Unable to find matches, he turned to his brother. "You got a light?"

Judd reached into his front pocket and tossed a lighter to Rebel. "I'm really happy for you, bro." He extended his hand. "Truly."

Rebel took a long drag on the cigarette and shook his brother's hand. "Thanks."

"You tell Blackie yet?"

Rebel grinned as he nodded. "I talked to him yesterday. He said women are nothing but trouble and wished me luck."

Judd laughed. "Sounds like you caught him in a good mood."

"Yeah."

"Don't worry, bro. He'll love Gypsy once he gets to know her. Just like we all do."

"I'm not worried about him liking my wife, Judd."

"Then what is it?"

"He told me he's got a parole hearing in a couple of weeks, said it looks like he'll get out this time."

"Already?" Judd sounded surprised.

"It's been three years."

"I guess it has." Judd squinted at his brother. "So what's the problem?"

"Wherever Blackie is," Rebel said, taking another long drag on his cigarette, "trouble's never far behind."

"You worried about Gypsy?"

"Concerned."

"He wouldn't do anything to put her in danger."

"Not on purpose."

"What are you going to do?"

Rebel dropped the butt of his cigarette on the floor and crushed it with the heel of his boot. "What can I do? He's my brother, for Christ's sake. Our brother. I can't tell him not to come around; I want him here. But I can't afford to take chances by getting involved if he gets himself in trouble again. The last two times won me a night in jail, and I don't want to leave Gypsy alone, even for a minute. At least until we settle this thing with her father."

"Don't worry about Gypsy, Rebel. You can count on me for help if you need it."

Rebel studied his brother and knew he was sincere. "I appreciate that. Let's just hope I don't."

Judd raised his right fist to Rebel, who lightly touched it with his own. Then the brothers embraced. It'd been a long time since they'd hugged one another; probably since the first and only time they ever got lost in the woods. Judd was four, Rebel a couple of months away from turning four. They'd been out all night before Frank found them the next morning huddled together under a tree. It had felt good for each of them to know they weren't alone then, and it felt good now.

"I really am happy for you," Judd told his brother. "You got yourself a hell of a woman. Maybe I'll find me one just like her someday."

Rebel bent down and began unlacing his boots to try and hide his surprise. That was the first time in Judd's thirty-one years that he'd said anything about wanting to settle down. He'd always been just as adamant as Blackie about women being trouble. The only difference between Rebel's two older brothers was that Blackie stayed away from women all together, except to use them for sex, but there were a handful of them that Judd had been slightly interested in over the years.

In the end, Judd, too, wound up only using them. But Rebel always thought Judd might get married someday…he liked to talk way too much to wind up old and unmarried with no one but the walls to listen to him ramble on about nothing.

"I know what I got when I found her," Rebel told Judd. "I just hope she doesn't bolt when she finds out what she got in return."

Judd grinned and gave Rebel a playful punch in the arm. "Deep down, she already knows. She's just too in love right now to care."

Rebel grinned in return. "I'm going to let that one slide…but only because I don't want to spend anymore time away from my new wife. Go home, Judd."

"I'm going, I'm going. You want me to take Outlaw?"

Rebel looked over at the sleeping German Shepherd. "Nah, I'll put him out front. He'll be fine until morning."

The brothers said their goodbyes, and Rebel locked up the garage before heading up to see Gypsy. When he entered their small apartment, she flew into his arms and greeted him with a long, slow kiss.

"Well, hey, darlin'. If I'd known I was going to get this kind of reception, I'd have thrown Judd out ten minutes ago."

She backed away and looked up into the blue of his eyes. "I missed you."

He leaned down and removed the boots he'd loosened earlier, then pulled his shirt over his head—a pair of blue jeans the only article of clothing left covering his body.

"Well, I'm here now," he told her, and she squealed in delight when he suddenly scooped her into his arms. "And I'd like to make love to my wife."

So with the shades closed tightly and all the lights off, Rebel and Gypsy spent the day in bed. They tasted and touched and explored each other's bodies until there wasn't an inch of either one of them that wasn't familiar. With their energy spent, the newly married couple fell into an exhausted, contented sleep.

* * * *

The sound of a striking match was what finally woke Gypsy. The room was darker now, the sun was down and night had fallen. She rolled onto her right side and propped her head on a pillow. "What time is it?"

"Ten-thirty. Did you sleep well?"

"Uh-huh," she said in a raspy voice, crawling out from underneath the covers. When she reached Reb, who was sitting on the edge of the bed, she rose onto her knees, wrapped her arms around his waist, and started kissing his back and neck.

Obviously aroused by her soft touch, Rebel hardened instantly. He turned and set his cigarette in an ashtray, then gently pushed Gypsy onto her back, kissing her neck in return. "You're going to wear me out, woman."

And they made love again.

"Reb?" Gypsy said when they were finished.

"Hmm?"

"I'm starving."

The chuckle came from deep in his throat. "Me too, but we have a problem."

"What kind of problem?"

"There's no food."

"None?"

"Cereal and beer," he told her, "but my guess is that you don't consider that a good meal."

Gypsy felt around in the dark for his T-shirt, found it, and slipped it over her head. "Guess again, Mr. McCassey. I'm desperate."

As she threw the covers off, Rebel turned on the small lamp next to him and grabbed her before she could get out of bed. "Don't leave."

"I have to," she said squirming, "I'm hungry."

He pulled her into his arms and began tickling her. "I'll make you a deal."

She was almost laughing too hard to answer. "What kind of a deal?"

"Stay in bed five more minutes, then we'll grab a shower, and I'll take you out to eat. Anywhere you want."

She caught her breath and looked at the digital clock on the dresser. "At eleven o'clock at night?"

"Shit." He sighed and rolled over onto his back. "I forgot it was so late."

"That's okay. How about hot dogs from the convenience store?"

"Seriously?"

"Sure, why not?"

"That's not much of a wedding day dinner."

"I don't care what kind of dinner we eat as long as we're eating it together. And besides, I could use a little fresh air. Can we go for a ride afterward?"

Rebel wondered how in the world he'd gotten so lucky.

Here it is her wedding night, and instead of expecting some formal expensive dinner, Gypsy was willing to eat hot dogs from a convenience store. "You're a hell of a woman, Mrs. McCassey." He sat up and held a hand out to her. "Care to join me in the shower?"

"You think we can both fit?"

"Only if we stand really, really close."

Chapter 12

After getting side tracked in the shower, it was another thirty minutes before Rebel and Gypsy left the garage. Dressed once again in his work boots and jeans, Rebel opted for a white tank top to keep him cool in the muggy, early August air. He shoved a pack of Marlboro's in his front pants pocket and held his hand out to Gypsy.

Dressed much the same, except in a gray T-shirt with McCASSEY'S GARAGE written in black script across the back, Gypsy had left her wet hair down to dry; the humid air transforming her curls into tight ringlets with more body than Rebel had ever seen.

Trying to suppress a laugh, Rebel reached out and brushed at one of her stray curls. "Humidity isn't really a friend of yours, is it?"

Gypsy smiled then laughed. "I know my hair has a tendency to get poofy when it's humid. Is it that bad?"

"Let's just say that you and your hair are going to have to go to the store by yourselves, darlin'. There's not enough room in the cab of the tow truck for all three of us."

"Well, in that case, I'll leave it down instead of forcing it into a ponytail. I'm rather enjoying the amusement on your face."

He laughed and patted her behind. "Suit yourself. But let's get going, I need food."

Rebel fired up the tow truck's diesel engine and turned on the air conditioner while Gypsy put Outlaw back into the garage. She quickly made sure the middle bay door was the only one left unlocked, then walked to the truck where her husband was holding the door open.

Gypsy climbed up and slid into the middle.

They stopped at the convenience store on the corner of Franklin and Cannon Streets and spent ten minutes in the store picking out snacks. When they got back to the tow truck, they heard Jimmy trying to get Rebel on the CB.

"How the hell did he know we were out here?"

Gypsy climbed up into the truck through the driver's side door and sat down in the middle of the bench seat. Rebel followed her in, closed the door and picked up the CB mic. "Yeah, Jimmy?"

"Where the hell have you been? I've been calling your apartment for the last ten minutes."

"We came out to get something to eat," Rebel said impatiently. "What's wrong with you?"

"There's trouble over at Diggers. Judd, Brady, Kane, Flynn, and a bunch of those Jenkins boys just got themselves thrown out of the bar. Now they're circling each other in the parking lot."

"Goddamn those guys!" he said, slamming the truck into first gear. "I'll be there in ten minutes."

Rebel put the CB mic back on its hook and pulled out of the parking lot. Torn between dropping Gypsy off at the garage and dragging her into a potentially violent situation at the bar, he decided to take her home. Leaving her alone was risky. But it was far riskier taking her somewhere she could get hurt, or have to watch something worse happen to him. "Sorry, Gypsy, the ride's going to have to wait. I'll drop you off at the garage but I don't have time to walk you in."

Gypsy's left hand touched his forearm. "Why can't I go with you?"

"Because this isn't a game. My family's been fighting with the Jenkins bunch since my grandfather was a kid. Most of them live down in Frederick now, which is about a half hour from here, so our paths don't cross too often. But when they do, it's always messy. Last time Flynn wound up in the hospital. It's too dangerous to take you there."

"Please?" she begged. "I'll stay in the truck."

When Rebel and his brothers and cousins were in junior high school, they actually invited girls to watch when they were going to fight someone. But that was when the most dangerous fighting they ever did was with their fists in the schoolyard.

Nowadays, the McCassey boys' occasional fighting was serious business, and the thought of Gypsy getting caught in the crossfire turned his stomach. He really didn't want to take her with him, but decided she shouldn't be left at home alone. Reluctantly, Rebel gave in to her request, making her promise to stay in the truck and to leave at the first sign of any real trouble.

"If anything happens, take the tow truck back to the garage and make sure to keep Outlaw inside with you. I'll meet you there later," he assured her as they pulled into the back part of Digger's gravel parking lot where a full fledged brawl was raging.

"Shit!" Rebel leaned across Gypsy and opened the glove compartment. In his haste to get to his family's aid, he missed Gypsy's stunned expression when he pulled out a handgun, cocked it, and jumped out of the truck.

* * * *

Rebel's gunshot sent an echo into the air that stopped the rumble immediately. The two families separated, McCassey's on one side, Jenkins on the other.

Watching out of the open window, Gypsy counted eleven people, not including Reb, every one of them staring at him in surprise.

"Jesus, Rebel," she heard one of the Jenkins boys say. "Put the gun away, man. We were just havin' a little fun."

Rebel turned and pointed the gun at him. "Fun's over, Davie. Take your brood and get out of here before I get angry."

"Look, man, you weren't here. This has nothin' to do with you." He took a step toward Rebel, who fired another shot into the air, stopping Davie Jenkins in his tracks.

"Wrong. My family has everything to do with me." Before Rebel finished his sentence, he was surrounded by McCassey's. Judd and Jimmy flanked him. Brady, Kane, and Flynn stood directly behind him.

As the men stared at one another in silence, Gypsy wondered why, after two gunshots, she didn't hear the high pitched screaming of police sirens. Didn't anyone in the bar care what was going on outside? Or were they just too afraid to interfere in any trouble that had to do with the McCassey's?

Davie put his hands in the air and backed off. "Okay then. Get rid of your piece, and let's make this a fair fight. Skin on skin."

Rebel smiled, tossed his gun to Judd, and punched Davie in the jaw before he knew what hit him.

The Jenkins boys all piled on Reb then, and Gypsy screamed inwardly when she saw him go down. Seconds later, he came up swinging and took out two guys with as many punches.

Judd and Jimmy got one guy each, and Brady, Kane, and Flynn, were pounding on the remaining three.

When it was over, all six McCassey's were still standing, their opponents quietly limping away from the battlefield. By the time their enemies were out of sight, Gypsy would've bet that Rebel's anger had reached the boiling point. When he walked a few feet away and turned on his family, she knew she was right.

"On my fucking wedding night?" he yelled to no one in particular. "What the hell is wrong with you guys?"

No one answered.

Rebel made his way back to the quiet group and stood directly in front of them. "I asked a question." He looked from Judd to Jimmy then glanced at Brady, Kane, and Flynn. "Somebody better tell me what the hell went on here tonight. Now!"

Jimmy finally spoke up. "Let's go back to the garage and discuss this, Rebel. The cops in this town may be lazy, but they're not stupid. Those gunshots aren't going to be ignored for long."

"Too late," Flynn announced, pointing to the opposite side of the parking lot. "We got company."

When Rebel saw the slow-moving sheriff's car, he sighed and raked a hand through his hair. "Terrific."

Gypsy noticed the sheriff at the same time she remembered the gun her husband had tossed to his brother. Judd was on probation, and if he was caught with it, he'd go to jail for sure.

Rebel had been keeping a close eye on her from where he was standing, but with his attention now focused on the sheriff, she was able to slip unnoticed from the cab of the truck.

The six McCassey's stood tall, shoulder-to-shoulder, as the car came to a stop and Sheriff Ben Johnson opened the door. Just before he got out, Gypsy snuck up behind the guys. Her small body hidden by their large sizes, she placed a hand on the waistband in back of Judd's jeans. He moved slightly, motioning for her to go away, but she ignored him. Finding what she was looking for, Gypsy lifted the back of his shirt, removed the gun, and tucked it into the waistband of her own pants.

She forced her way into line between Rebel and Judd just as the sheriff approached them. Rebel looked down and glared at her, and she knew he wasn't happy about being defied.

Wearing a smug look, the sheriff stopped only inches in front of Rebel. "Somebody reported hearing gunshots out here, McCassey. You know anything about that?"

Rebel's stone cold expression forced the sheriff to take a step back. "No sir, not a thing."

Frowning, the lawman turned his attention to Gypsy and greeted her. "Ms. Lance."

"It's Mrs. McCassey...Sheriff."

"You made a big mistake getting yourself mixed up with this bunch," he told her. "Now you're nothing but trash, just like the rest of them."

Gypsy felt Reb stiffen next to her. To divert his attention, she stepped forward. It was easy to tell that she'd surprised both her husband and the sheriff. "I'm proud to be a McCassey," she spat back. "You, on the other hand, are an embarrassment to law enforcement officers everywhere."

The sheriff's face reddened as chuckles and low whistles came from a few of the guys. "One of you has a gun, and I'm not leaving here until I find it." He waved his hand in the direction of the building. "All of you against the wall and spread 'em. Now!" He glared at Gypsy. "You, too…Mrs. McCassey."

Jimmy, Brady, Kane, and Flynn walked over to the side of the building, but Rebel and Judd stayed next to Gypsy.

She crossed her arms in front of her body and took a defiant stance. "You're not laying a hand on me, Sheriff. Unless there's a female officer present, you have no right to search me."

He stared at her in disbelief.

"That's right," she said smugly, "I know the law. So unless you're going to get on your radio and call for a woman to come up here, I'll be over by my husband's truck." Head held high, Gypsy turned her back on him and stalked off.

* * * *

Marveling at Gypsy's courage, Rebel and Judd watched her stroll away and sit down on the front bumper of the tow truck. Confident she was safely out of the sheriff's reach, the brothers started laughing. "Guess she told you, huh, Johnson?"

The sheriff pulled his gun from its holster and aimed it at the brothers. "Shut the fuck up, Judd. As I recall, your probation prohibits you from even thinking about firearms. If I find that gun on you, I'll drive you to prison myself."

Judd smirked and held his hands in the air. "No gun here, Sheriff. But you're welcome to look."

"Against the wall, Judd." He waived the gun in the direction of their cousins. "You too, Rebel. Move."

The six men turned to face the wall. Arms and legs spread, they stood still as Sheriff Johnson made his way down the line, thoroughly searching each one. After finding nothing, he told them they were free to go.

"But I'll be watching," he said and turned to leave. Halfway to his patrol car, he stopped. "I suggest you keep a close eye on your wife, Rebel. And teach her some manners while you're at it. Next time, I won't be so tolerant of that sharp tongue."

Using every ounce of restraint he could muster, Rebel ignored the comment. "Have a nice night...Sheriff."

Lined up next to each other once again, the McCassey's watched the sheriff's car pull out of the parking lot. When it was out of sight, Gypsy rose and made her way over to the guys.

Rebel turned and gave his closest relative, which happened to be Judd, a hard shove. He flew backward and landed in the dirt. "Somebody better tell me what the hell went on here tonight!" he yelled. "And where's my goddamn gun?"

"I have it."

Rebel whirled around at the sound of his wife's voice.

"Here." She reached behind her, pulled the gun out of the back of her jeans and handed it to him.

Rebel snatched the .38 Special from Gypsy and unloaded it; shoving the bullets into the front pocket of his jeans. "I told you to wait in the truck," he reminded her, fighting to control his anger.

"I was just trying to help Judd," she explained, and Rebel's anger faded immediately. He couldn't hold it against her that she wanted to help his brother.

"I know," he told her as he leaned in and kissed her forehead, "and I'm proud of you. But we'll talk about it later." He draped his right arm around Gypsy and turned to his family. "Start talking boys."

Jimmy began the story with how the five of them were sitting in the bar minding their own business when the Jenkins boys approached them.

"We haven't had trouble with them for years," Rebel said. "Why all the sudden would they start something?"

"Who knows? But Davie came right over and started in on Judd, knowing he's always the first one to lose his temper. They were definitely looking for a fight."

Rebel shook his head. "Something's not right."

"You think they had something else in mind besides just giving us a little trouble?" Judd asked.

"I know they did."

"How?"

Rebel turned to his brother. "Judd, you remember what happened the last time Johnson and his men showed up during one of our fights with the Jenkins boys?"

Judd laughed. "Yeah, we all got hauled in, and they had to put the families in separate cells."

"And what happened this time?"

It seemed to dawn on all of them at the same time.

During the last fight, the sheriff and his deputies grabbed all the McCassey's and chased down every last Jenkins who tried to run and hide in the woods. Tonight, not only did the sheriff show up alone and let the other family go without a chase, but he didn't arrest a single McCassey.

"Let's get back to the garage," Rebel told them. "Flynn," he called, to his inquisitive younger cousin, "I got a feeling the

Jenkins were sent here to start something with you boys. The question is, why? And by who? Go back inside and ask around, see if you can find out anything. Brady...stay with him." Rebel looked at his watch. "It's twelve-thirty. If you two aren't back at the garage in an hour, the rest of us will come looking for you. Be careful."

Slick and sneaky, Rebel knew that if anyone could get the information they needed, it was Flynn. Just after he and Brady re-entered the bar, Rebel led Gypsy over to the tow truck. He opened the door and lit a cigarette as she climbed inside.

"Are you going to yell at me?" she asked, nervously, after he'd gotten in.

"No." He released the smoke from his lungs. "I'm going to very calmly explain that when I tell you to do something, it's for a good reason. You got lucky tonight, Gypsy. Next time, and believe me, at some point, there will be a next time; you have to promise you'll do exactly as I say, no matter what."

"I'm sorry I didn't listen, I just wanted to help Judd," she said again, her voice cracking. "I didn't even know you kept a...a...gun...in the truck." Then suddenly, she burst into tears.

Since it was uncommon for Gypsy to be so emotional, her tears took Rebel by surprise. He immediately tossed his cigarette out the window and gathered her into his arms. "Shh, it's all right," he said, tenderly, "it's over now."

"But you weren't even scared." She sobbed. "How come you're not afraid of anything?"

"I've been involved in things like this my whole life Gypsy. I'm used to it...we all are. But that doesn't mean I'm not afraid of anything. You know what?"

She sniffed. "What?"

"You've got more guts than any woman I've ever met. That was a brave thing you did, sneaking the gun away from Judd and challenging the sheriff to find someone to search you. I'm not happy about you taking a chance like that, but I'm damn impressed that you did. And the way you stood up to Johnson when he called us all trash. That took balls, girl. How'd you know it was against the law for him to search you?"

She sat up and wiped at her tears. "I heard it somewhere once. I didn't even know it was true until I saw the look on the sheriff's face."

Reb chuckled and sat up. "You sure are something."

He started the truck and leaned over to give her a kiss. "You'll feel better once we get back to the garage."

She nodded, curled both her arms around his right one, laid her head on his shoulder, and fell asleep almost instantly.

Judd, Jimmy, and Kane were inside the garage waiting when Rebel pulled into the parking lot. He gently lifted Gypsy down from the truck. She didn't stir once as he carried her past his awaiting family, up the stairs, and tucked her into bed. Just in case she woke up, he turned on the small light sitting on the dresser and left a note next to it saying he was downstairs.

"Gypsy okay?" Judd asked when Rebel joined them at the table.

"Yeah, a little shook up is all. I don't think she realized what she did tonight until it was all over."

"I can't believe the way she stood up to Johnson. She must really love you, bro."

"She loves *us*, Judd. She took the gun to help you. I'm

sorry. I never should've thrown it to you."

Judd rolled his eyes. "It's not the first time I've touched a gun since I've been on probation. There was the time——"

Rebel put his hand up and stopped his brother in mid-sentence. "I don't want to know about it."

Before Judd could continue teasing his brother, Flynn and Brady walked in.

"Well, what'd you find out?"

"You were right, Rebel. Something's definitely up."

Rebel grabbed a chair from the table, turned it around backward and straddled it. "Well, spill it already."

"Ten minutes after you all left, Davie Jenkins's younger brother, Byron, came back into the bar alone. He slid into our booth and just started talking."

Rebel was agitated. Flynn might be good at gathering information, but getting him to tell you what he found out was almost impossible. "Well, did he have anything interesting to say or not?"

Flynn raised his eyebrows and nodded. "Yeah, get this. About a week back, Davie gathered his brother and cousins and told them they were coming up here to give us some trouble."

"We haven't tangled with them for years, and they've never beaten us," Rebel reminded him. "Why would they want to start something now?"

"Byron didn't know. But he did say that he thinks Davie was blackmailed into doing it."

"Blackmailed? By who?"

"Byron didn't know that, either. He said he tried to get Davie to tell him what's going on, but Davie refused to talk."

Rebel had a feeling there was more. "What else?"

Flynn stared at his cousin. "Davie made it clear to his boys that they weren't to start anything with us unless you were there."

"Why me?"

Flynn shrugged.

"But I wasn't there tonight."

"They thought you were. Somehow, Davie found out you and Gypsy got married today. They thought we took you to Digger's to celebrate. When they realized you weren't there, they started with Judd and got us all thrown out of the bar on purpose. You're our leader, man. I guess they knew you'd show up sooner or later."

Rebel didn't feel very much like a leader right now. In fact, he found himself wishing Blackie was out of prison and sitting in the garage with them. His oldest brother was wild, impulsive, and hopelessly irresponsible, but he was also always good for an idea. Judd, Jimmy, and the rest of the guys watched him stand up and pace the floor for five minutes before he stopped and sat down again. "Did he mention anything about Gypsy?"

"Nope, Byron never said a word about her. Almost like he just assumed she wouldn't be there."

"Why the hell wouldn't my wife be with me on our wedding night?"

Flynn shrugged. "You want to know what I think?"

Reb nodded.

"Everyone knows you put family first, Rebel. Maybe the Jenkins thought you wouldn't turn us guys down if we wanted to take you out for a beer. Or they could've assumed Gypsy wouldn't want to go. Digger's Bar is a rough place. His sister, Angel, is one of the only women I've ever seen inside. She's a tough, smart ass bartender and can handle just about anything. Excuse me for saying so, but Gypsy's not like that. Maybe the Jenkins had seen her in the diner and thought a girl like that wouldn't want to go into a wild bar; they probably figured she'd pass on the beer and want to stay home."

The revelation washed over Rebel like a wave. "That's it! Someone wants us out of the way."

"What are you talking about?" Judd asked. "Who wants us out of the way?"

"That's what I'd like to know."

Judd looked skeptical. "But why would—"

"Because someone's after Gypsy, you moron!"

"Her father?" Jimmy asked.

"That's the only person I can think of. I'm not sure how her father would know the Jenkins, though. Gypsy doesn't think he's ever been out of Baltimore City, but there's a chance she could be wrong." Then he shook his head in frustration. "Aw hell, I don't know. The Jenkins boys stick pretty close to Frederick. It'd be almost impossible for them to know each other."

"So you think this is it?" Judd asked. "You think Gypsy's father's after her?"

Rebel shrugged. "It's the only thing that makes sense right now. Why else would someone want all of us, especially me, out of the way? The only reason I can think of is so that they'd have an easier time grabbing Gypsy."

"How do you think he found out where she is?" Kane asked.

"Blackie and Johnny Cooper, Gypsy's father, are in the same prison. When I talked to Blackie the day after the tornado, he said he read the article about Judd and me rescuing

Gypsy in The Baltimore Sun. Chances are Cooper read the same article. His parole hearing is supposedly sometime this month, so the timing's perfect. The person after Gypsy could very well be her father."

Judd got up and went in search of a cigarette. He took the pack from the top drawer of Rebel's tool cabinet and lit one for himself and his brother. "What about asking Blackie if he knows Cooper?"

"I already did. Months ago. He'd never heard of a Johnny Cooper, but asked around and did eventually find out who he was. As of last week, Cooper was still inside. Blackie didn't say anything about him when we talked yesterday."

"What are you going to do?" Judd asked.

"I'm not going to let Gypsy out of my sight for a second. That's for damn sure."

"What about us, bro? What do you want us to do?"

"Keep your eyes and ears open but play dumb, just in case whoever's after her is roaming around town. Pay close attention to people you don't recognize. And no one, no one, comes into this garage. All customers, no matter who they are, stay in the waiting area. I don't want anyone having easy access to my wife."

"Are you going to tell her?"

"I have to, Judd. I can't keep something like this a secret."

"What do you think she'll do?"

Rebel remembered the way Gypsy tried to run away from Pizza Hut and shrugged. "There's only one way to find out." He extinguished his cigarette and headed up the stairs, leaving his family to lock-up behind them.

The walk from the garage up to his apartment was the longest one Rebel had ever taken. How in the world was he supposed to tell his wife that he thought her worst nightmare was coming true? That the father who'd promised to kill her eleven years ago was out of prison and coming to get her?

Worry kept Rebel from getting any sleep. He lay awake all night trying to figure out the possible connection between Davie Jenkins and Gypsy's father, what to do about it and how to keep her safe.

He'd hoped to get a chance to let her know what was going on before his uncles and cousins showed up at the garage the next morning. But she slept until the loud sounds of Frank and Jimmy opening the bay doors woke her.

* * * *

It wasn't until Gypsy sat up and realized she was still in her clothes that the events of the night before came slamming back into her memory: Reb's gun, the fight, Sheriff Johnson. "I'm sorry I fell asleep."

Rebel rolled over and pulled her into his arms. "I'm not. You needed the rest."

"Were you up late?"

"Yeah, the boys and I had a little meeting after I put you to bed. Flynn came across some interesting information."

The tone of his voice made the tiny hairs on the back of her neck stand up. "Anything I should know about?"

"Unfortunately."

For the next twenty minutes, Rebel told his wife all the information Flynn got from Byron Jenkins, and the conclusion he came to that Gypsy's father was after her.

"You're taking this a lot better than I thought, Gypsy. Please say something."

She gave a short laugh. "I guess you were expecting tears, panic, or maybe even surprise, huh?"

"Any one, hell, even all three of those emotions would be normal for you to have. But that glare you're giving me is one borrowed from a page in my book, darlin', and that's scary as hell. Talk to me."

"All I want to know is what you think I should do. I'm not some dainty, fainting flower, Rebel. You don't have to keep secrets or treat me like I'm going to break. I've known for a long time that something like this was going to happen."

"I told you everything I know, Gypsy. All we can do now is wait."

She sighed, her shoulders slumping in defeat. "That's the hardest part."

"Tell me about it. I'm not going to sleep until I figure out what we're up against here. Going to the sheriff for help is out of the question. I don't trust Ben Johnson, and I'll be damned if I'm going to give him the satisfaction of knowing a McCassey needs help."

It was up to Rebel alone to protect his wife. Now all he had to do was figure out how the hell he was going to keep her safe.

Chapter 13

Gypsy was surprised by how normal everything was around the garage that morning. She figured everyone would be on edge waiting for something to happen. Lord knew she was. But everything was pretty much the same. Customers and cars came and went, Judd bought lunch Monday, Jimmy on Tuesday, Brady and Kane goofed off and got on everyone's nerves, and Rebel spent the days with his head buried in the engine he was trying to finish rebuilding.

Wednesday was the day her world fell apart.

The demolition of what was left of the diner was complete, and the construction company that had been camped across the street for the past two weeks was in the process of loading their heavy machines onto flatbed trailers. It'd been pouring down rain since dawn, and they were working as fast as they could to get their equipment loaded before the mud became too deep for them to maneuver around.

Just before ten o'clock in the morning, the construction crew ran into a problem and their foreman came over to the garage asking for a hand. Since the workers were around all the time, they'd gotten to know Brady and Kane, whom they'd run into several times over the past fourteen days at

Digger's Bar.

"We got a backhoe hung up in the mud pretty bad. Can you tow it out?"

"Nah," Kane told him. "Judd's out on a call with the truck. But we could probably push you out."

Kane, Brady, Jimmy, and Flynn set their tools down and started to leave the garage.

"You coming, Rebel?" Flynn asked.

"In a minute." He closed the hood of a car and wiped his hands on a white rag. "I want to run upstairs and check on Gypsy first."

Because she wasn't feeling well that morning, Rebel had made Gypsy eat a handful of crackers and talked her into staying in bed. She hadn't been happy about it. In fact, she'd put up a hell of a fight. However, when she stood up and became dizzy, she changed her mind and crawled back in bed.

Rebel quietly opened the door to their apartment and walked in. With the lights off and shades drawn, the small room was dark as night. Not sure if his wife was awake, he tiptoed to the bed and gently sat down.

Once his eyes adjusted to the darkness, he saw that Gypsy was sound asleep. The covers he'd pulled up to her chin earlier had slipped to her shoulders, partially revealing the threadbare T-shirt she insisted on using as pajamas, even after he'd offered to buy her new ones.

"What do I need new pajamas for?" she'd questioned seductively. "It's not like I wear the old ones very long once we're in bed." Her little statement had been cute at the time, but now Rebel was sorry he'd listened to her. Winters in the western panhandle of Maryland were sometimes frigid, and when the cold weather came, she was going to be wearing something warmer than a ratty old T-shirt whether she liked it or not.

But then Rebel smiled to himself as he thought about how they'd made love every night, sometimes several times, since he'd taken her virginity in the woods. Warm, willing, and not the least bit shy, Gypsy was an eager student when it came to learning about love-making. She trusted him unconditionally, and that alone caused his love for her to grow by the minute.

Because he was happier than he felt he had a right to be, Rebel worried about Gypsy constantly. Just that morning, when she'd woken up pale and nauseous, he'd been terrified. Keeping her safe from someone who wanted to harm her was one thing, but an illness was something else. There was nothing he could do to stop it, nothing he could do to make her feel better except force her to take it easy. And force was exactly what he'd had to do that morning after she'd protested his order to stay in bed.

"I can rest just as easily sitting at a desk in the office helping Rose," she claimed.

Both impressed and annoyed by the obsession Gypsy had to pull her own weight, Rebel crossed his arms and leaned against the bedpost grinning. "How the hell do you expect to get any rest down in the office answering the phone?" Before she could answer, he added, "Better yet, how do you expect to get to the office? It's a long trip down that flight of stairs for someone who could barely get out of bed just now."

"If you could just carry me—" she started to suggest, but stopped in mid-sentence when he arched his brows.

He could tell that despite her body not feeling well, there was nothing wrong with Gypsy's temper. She lifted her head from the pillow and pointed a finger at him. "Rebel

McCassey—"

Rebel laughed and shook his head, wondering just where inside her tiny body all that spit and vinegar came from. "Uh-uh, darlin'. Don't even think about unleashing that red-headed temper on me. If you can't make it downstairs by yourself, you're not going."

"Oh, what's the big deal? Just take me down. If I start to feel bad, I'll come back up, I promise."

Rebel admired her efforts, but wasn't giving in. "The bottom line is that you're too sick to work. And it doesn't matter how angry it makes you, I'm not letting you out of this apartment until I'm damn sure you're well enough."

Gypsy tried changing her tactics from anger to pouting and gave him the saddest look she could come up with.

"Forget it, darlin'. It won't work," he said as he tucked her in. "I'll be back to check on you at lunch."

* * * *

As gently as possible, Rebel brought his hand up and brushed a stray curl from Gypsy's face. He was apparently trying not to disturb her, but when he lightly kissed her forehead, she stirred.

"Hey," she said groggily. "Is it noon already?"

"No," he whispered, "it's just after ten. How do you feel?"

Gypsy took a deep breath and felt her stomach turn over. Grateful Reb had made her stay in bed, she closed her eyes and grabbed for his hand, drawing comfort from his touch. "The same. It's probably just a twenty-four hour bug or something. I'll be fine."

Rebel frowned. "Gypsy, I think I know what's causing you to feel sick."

"You do?"

"I don't know any other way to say this but to just spit it out." He paused and then said, "Has it occurred to you that you could be pregnant?"

"What?" she asked, more than a little surprised by the question. "Why would you think…"

Gypsy stopped, did some quick figuring in her head, and answered her own question. She hadn't had her period, which had always been a little irregular, since three weeks before the tornado. Five weeks ago.

Dizziness. Nausea. No period for eight weeks.

She had to be pregnant.

The very thought of Rebel's baby growing inside her made Gypsy want to leap out of bed and dance around the room, but the queasy feeling in her stomach forced her to stay where she was.

"Well?" he asked, anxiously, "are you?"

She had to tell him, but would he be happy? "I don't know," she said tentatively, "my period has always been irregular, but I've never gone eight weeks without one. It could be a little early to tell, but…I think I might be."

"I love you," he whispered.

"You mean you're happy?"

"Of course I'm happy, Gypsy. Why wouldn't I be?"

"Because it's so soon. We just got married. I thought maybe—"

"I know where you're headed darlin' but don't even go there. There's no greater gift you could ever give me than a baby. Today, tomorrow, next week; it could never be too soon."

Her dizziness and nausea temporarily forgotten, Gypsy

sat up and threw her arms around her husband as tears of joy sprang to her eyes. "Oh, Reb."

Rebel drew her close and buried his face in her hair. After a minute of tender silence, he said, "I think we should get a test or maybe take you to the doctor. Just to be sure."

"Okay," she agreed. "Just not today. I don't feel much like going anywhere."

Rebel kissed her on the lips and eased her head back down onto the pillow. "I'll call and make you an appointment for later in the week," he told her. "That way, I can go with you."

That was unexpected. "You'd really go with me?"

"I wouldn't miss it," he said, standing up. "But right now I have to go. Kane's new friends from across the street have a backhoe stuck in the mud, and he was nice enough to volunteer us to push them out. I'll be back as soon as I can. Frank and Rose are in the garage if you need anything."

"Okay."

"I'll come up and check on you when I get back," he said and bent over to give her a kiss.

She tightened her grip on his hand as he tried to walk away. "I love you."

He gave her hand a careful squeeze and tucked it back under the blanket. "I love you, too, darlin'. Get some sleep."

The door to their apartment clicked shut and Gypsy listened to the sound of Rebel and his heavy, steel-toe work boots thundering down the metal stairs. She heard the clank of a big bay door opening, followed by Outlaw's loud barking and obnoxious shouts and laughter as her husband and his cousins left the garage. Sometimes, she thought, they were no more mature than a bunch of ten-year-olds.

Thinking about kids caused her mind to wander to the tiny life growing inside her. Besides her mother, this baby would be the first blood relative she ever had. She'd love to have a little boy that looked exactly like Rebel, jet-black hair and those McCassey royal blue eyes. But no matter what it turned out to be, Gypsy knew she and Reb would make sure the baby knew how much it was loved.

Still dizzy, Gypsy flipped off the covers and slowly sat up, figuring as long as she was awake, she might as well use the bathroom. Even though it was only ten feet down the hall and everyone but Frank and Rose had gone across the street, she pulled on a pair of cutoff jean shorts anyway, just in case. Her long white T-shirt completely covered them, but she felt more comfortable not being half naked.

As she passed the door to the fire escape halfway to the bathroom, Gypsy thought she heard a noise on the metal steps. Before she could check it out, her stomach lurched and she barely made it to the bathroom before throwing up the crackers Reb had talked her into eating earlier.

Twenty minutes later, Gypsy emerged from the bathroom no longer nauseous, but not even close to feeling normal. She'd managed to relieve herself and brush her teeth without much of a problem, but wasn't up to taking a shower and couldn't wait to crawl back into bed.

The well-worn planks of the wooden floor were soft against the bottom of Gypsy's bare feet as she made her way down the hall. Once inside the apartment, she closed the door behind her. But before she had the chance to lock it, someone grabbed her from behind, a hand inside a leather glove clamping tightly over her mouth. Swallowing the bile that had risen in her throat, Gypsy began to struggle.

When she felt the cold steel of a gun touch her temple, her mouth went dry, she broke out into a sweat, and her body went deathly still.

"That's a little more like it," an unfamiliar male voice said when she stopped struggling. "You give me any trouble, the couple downstairs is history. Understand?"

Gypsy nodded.

"Come on." His gloved hand quietly opened the door, and he half dragged Gypsy into the hall.

Who was this person? And how did he get into the garage without being seen?

When her captor stopped midway down the hall in front of the door leading to the fire escape, Gypsy's stomach did another flip and she almost threw up again as she realized how the man had gotten in. The noise she'd heard earlier must have been him climbing up the fire escape. She didn't know how he'd managed to get the door unlocked, but that didn't seem to matter now. He was in, holding her at gunpoint, ready to kill, or have someone else kill Frank and Rose if she made any noise.

Gypsy began to panic. What was she going to do? There was no way she'd risk two innocent lives by trying to alert them to the intruder's presence. And since she was barely dressed, she didn't have anything to drop to leave a trail for Reb to follow. All she had was her wedding ring, which would make noise upon landing on the wooden floor. Gypsy didn't really want to part with it anyway. For all she knew, it was the only part of her husband she would ever see again.

* * * *

For two, muddy, rain-soaked hours, Rebel, his uncle, and cousins worked to free the sunken backhoe. After handshakes and thanks, the construction foreman offered to buy lunch, but the five exhausted McCassey's declined and trudged back across the street. They stopped in front of the office door and stripped off their polyester coveralls and work boots, which were sopping wet and covered in mud.

Rose was waiting with an armload of dry towels and generously handed them out as the men came back inside.

"Thanks, Rose," Rebel said, taking one to wipe his face. "Has Gypsy been down?"

Rose shook her head. "She was in the bathroom for a while just after you boys left but didn't come downstairs. I haven't heard a peep out of her since. Maybe you should go check on her."

Rebel tossed his towel into the barrel they used for dirty rags. "I'm headed up now." He turned to his cousin. "But first I want to thank Kane for volunteering our services. It's not like I had any real work to do today."

"Sorry, man," Kane said, sounding not only surprised, but also grateful to hear the slight hint of humor Rebel had put into his statement. "But you know you would have gone over and helped whether I volunteered you or not."

"Yeah, right," Rebel said sarcastically, throwing his cousin two twenty-dollar bills. "It's my day to buy lunch but you're going to pick it up. I'm worn out."

Kane started to protest then closed his mouth. "Hey!" he said, obviously trying to lighten the mood a little more. "I can't help it if something I was sure would take no more than fifteen minutes wound up wasting the entire morning. The hole that backhoe was stuck in couldn't have been any deeper if someone had taken a shovel and dug it themselves."

"You're treading on thin ice, Kane," Rebel warned, no

longer in the mood to fool around. He felt like a drowned rat, and wanted nothing more than get cleaned up.

Kane changed the subject immediately. "What do you want to eat?" he shouted, as Rebel turned and headed toward the stairs.

"I don't care," he shouted back, "something hot."

Instead of walking into the apartment filthy and wet, Rebel detoured into the bathroom to take a shower first.

Standing under the hot water, he thought about how much his life had changed. Less than six months ago, he hadn't even been dating anyone. Now he had a wife, and together they were going to have a baby. Even though babies born into his family had an immediate strike against them because they were McCassey's, Rebel vowed that his children would have a better life than he did. And they weren't going to grow up around violence or be beaten the way he and his brothers were. Any kids he and Gypsy brought into the world were going to know from day one that they were wanted and loved by two parents who loved each other.

Thoroughly excited about the idea of becoming a father, Rebel finished his shower and dried off. Thankful for the extra change of clothes he kept under the bathroom vanity, he dressed in the old blue jeans and white sleeveless shirt.

He debated about whether or not to disturb Gypsy, but he'd promised to check on her when he got back, so he decided to see if she needed anything.

The inside of the apartment was still too dark to see. He turned on the small kitchen light. When he glanced at the bed and noticed it was empty, he became alarmed. "Gypsy?"

When there was no answer, he realized she must be in the garage, and headed downstairs.

"Gypsy?" he called when he reached the bottom of the metal steps.

Rose walked out of the office. "Rebel, I told you she hasn't been downstairs all morning." She frowned. "Didn't you check on her?"

"You mean she didn't just come down here?"

She shook her head. "No."

He put his hands on her shoulders and squeezed a little harder than he meant to. "Are you sure?"

Rose winced, and he let go immediately. "Yes, I'm sure. I can see the stairs from my office window. I've been in there all morning, and Gypsy hasn't been down."

Rose took a deep breath and backed away. "Frank!" she called to her husband frantically. "Frank!"

Frank walked around the corner with a greasy rag in one hand and ratchet in the other. "What is it?"

Instead of answering her husband, Rose raised her arm and pointed at Rebel, whose face had gone completely white.

Frank took a step forward. "Good Lord, boy, what's wrong?"

Struggling to keep calm, Rebel told him, "Gypsy's missing."

Upon hearing that, everyone in the garage dropped what they were doing.

"What do you mean missing?" Frank asked. "She couldn't have gone anywhere, Rebel. She never came downstairs. Not once."

"Well she's not upstairs, either."

"Are you sure?"

"Yes, I'm sure, Frank! This is a small place; it's very hard to miss someone!"

Hot with a mixture of anger and fear, Rebel began searching his tool cabinet for a pack of Marlboro's.

Judd, who'd returned just fifteen minutes before they'd gotten the backhoe free, was suddenly by his side. He put a comforting hand on his brother's shoulder and handed him a lit cigarette. "Tell us what happened, bro."

In less than a minute, Rebel spit out the whole story, beginning with Gypsy feeling sick that morning and ending with finding the bed empty after his shower.

"You don't think she just went for a walk or something?" asked Kane, who had just returned with lunch.

"In the pouring rain?" Rebel was glaring in such a threatening way that Kane actually took a step back.

Judd stepped forward and suggested they take a few minutes to search for her. "Maybe she just needed some air."

Rebel whirled around and yelled, "She's pregnant, goddammit! She wouldn't take a chance on getting sick by walking around outside in a downpour."

Judd froze. "Gypsy's pregnant?"

Looking shocked, everyone watched as the man who was usually more calm than anyone in a desperate situation sat down in a chair, bent his head, and sighed. "Yes."

"How far along is she?"

"I don't know, a few weeks." He raised his head and looked at his brother. "She was too sick to get out of bed this morning, Judd. There's no way she left here on her own."

"What about Outlaw? He would've barked if anybody strange was sniffing around."

"He was across the street with us," Jimmy said from a few feet away.

Rebel didn't need to hear the sound of Kane throwing up

into a trashcan to know his cousin was feeling more than a little guilty. He also knew that Kane would be useless in their search for Gypsy unless he was sure Rebel wasn't mad at him. "It's not your fault, Kane," Rebel said, flatly. "If someone was able to sneak Gypsy out of here while the garage was quiet without Frank and Rose hearing anything, they could've gotten her out from under our noses, too."

"Not fucking likely. Nobody's ever pulled one over on you, Rebel," Kane reminded him, "nobody. You're too smart for that."

"Yeah, well, this time I wasn't."

Kane walked over and held a hand out to his cousin. "I'm sorry I let you down, man. Really. If I thought for one minute something was going to happen while we were gone, I would've told those guys to dig their machine out themselves, Rebel. I swear."

Rebel gave his hand a quick shake. "What's done is done. It's not your fault."

"Thanks."

Ignoring Kane, Rebel stood and began talking to no one in particular. "The only way someone could enter or leave the garage without being noticed is through the fire escape."

Followed by Judd, Kane, Brady, and Flynn, Rebel took the metal stairs two at a time. When he reached the door to the fire escape, he held his breath and wrapped his large hand around the doorknob, praying it was still locked. When the knob twisted and the door opened, the five men stared in shock at the muddy footprints leading up and down the steps.

"Son of a bitch!" Reb yelled.

No one spoke.

"Whoever grabbed her took a lot of care not to leave

footprints anywhere else but here in the stairwell. There's none in the hall or my apartment."

Before the others knew he was moving, Rebel had pushed passed them and walked into his apartment. They followed, catching him just as he sat down to put on his boots.

"What are you doing?" Judd asked.

Rebel stood and opened a dresser drawer. "Going to find my wife." He pulled out a .22 caliber pistol, checked the clip, then reached behind his back and put it in the waistband of his pants.

Judd stepped forward and grabbed his brother's arm. "I'm not letting you go alone."

Rebel yanked his arm from Judd's grasp and made his way to the door. "You don't have a choice."

"You don't even know where she is!" Judd yelled as he and the boys chased Rebel down the stairs.

"Well, I'm not going to find her standing around here arguing with you!"

Rebel raced down the stairs, the four men close on his heels. Halfway across the garage floor, he stopped short at the unexpected sight of his oldest brother, Blackie. Arms crossed, the man with waist length, wavy, dark brown hair was leaning with his shoulder resting against the wall, cigarette dangling from his lips. The shaggy, dark colored five o'clock shadow was new. So was his enormous muscular build; twice what it had been the last time Rebel had seen him. What hadn't changed was the cocky tilt of his head and come-on-I-dare-you look on his face.

Paying no attention to where they were going, Judd, Brady, Kane, and Flynn slammed into Rebel.

"Back off!" Reb yelled, still staring at Blackie.

Muffled apologies came from behind him just as Blackie began laughing. "I see you four assholes are still playin' follow the leader; never could figure out what made you the fuckin' Pied Piper, little brother."

Rebel smirked at his oldest brother. "Nice to see you, too, Blackie."

Ignoring his other brother and cousins, Blackie took one last drag on his cigarette and dropped it to the floor. Without bothering to extinguish the butt, he pushed away from the wall and walked to his youngest brother. They embraced then Blackie backed away. "I got some information you might be interested in."

Rebel shook his head and went to his tool cabinet in search of his truck keys. "I don't have time to screw around, Blackie. My wife's missing."

"How long has she been gone?"

Something about the seriousness in his brother's voice made him stop and look up. "A few hours at the most. Why?"

"Then you might want to listen to what I have to say."

Squinting suspiciously, Rebel took a threatening step toward his brother. "What do you know about Gypsy?"

Blackie grinned. "You ain't changed much." Rebel was a big man now, but thanks to constant weightlifting, Blackie was, and always had been, much bigger. His size was intimidating, but even as a scrawny kid, Rebel hadn't been afraid to challenge his oldest brother; though he usually wound up getting his ass kicked for doing it. By never showing any fear, Rebel had earned a lot of people's respect, including Blackie's. And despite the fact that they looked at just about everything completely different, the brothers were very close.

"Only what you told me on the phone," Blackie replied,

"but I know plenty about her father."

Rebel stared at Blackie.

"I guess you want to listen now, don't you?"

"Shut the fuck up. Keep your sarcasm to yourself and tell me what you know."

Blackie walked to the table in the middle of the room, turned a metal folding chair around backward, straddled it, and sat down. "You got a smoke?"

Following his brother's lead, Rebel sat down opposite Blackie and not-so-gently tossed a book of matches and half empty pack of Marlboro's across the table. "Talk."

He chuckled. "I got a story you ain't never gonna believe, little brother."

Rebel lifted a brow and Blackie finally started talking. "Okay, so after you asked me about Johnny Cooper, I did some askin' around and found out who he was. After watchin' him for a few weeks, I decided to find out who his cellmate was and talk to that guy instead of Cooper, just so Cooper wouldn't get wind I was lookin' for information on him.

"So one day in the yard, I make sure Cooper ain't around and approach his cellmate. Man did that guy hate to see me comin'." Blackie paused to laugh. "He turned white as a ghost. . Probably thought I was bein' sent to kill him or somethin'."

Blackie finished his cigarette and lit another one before repeating, word for word, the conversation he had with Cooper's cellmate...

* * * *

"I'm lookin' for a guy named Johnny Cooper," Blackie announced. "You know him?"

The man, who was probably a good nine inches shorter than Blackie, didn't do much to hide the fact that he was very afraid. "Yeah, I know him. We been sharin' a cell since I got here."

"How long is that?"

"'Bout ten years give or take. What do you want with Cooper?" the man asked, nervously. "He done somethin' to you?"

Blackie tossed the man a pack of cigarettes. "I need some information."

"I'll tell you anything you want to know, man."

"Cooper ever mention that he's lookin' for someone?"

"Funny you should ask that. Up until a couple of weeks ago, Cooper hadn't said more than ten words to me or anyone else the whole time he's been in The Joint."

"What happened to make him start runnin' his mouth?" Blackie asked.

"Cooper likes to read a lot. Newspapers mostly. One day at the end of July, he's readin' The Baltimore Sun, and just like that, out of the blue, starts laughin'. Since he seemed happy, I took the chance he might want to talk and asked him what was so funny."

"What'd he say?"

"He said that he was finally gonna get revenge on the person who'd ruined his life. He said he'd been searchin' for eleven years."

"Eleven years is a long time," Blackie commented. "Who's he searchin' for?"

"I asked him the same thing. I said, 'Hey Cooper, what'd this guy do to you that you been searchin' for him eleven years?' That's when he told me it wasn't no guy he was lookin' for, it was a girl. After hearin' that, I lost interest and didn't ask no more questions. I figured it was just some girl who'd fucked him over or somethin'. Bullshit as far as I'm concerned."

Shit like that was bull as far as Blackie was concerned, too. "You ever find out what that article was about he was readin'?"

"Somethin' about a tornado they had somewhere out west. Hagerstown, I think."

Blackie nodded. Cooper's cellmate had told him exactly what he wanted to know, that Cooper was planning on going after Gypsy the minute he was released from prison.

"I heard Cooper's got a parole hearin' comin' up. Any idea when it is?"

The man shrugged. "Any day now. Cooper don't even know for sure."

Blackie nodded again. "You'll keep quiet about our conversation?"

Cooper's cellmate eyed Blackie from head to toe. "Sure thing, man."

Blackie tossed the man another pack of cigarettes and walked away.

* * * *

Rebel's stomach tightened into a knot. "You ever get a chance to talk to Cooper?"

"No, but I followed him around for a few more days, watched him make a mess of phone calls the last week or so he was there, traded nearly everything he had to other inmates for their phone privileges."

"Is that it?"

"Nope. Someone he knows owns an old two-story huntin' cabin on the outskirts of Frederick. I overheard him repeatin' the directions to whoever he was talkin' to on the phone the day before he was released. I'll bet you a carton of smokes that's where your wife is."

A million thoughts were running through Rebel's head as he stared at his oldest brother. Had Cooper himself snuck into the garage and taken Gypsy? If not, then who? Rebel thought for a minute that maybe the person who owned the cabin in Frederick lived in Hagerstown. That made sense, because whoever took her had to be familiar enough with the garage to know they'd need tools to cut the locks off the fire escape door. But how would Cooper know anyone in Hagerstown? Rebel recalled Gypsy saying she didn't think her father had ever been out of Baltimore City. Was she wrong? Shit! He didn't have a single answer for any of his questions.

"Well come on, Rebel." Blackie stood suddenly and swung his right leg over the chair, turned it around, and pushed it back under the table. "Let's me and you go get your wife."

"Let's go get my wife?" he repeated, borrowing some of Blackie's sarcasm. "Just like that?"

"Yeah, little brother, just like that. The cabin ain't more than twenty miles from here. You got any of my guns handy?"

"You're on parole," Rebel reminded him. "And half of them," he swept an arm in front of the group of cousins gathered behind him, "are on probation. I can't ask anyone to risk being thrown in jail. I have to do this alone."

"Fuck that," Blackie yelled. "Mess with one of us, mess with all of us. Right boys?"

Every man standing behind Rebel shouted in agreement.

Blackie moved around the table and put an arm around Rebel's shoulders. "But we don't need their help, little brother. Just you and me this time. Besides, whoever's got your wife ain't gonna try and chase us away with sticks. We're gonna need firepower."

Rebel momentarily considered what Blackie had said and knew his brother was right. "Your guns are up at Ten Acres. My .38 Specials are in the tow truck, they're much better than this," he said, setting his .22 on the table.

"The rest of you boys go up to Ten Acres and wait for us," Blackie instructed, as he and Rebel started to leave. "We'll meet you there sometime tomorrow and figure out what to do next." On their way out the door, Blackie stopped in front of Rose. "Pack a bag for Gypsy—a couple of changes of clothes, a pair of shoes, and whatever else you think she might need. Give it to Judd before he leaves." Then he turned to Frank and tossed a tiny scrap of white paper in his lap. "The address to the cabin," he whispered, "in case we don't come back."

Chapter 14

Soaking wet, Gypsy shivered uncontrollably as she curled into a ball and tried to keep warm. There was no doubt in her mind that her father was responsible for her kidnapping. At least she could be thankful none of the McCassey's had gotten hurt when she was taken.

At least she didn't think anyone had been hurt.

Shuddering, Gypsy wished she'd been wrong when she told Reb that her father would someday catch up to her. And wishing, too, that he'd been wrong the other day when he said he believed her father was now after her.

Rebel, more than likely, had discovered by now that she was missing. Her heart ached for him, knowing he must be going crazy wondering where she was. She just prayed he'd figure out that she hadn't run away this time, but instead, was taken against her will.

A single tear slid down her cheek when the reality of the situation sunk in. "He won't even know where to look for me," she cried out loud, convinced the chances of seeing her husband and his family again were slim to none. Her father had wanted to kill her for eleven years, and now he had his chance.

She'd probably be dead before nightfall.

Lying at the foot of the bed, Gypsy closed her eyes and

tried to recall everything that had happened since she was taken.

Whoever grabbed her from the apartment had carried her down the fire escape and into the woods behind the garage. Blindfolded, she was handed off to a man waiting on some kind of all-terrain vehicle. After a long ride through the pouring rain; wet branches slapping and scraping her face, they stopped and she was thrown into the back of a car and driven to the place she was now being held.

The man driving removed her blindfold when they arrived, but Gypsy didn't get much of a chance to look around before she was dragged inside a small, dilapidated two-story cabin. Once through the front door, she was ushered up the stairs and into the only room on the second floor. The spacious area had just one window and one piece of furniture, a bare single mattress on top of a rusty metal frame.

"Sit," the tall, skinny man demanded.

Thinking about what would become of the tiny life growing inside her if she made the man angry, Gypsy obeyed and sat on the edge of the bed.

She gasped in fear when he suddenly grabbed her legs and swung them up onto the mattress, but was relieved when all he did was reach under the bed and pull out a pair of shackles, realizing his only intention was chaining her to the frame.

The man worked quickly, silently. He closed the shackles tightly around each of Gypsy's ankles, wrapped the chain around the frame of the bed several times, and secured it with a padlock. With his task complete, he turned and left the room without another glance at his prisoner.

The second the door closed, Gypsy sat up and tugged on the shackles and chains.

Nothing budged.

"I'll never get out of here," she said as she lay down again. Trying frantically to get a handle on the flood of emotions running through her, Gypsy fought the tears and hysteria that threatened to take over. In the end, the tears came anyway. She cried for everything from her unborn baby to the mother she'd lost and everything in between, missing the comfort and safety of Rebel's big, strong arms, the sense of home she'd felt at the garage, and because she just didn't feel good. Then she prayed that somehow Rebel would find out where she was being held, and come for her so that they could be together again.

Gypsy had tried to be strong her whole life—mostly because if she didn't take care of herself, no one else would. But all the time she'd spent with the McCassey's the past few months had shown her what it was like to be part of a family. Gypsy didn't want to lose that. And she didn't want to lose Rebel.

So she made up her mind that if given a chance to face her father, she would be brave. She would stand up to him, for herself and for her mother, who never got the chance. She may have been scared and weepy now, but not for long.

She was going to fight for her freedom.

Just as soon as she got the chance.

* * * *

The slamming of the bedroom's heavy, wooden door caused Gypsy to wake with a start. When she turned toward the noise, she focused on a slim man whose dark brown eyes were boring into her.

A few inches shy of six feet, he was dressed in work boots, faded black jeans, and a threadbare grease-stained T-shirt that probably, at one time, had been white. His short red hair was sprinkled with the same small patches of gray as his disheveled beard, and was as filthy as the shirt. He flashed an evil grin, revealing a mouth missing more than half the number of teeth he should've had. Those that remained were badly decayed and yellowed.

"You know who I am, girl?" he asked in a low, raspy voice.

When Gypsy said nothing, the man's grin widened. "You do know, don't you bitch?"

Gypsy's eyes widened in terror. This was her father. This was the man who'd murdered her mother in cold blood then threatened to kill her, too.

And he was standing ten feet away.

Although she tried to remember her vow to be brave, the fear of this man she'd been afraid of seeing again for so long paralyzed her. Barely breathing, all she could do was stare as he came closer.

His first backhanded slap caught her on the right side of the face, sending searing pain through the scratches she'd gotten from the wet tree branches. He immediately gave her another vicious slap, and after a third brutal backhand, Gypsy's entire face went numb.

Dazed, Gypsy fought the darkness that threatened to take over, forcing herself to remain awake and alert by thinking of Rebel and their unborn child. Trying desperately to block out the throbbing pain in her face and ignore the ringing in her ears, she remained focused on her father. He was laughing at her efforts to stay upright.

"Don't give up, do you, girl?" He cackled, watching her struggle to remain conscious. "That comes from me. Your mother was weak. One little slap and that was it, bam, she was dead. That little incident was damn inconvenient, too. She died before I could find out where she hid my key."

Tears threatened at the mention of her mother, but she fought them off, vowing not to give this man the satisfaction of knowing he'd upset, hurt, and scared her. She stared at him in silent defiance for several minutes before he stepped forward, pulled back his arm and struck her with a blow that would have sent her flying off the bed if her ankles hadn't been chained to the frame.

"I'm in charge here," he said sternly, "not you."

Did he actually think she was trying to play mind games with him? All she wanted to do was stay conscious, a feat that was becoming more and more difficult by the second.

"I should've wasted you the same day as your mother."

Wide-eyed, Gypsy stared at him.

Wearing the same toothless, evil grin as before, he took another step forward. "I spent almost eleven years in prison because of you, you little bitch. I had to keep quiet and put up with a lot of shit for a long time to be able to make parole on my first try. But it was worth it. You know why? Because the whole time I was in The Joint, all I thought about was you."

Gypsy hoped the terror she felt wasn't showing on her face.

"That's right. I thought about getting the key your whore of a mother stole from me, because I know you have it. And I thought about how I was going to kill you once you gave it to me. I think the best way would be for me to torture you…slowly. That should almost pay me back for the torture I suffered in prison trying to behave myself.

"I got through a lot of those days by reading the newspaper, hoping that one day I'd see your name in there, maybe pick up a clue where to find you when I got out. I almost couldn't believe it when I finally struck gold; that was a real nice story the reporter wrote about those McCassey boys pulling you from a collapsed building. The article said you would've died if they hadn't gotten you out." He knelt in front of Gypsy, raised his left hand, and grabbed a bunch of her hair that had escaped her ponytail. "It's too bad they wasted their time, because this time tomorrow night, you'll be dead."

Cooper reached under the bed with his right hand and pulled out a .22 pistol. He cocked it, put his finger on the trigger, and pressed the end of the gun to her lips. "That key is going to make me a rich man. So tell me where it is, and maybe I'll take mercy on your pathetic soul and just blow your brains out, quick and painless like. Refuse, and I'll torture you slowly and painfully until you tell me where it is. Either way, you're going to die. But how it happens is up to you."

Johnny Cooper let go of his daughter's hair and walked to the door. "It's getting late and I got some business to tend to before dark." He pointed the gun at her, tilted it slightly upward, and fired. The bullet tore into the cabin's wooden wall just above her head, sending splinters flying into Gypsy's already battered face. Her father flashed a grin that made Gypsy's blood run cold. "You think about what I said, girl. I'll be back first thing in the morning expecting some answers."

He turned and disappeared through the door, and Gypsy passed out.

* * * *

Rebel and Blackie crouched in the woods behind the

cabin, squinting against the rising sun, grateful it had finally stopped raining. They'd been watching the area for hours trying to figure out what they were up against. There hadn't been much activity outside the cabin all night, but that didn't mean there wasn't an army of men inside.

"I've had it with sitting in these damn trees," Reb whispered to his brother. "We've been out here all night, and the only thing that's moved has been that old man every time he comes outside to take a piss."

"So?"

"So that tells me there's no indoor plumbing. If anyone else besides Gypsy was in that cabin, they would've been coming out here to do the same thing the old guy's been doing. He's probably the only one here guarding her."

"Well, what do you wanna do, little brother?" Blackie asked. "It's your call."

Rebel splayed the fingers on his right hand and ran it through his still damp, jet black hair. "Let's take out the old guy first. Once he's out of the way, we'll do a quick sweep of the first floor to make sure no one else is here. My guess is that Gypsy's in that room upstairs."

The brothers glanced simultaneously at the lone window on the second floor.

Rebel started to rise, but Blackie grabbed his arm and pulled him back. "Wait here," he whispered, "I'll take care of the guard."

Blackie got to his feet. When Rebel started to follow, his older brother pointed a loaded gun in his face. "I said stay," he repeated, low and threatening, "I'll signal when I'm ready for you."

Knowing Blackie would knock him out, or at least try if

he didn't obey, Rebel nodded, cursed under his breath, and returned to his crouched position. He wasn't happy about being left behind. As Gypsy's husband, he felt it was his duty to rescue her. But he'd be dammed if he was going to get shot by his own brother doing it.

Rebel waited silently at the edge of the woods for Blackie's signal. When his brother finally stepped around the corner and waved him over, he took off like a shot.

"Well?" he asked in anticipation when he reached Blackie. "What happened?"

"Ain't no one else downstairs," was the only answer his brother offered.

Confused, Rebel stopped short of entering the cabin. "Where's the guard?"

"Dead," Blackie said matter-of-factly. "Now go get your wife."

Rebel stared at Blackie in disbelief. He'd always wondered if his older brother had enough self-control to stop himself from killing someone. Now he knew.

"I ain't gotta explain myself to you," Blackie said, giving Rebel a shove toward the door. "Get your ass inside and find Gypsy before company shows up."

Knowing his brother was right, Rebel drew his gun and entered the house. Quietly taking the stairs two at a time, he stopped in front of the bedroom door and listened for any signs of life inside.

Everything was quiet.

Knowing there could still be guards lying in wait, Rebel readied himself and gently turned the knob.

* * * *

Gypsy's breath caught in her throat the instant she heard

the clank of the metal doorknob turning. The man guarding her from the wooden chair just inside the door took a long swig from his beer bottle and smirked. "You're in for it now," he whispered.

Assuming the person coming in was her father, Gypsy lay down on the mattress and turned away from the door. It wasn't until she heard her guard's chair crash to the floor that she turned back around to see what was happening. Her eyes widened in amazement when Rebel appeared in the doorway.

Rebel spotted the guard immediately and fired his gun into the man's stomach. At the same time, the guard managed to shatter the half-empty beer bottle across Rebel's temple. Gypsy's scream died in her throat as both men fell to the floor.

Unable to take her eyes off her husband, Gypsy struggled to sit up. What was Reb doing here? How had he found her? How was she going to help him?

Her train of thought was suddenly broken when a large man burst into the room. Frightened by his size, Gypsy wrapped her arms around her half-naked body and curled into a ball, inching into the corner as far as the shackles would allow.

A good four inches taller than Reb, the stranger's long, shaggy, dark brown hair fell around his face, which was covered in a few days growth of dark stubble. Assuming he was coming for her, Gypsy was surprised when he focused his attention on Reb instead. Kneeling, he ran his large hands along Reb's arms and legs. She could've sworn he was checking for broken bones, and knew she was right when she heard him sigh with relief when he found none.

Taking a deep breath, he carefully shifted around tufts of

Reb's hair until he found the source of the blood. After close examination, he said, "You're gonna be fine, little brother."

Little brother? Gypsy squinted and took a closer look at the man who was now slowly rolling her husband onto his back. When he turned his head in her direction as he scooped Reb into his arms, Gypsy wondered why she hadn't recognized him sooner. He was taller, more muscular, and his hair was much longer than in the picture taken fifteen years earlier, but she knew she was staring at Blackie McCassey.

"Blackie?" she said, not realizing she'd actually uttered his name out loud.

He froze, then turned and looked at her as if just realizing she was there. "Holy shit!" he rushed over, depositing his brother on the mattress next to her. "I almost forgot about you."

"I'm Gypsy."

"I know who you are, girl," he said, taking in her bruised and swollen face, along with the bloody scratches covering her arms and legs. "We waited outside all damn night in the rain to come in here and get you." He knelt down to feel her limbs for broken bones the same way he did to his brother, but when he went to touch her, she flinched and tried to move farther into the corner.

He backed away immediately. "I ain't gonna hurt you, Gypsy. I just wanna make sure you're okay."

"I'm fine," she said just a little too quickly, drawing a suspicious glance from Blackie. To avoid the questions she knew Blackie was about to ask, Gypsy changed the subject. "What about Reb?"

Blackie looked down at his unconscious brother. "He's okay. But he's gonna have a hell of a headache when he wakes up."

Hearing that, Gypsy burst into tears.

"Hey!" Blackie shouted as if he was angry, "don't do that!"

Gypsy looked at him and continued to cry, tears silently rolling down her cheeks.

"My lovesick little brother ain't quit talkin' about you since we left the garage," he told her. "He said you been through a lot and don't get upset easy. So why the hell are you cryin', girl? I just said he's gonna be fine."

She wiped at her tears. "I'm sorry. I just didn't know how bad he was hurt. I was afraid he was going to die."

Blackie took a closer look at Gypsy. "You know, with no make-up and your hair in a ponytail like that, you look more like someone's little sister than my brother's wife."

Was he for real? Her husband, *his brother*, was lying in front of them unconscious, and all Blackie could say was that she looked like a little kid? "What?"

He sighed. "Gypsy, I can tell how much you love Rebel, and I'm sorry for yellin' at you. It's just that I don't deal well with cryin' females."

When Gypsy's only response was a loud sniff, Blackie, looking very much like Rebel as he ran a hand through his long hair, squatted in front of her. "Look," he explained calmly, "I may be a lot of things, but I ain't no liar. Rebel's gonna be fine. One good slap in the face, and he'll be wide-awake. Okay?"

"A slap in the face?"

"Yeah. It always worked when he was a kid."

She shrugged, knowing full well that Rebel wasn't going to be happy about his brother slapping him in the face. "Okay," she agreed, expecting to have to dive for cover when

Reb came to and realized who'd hit him.

"Good." He flashed a quick grin, revealing perfectly straight teeth. "Now let's get the hell out of here before someone discovers the dead guard downstairs."

"Dead?" Her eyes widened a little. "You killed him?"

Blackie shrugged, showing no remorse. "It was him or me, honey. And I ain't much good to you and my brother dead. Am I?"

"No."

"Right, now let's go."

"I can't," she told him, pointing to the shackles around her ankles and the chains locked to the bedpost.

"Shit!" Blackie bent down to examine the chain and ran his hand along the thin metal. "I ain't got nothin' to cut these off."

"It's okay," she said. "Just get Reb out of here before they come back."

Blackie looked at her in amazement. "You really would sacrifice yourself for my brother, wouldn't you?"

She nodded, and he changed the subject. "How many of them are there?"

"I'm not sure exactly. One guy grabbed me from the garage, there was one on an ATV, one driving a car, the two guards, and my...and Johnny Cooper." She paused to look out the window at the rising sun. "He said he'd be back first thing this morning. Please hurry and get Reb out of here, Blackie. He got hurt trying to help me, and I'll never forgive myself if something else happens to him."

"And he'd never forgive me if somethin' happened to his wife." He looked her dead in the eye. "I ain't leavin' you behind."

Blackie took a quick look around the room. Seeing nothing to cut the chains off Gypsy's ankles, he reached behind his back and pulled out the pistol. "There ain't no other choice, I gotta shoot the chains off." He quickly removed his T-shirt and handed it to her. "Cover your head with this. I don't want no metal ricochetin' into your face."

She started to lift the shirt but he put a hand out to stop her. "One more thing," he said. "The sound of this gun goin' off is probably gonna attract some attention, it not bein' huntin' season and all. So we're gonna have to run like hell if we want to get out of here unnoticed. Can you make it?"

Gypsy looked down at her bare feet and bruised, swollen ankles, not even sure she could walk. "I can do it."

"Good deal." He looked down at Rebel's large, still form and shook his head. "I'm gonna try and rouse him one more time before I fire this gun, 'cause it's gonna be a long walk outta here if I gotta carry him. My baby brother ain't as little as he used to be."

Blackie turned away from Gypsy and knelt in front of his brother again. With an open palm, he not-so-gently tapped the side of Rebel's face until he began to stir. "Nap time's over, little brother, wake up."

Rebel's eyes went wide when he opened them. "What the hell…"

"Your head lost a fight with a beer bottle. You got a hell of a knot."

* * * *

Rebel's hand flew to the left side of his head, and he groaned when it came in contact with a baseball-sized lump and warm, sticky blood.

Wiping the area with the bottom of his shirt, Rebel sat up

and took a good look at Gypsy's face. She'd been beaten, that much was obvious. But what else had they done to her? The clothes on her body, scant as they were, seemed to be intact; no rips or tears, and there wasn't any blood on the mattress. It didn't appear as though she'd been raped, and Rebel thanked the Lord for small favors.

Careful of any wounds she may have that he didn't notice, Rebel cautiously pulled his wife close. "Are you all right? He didn't hurt you too bad, did he?"

Too choked up to talk, she shook her head to tell him no.

"Don't worry, darlin', we'll get you all fixed up when we get out of here."

"We got somethin' else to worry about first." Blackie moved out of his brother's line of vision to reveal Gypsy's ankles; black and blue, chained to the bed.

Rebel let loose with a string of profanities and jumped up to examine her ankles. "Good God." He sat on the bed next to her and raised his hands, wanting to pull her into his arms again. "What did he do to you?"

She took a deep breath and managed a smile. "It's not as bad as it looks. I'm just glad you're okay. I thought you were going to die."

"Sorry, Gypsy, I'm afraid you're stuck with me."

"Ahem," Blackie cleared his throat to get their attention. "This is real sweet and all, but we need to get those chains off and get the hell outta here."

"How?" Rebel asked. "There's nothing here..." Then he noticed the .38 in his brother's hand. "Good idea."

Blackie grinned, reached into his waistband, and pulled out the gun he picked up off the floor. He tossed it to Rebel. "The clip's full. Ready when you are."

Rebel returned his brother's grin. "I'm glad you're back."

"It's good to be back, little brother," he aimed his gun at the chain on Gypsy's right ankle. "Let's get this over with."

"Cover your face, darlin'," Rebel said after giving her a quick kiss. "This'll only take a second."

Gypsy put the T-shirt over her head and squeezed her eyes shut. The brothers fired two shots each and she was free.

She swung her legs over the edge of the bed, wincing when the shackle still attached to her left ankle struck the metal frame. Planting her feet on the floor, she stood.

"No shoes?" Rebel asked.

She shook her head.

"It's okay," Rebel offered reassurance by touching her shoulder. "Can you walk?" he asked.

"I think so."

Blackie looked out the window to check for anyone who might have heard the shots. "It's clear," he said. "I'll go out first. If somethin' happens and I go down, leave me. Don't take a chance on gettin' caught by these guys again." Blackie took a deep breath and checked the window one last time. "Don't forget, the truck keys are still in the ignition. You two ready?"

Rebel looked at Gypsy, who nodded. He took her right hand in his left. "Ready."

All three moved toward the door as one. Blackie reached for the knob, but before turning it, he made a fist with his left hand and held it out. Rebel let go of Gypsy and touched his fist to his brother's. The men nodded to each other, Rebel took hold of Gypsy's hand again, and they left the room.

Guns drawn and ready, Blackie and Rebel led the way down the stairs of the small cabin followed closely by Gypsy, who was clinging to Reb's left hand and trying to keep the few links of chain still attached to her shackles from clanking together. When they reached the bottom, Blackie put a finger to his lips. He peeked around the corner and noticed that the guard whose neck he'd broken earlier was still on the floor. There was no sign that any one else had returned.

"The cabin's empty. Rebel, you and Gypsy go out first. If it's clear, send her ahead of you to start the truck." He turned to Gypsy. "Once you get it runnin', honey, slide into the middle. I'll drive."

Blackie twisted the knob on the front door, backed away, and kicked it open. There were no sounds outside. "On the count of three," he whispered, "you two take off." He put his left hand in the air, raised one finger, two, then put his hand on Rebel's shoulder and pushed him out the door.

All was quiet until Rebel and Gypsy were halfway to the truck. Someone fired a gun at them, the bullet hitting the side of the cabin just above Rebel's head. "Go!" he yelled to Gypsy, pushing her toward the truck.

She took off running while Rebel and Blackie returned fire, the sound of their guns deafening.

Rebel's pickup truck was right where Blackie said it would be. Gypsy opened the door and jumped into the driver's seat. She grabbed onto the key and turned the ignition but nothing happened. Again and again she tried, but the engine refused to turn over.

The sound of gunfire was getting closer as Rebel and Blackie made their way to the truck. "Oh, you stupid truck!" she yanked the keys from the ignition and tossed them to the floor. Left with no other choice, Gypsy reached under the steering column and pulled out the wires. She took the ignition wire in one hand, battery wire in the other and closed her eyes, praying she was doing everything right. "Please let this work." She brought the wires together and the engine roared to life. Gypsy slid into the middle seat just as the brothers reached the vehicle.

Rebel jumped into the passenger seat and leaned out the open window. He continued firing as Blackie got behind the wheel, slammed the truck into gear, and took off down the dirt road.

They were a good quarter mile away before Rebel stopped firing. He ducked back into the truck and turned his attention to Gypsy. "Are you okay?"

"I'm fine," she told him, then noticed the blood running down his right arm. "You're bleeding!" she cried, beginning to panic.

"It's just a flesh wound. See?" He leaned closer and showed her where the bullet had grazed his bicep. "I'm fine."

Gypsy took a deep breath and looked at Blackie, who was also bleeding. She started to touch the spot on his thigh where blood was seeping through his blue jeans, but his right hand left the wheel and caught her wrist in mid-air. "Uh-uh, honey. That ain't no flesh wound." He released her almost immediately and grabbed the steering wheel again. "It hurts like hell, so don't touch."

"Sorry." Her voice cracked, giving away exactly how unnerved she really was.

* * * *

Rebel took one look at Gypsy's face and knew she had to be close to tears. His young wife was tough, but in less than twenty-four hours, she'd been kidnapped, beaten, and caught in the middle of a gun battle. Now she was sitting in a truck between two bleeding men, one with a bullet in his thigh. "Come here, darlin'." Rebel lifted his left arm and she leaned into him, lying quietly until Blackie found his voice again.

"Who-wee, little brother, you ain't lost a thing!"

Rebel tried not to smile, but failed. He shot rifles all the time when he went deer hunting, but had only shot a .38 a handful of times since he was a teenager. It felt great to know his aim was still just as true. Out of the three men shooting at them, Rebel hit two, plus shot out all four tires on their truck; which was why no one was chasing them. "No, I guess I haven't."

* * * *

Gypsy sat silently as the brothers talked, amazed that neither one of them seemed the least bit affected by the fact that they'd just been in a gunfight. A gunfight! They didn't seem worried about the police, or that they were both in need of medical attention.

"How did you find me?" Gypsy finally asked.

Blackie pulled over to the side of the road, and the two men filled Gypsy in on everything they knew. By the end of Blackie's story, she was barely able to breathe.

"You followed my fa—" She started to say *father*, but Johnny Cooper had never been a father to her. "You followed Cooper around the prison just to find out if he planned to come after me?"

Wasn't that dangerous? Couldn't that have started some kind of trouble if Cooper had noticed he was being watched? Blackie had put himself in danger for her. Twice.

"Damn good thing I did, too. Otherwise, girl, you'd have been long dead before anyone knew where to look for you."

The truth of Blackie's statement hadn't escaped her. Neither did the fact that she'd yet to thank the man she knew was responsible for saving her life. She gently touched her brother-in-law's muscular forearm with her small hand. "Thank you, Blackie."

"For what?"

"Saving my life. If you didn't love Reb so much, I'd still be chained to the bed in that cabin."

Apparently not a bit uncomfortable accepting thanks and praise from a woman, Blackie smiled and leaned down to kiss Gypsy's cheek. "No worries, girl. You're a McCassey now. And we take care of our own. Plus," he added with a wink, "I think I'm gonna like havin' me a little sister. I ain't had no one to pick on since this one," Blackie motioned toward Rebel, "grew big enough to do some damage when he was fightin' back."

Gypsy smiled up at him and snuggled closer to Reb.

Comfortably settled, she was about to close her eyes when she caught the look Blackie threw Rebel. "What is it?"

"There's something else we have to tell you."

There was no mistaking the seriousness in her husband's voice, just like there was no mistaking the rising panic in hers when she asked what was wrong.

Rebel wrapped his arms tightly around his wife. "We still don't have any idea who's helping Cooper."

Instantly, her body went rigid. "There's someone else after me, too?" She tried to sit up, but Reb just tightened his hold. "We're not sure if this person is actually after you or if they were just helping Cooper get to you. But we think it's someone in town because whoever took you from the garage knew how well we kept the door to the fire escape locked up. They were prepared with all the right tools to break in."

"What do we do now?" she asked.

"We're heading up to Ten Acres. The rest of the boys are there waiting for us. We need to let them know what went on here and come up with a plan on what to do next."

"What about the police?" she asked. "Shouldn't we call them?"

Rebel and Blackie exchanged glances. "No," Reb told her, "we'll handle this on our own."

"But there are two dead men back there. Won't there be some kind of investigation or something when the police find their bodies?"

"Correction, girl," Blackie said. "There are two dead criminals back there. The police ain't never gonna find their bodies, 'cause their criminal friends are gonna sink them to the bottom of Antietam Creek as soon as they find them."

"Blackie's right, Gypsy," Rebel said. "And there's no need to worry about the cops. They tend to stay away from any problems they think may be family feuds. Not only that, I wouldn't give Sheriff Johnson the satisfaction of knowing we needed help. He'd enjoy it too much."

"So what about Cooper?" Blackie cut in. "Did he talk to you? Say anything about why he's so angry with you?"

She shrugged. "He didn't tell me anything I didn't already know. He threatened to kill me eleven years ago if I went to the police, which I did, so I just assumed that's why he had me kidnapped."

"But why would he kidnap you if all he wanted was to kill you?" Blackie asked. "Why not just hide behind a tree and shoot you or run you down with a car? Why go to all the trouble to involve at least six other people if there was nothin' in it for them? We're missin' somethin' here."

Then it dawned on her. "He wants the key."

"A key?"

"Yeah," she confirmed. "Some kind of safe deposit box key he said was going to make him a rich man. He's convinced I have it."

"Do you?"

"Of course not."

"Than why does he think you do?"

"How the hell should I know?" she snapped, annoyed that he didn't seem to believe her.

The corners of Blackie's mouth lifted into a grin at the brief show of Gypsy's temper.

Breaking his temporary silence, Rebel jumped in and said, "Don't even think about it," when he noticed his wife and brother eyeing each other. "I know what the both of you are made of, and we don't have time to sit here while you," he pointed to Gypsy, "spit your angry fire at him while he," Rebel pointed to Blackie, "talks us to death. If you two want to go a few rounds, save it for when we're not being hunted by killers."

Blackie winked at Gypsy, who responded by cocking an eyebrow, but they both remained silent.

"Now," Rebel said, turning his attention to Gypsy. "Didn't you tell me that your parents had a fight about a key the night your mother died?"

"Yeah, she'd stolen it from him and refused to give it back. That's part of the reason he was so mad at her."

"Okay." He loosened his hold on her and sat up straight. "Now we're getting somewhere. So far we know that Cooper's looking for the key to a safe deposit box holding something that's going to make him rich. The question is...why would he think you have it?"

"Well, the police gave my social worker a small box of things they gathered from our apartment after my mom died, things they thought might be of value. It could've been in there."

"Bingo," he said. "Where's the box now?"

She frowned. "I don't have it anymore. It was stolen from my apartment the same day my social worker gave it to me. I never even got to look inside."

Rebel leaned against the passenger side door.

"What are we going to do?" Gypsy asked in sudden desperation, the playful moment she'd just shared with Blackie forgotten. "We can't go to the police for help and Cooper won't give up until he gets that key. A key I don't have! And even then he won't leave me alone. He wants me dead because I turned him in to the police."

Rebel kissed the top of Gypsy's head and began stroking her hair. "I need time to figure out our next move, and we need to put some distance between us and Cooper's cabin. Let's get up to Ten Acres, Blackie." He motioned for his brother to start driving again. "We need to find out more about Cooper and whoever the hell's been helping him before they realize we escaped and took out their men. Once they know Gypsy's gone, we won't have much time before they come after her again."

Rebel watched Gypsy as she settled herself against him again and closed her eyes. She'd had a hell of a couple of days and had kept herself together much better than he'd expected. She deserved to fall apart, but to her credit, seemed to be handling everything pretty well...so far.

Blackie put his hand on the ignition to start the truck and

suddenly realized it was still running. "Where the hell are the keys?"

Gypsy opened her eyes, winked at Blackie, and closed them again.

Blackie turned to his brother, who was beaming with pride. "You taught her to hotwire the truck?"

Rebel grinned. "Just like you taught me."

"Damn, little brother," he said, pulling back out onto the dirt road. "You got yourself one hell of a woman."

Chapter 15

Four men, their faces lined with worry, jumped to greet the battered trio as they entered the dark hunting cabin on Ten Acres.

Judd, Brady, and Kane began firing questions the second Frank struck a match and lit the wick on an oil lantern. But as the room brightened and the group got a good look at Blackie, Rebel, and Gypsy, who looked as if they had been through a war, each one became silent.

Following Rebel as he took her hand and led her past the curious gazes of his family, Gypsy looked around the rustic, one-room, dirt floor cabin, which was complete with a wood-burning stove. The lantern resting on the kitchen counter did more to light the room than the numerous, small windows, which were all open in an effort to get the thick, humid, August air to circulate.

To Gypsy's left, she noticed a red water pump aimed into a large tub mounted on the wall, and canned goods were neatly stacked on the custom made shelves above. All eight cots lining the middle of the far wall were neatly made, blankets folded into thick squares at the bottom of each, making them look as if they belonged in an army barrack. The line of beds was flanked on each side by large pine bookshelves filled with everything from bars of soap, clean towels, and first aid equipment, to sheets, boxes of ammunition, and an abundance of clean neatly folded clothes. In the center of the room was a long wooden table surrounded by eight chairs. It was here that Rebel stopped and motioned for Gypsy to sit down.

Frank rushed to her when he noticed the shackles. "Good Lord, girl, what happened to you?"

"I'm okay, Frank." She waved him off. "Help Blackie first, he's been shot."

Frank moved over to his nephew, and the men embraced. "You really came through for your brother," he said to the man infamous for being reckless and irresponsible, "and for Gypsy, too. We're all really glad to see you."

Blackie smiled. "It's good to be seen, old man. Now dig this hunk of lead out of me, will ya?"

Five minutes later, Blackie was sitting on one of the cots drinking moonshine from a small flask. Brady and Kane were holding him, trying to stop his flinching as Frank dug the bullet out of his thigh.

Ten feet away, Rebel and Judd had removed the chain links from Gypsy's ankles with bolt cutters and were now working on the shackles with hacksaws. They stopped when she flinched.

"You okay?" Judd asked.

"I'm fine."

"Hang in there, darlin'," Rebel shouted over the noise of his saw. "We're almost done."

"Okay."

Her ankles were free within minutes. While Judd collected the shackles and began to inspect them, Rebel carefully brushed the metal shavings from Gypsy's legs onto the floor and lifted her off the chair. He walked to the row of cots and deposited her petite body on one at the end of the row.

"Let's get you cleaned up."

She nodded and sat still while he drenched a cotton ball with peroxide and went to work cleaning the scratches on her face. They were swollen, dirty, and covered in dried blood. Rebel told himself to ignore the unshed tears that appeared in her eyes. He knew the antiseptic was probably making the cuts on her face sting like hell, but they needed to be cleaned.

"I'm almost done, darlin'," he kept saying. "I'm almost done."

Judd waited until Rebel was finished taking care of Gypsy before bringing him the bag their aunt had packed for her. "Blackie had Rose put a few things together for Gypsy," he said, handing the bag to his brother. "Me and the boys'll clear out so she can change."

Everyone, including Blackie, who was a little unsteady on his feet, stepped outside for a smoke to give Gypsy some privacy.

"Come on," Rebel said, helping Gypsy stand up. "Let's get you washed and into some clean clothes."

He unzipped the blue nylon bag from Rose and rummaged through it until he found what he was looking for; fresh undergarments, a T-shirt, and pair of shorts. There were socks and tennis shoes, too, but from the look of Gypsy's ankles, she wasn't going to be able to wear them.

"Do you have to use the bathroom before you change?"

Relieved, she said, "I thought you'd never ask."

"There's no indoor plumbing," he told her, "but there is a portable pot behind that curtain." Rebel pointed to the corner of the kitchen where a plastic shower curtain hung in a doorway. "Just do whatever you have to do and leave it there. I'll empty it later."

Red faced, Gypsy turned to him. "But…"

Rebel sighed. They'd made love a hundred times and knew every inch of each other's bodies. Why was she picking now to start being modest? "It's nothing I haven't seen before, Gypsy, darlin'. So please, just go take care of yourself, so we can get you into some clean clothes. Okay?"

Gypsy turned away and disappeared behind the curtain. She made quick work of what had to be done and reappeared just as Rebel took a fresh bar of soap, washcloth, and towel off one of the shelves and placed them on the table next to a metal basin filled with water.

"Feel better?" he asked as he strode to the table.

"Much."

He smiled and reached for her. "Good. Come on over here and have a seat."

Gypsy sat down and watched as he dipped the washcloth into the water and lathered it with soap. "It's not a shower," he told her, "and the water's ice cold. But it's the best I can do."

After helping Gypsy remove her shirt, Rebel gently but quickly washed her upper body with the cloth and dried it. Then he hooked her bra for her and pulled the clean shirt over her head. Because the water had been so cold, she was shivering despite the heat as he unbuttoned her jean shorts. He slid them, along with her underwear, down her leg.

She stepped out of the clothes so Reb could pick them up and shove them into the bag. Then he washed the lower half of Gypsy's body.

When she was finally dry and dressed, Reb led her to the pump in the kitchen and washed her hair as quickly as he could. By the time they were done, she was shivering again. "You ought to bottle that stuff and sell it," she told him through chattering teeth. "It's freezing."

"That's because the well is down so deep," he explained. "Sometimes it comes in handy, though. When I was seventeen I sliced the palm of my hand open gutting a ten-point buck. Judd had taken the truck and run into town for more ammo and Frank and I were here alone. He couldn't take me to the hospital until my brother got back, so he filled the sink with water and made me put my hand in it. I was numb in less than a minute."

Rebel put clean sheets on one of the cots as Gypsy towel dried her hair. When she was done, she draped the wet towel over one of the chairs at the table and crawled onto the cot. Rebel knelt down and covered her with the top sheet as she rested her head on a soft feather pillow.

"Try and get some rest, okay?"

She grabbed onto his wrist before he could move. "Don't leave me here."

The look of fear on her face twisted his gut. But she needed rest and he needed a smoke. "I'm not leaving, darlin'. I'll be right outside the door, I promise."

He leaned in and kissed her lips, then went to the bookcase for a flashlight. After turning it on and off several times, he set it on the floor beside her. "This place was built over a hundred years ago and has no electricity," he told her. "It's so dark without the lantern because the trees block out most of the sunlight. I'm turning it out, so if you need to see, turn on the flashlight."

"But I thought you were just going out to smoke a ciga-rette."

"I am. But the guys and I need to come up with a plan and figure out our next move."

She tried to sit up. "I should be in on that. Don't you need some information from me or something?"

Rebel put a hand on her shoulder and forced her back down. "You already told us everything you know. And what I really need is for you to relax and take it easy for a while. This place has been in my family for over a century, and it's no se-cret that my cousins and I hang out here. You can bet your life someone knows where we are, and because of that, there's a chance we may have to move out fast. I want you rested and ready…for anything. And I don't want something happening to the baby. So please do as I ask and lie down for a while."

Gypsy fixed her green eyes on his blue ones and took a deep breath. "Can I say something?"

Rebel knew the look in Gypsy's eyes. It was the same one he'd seen the day she shook the oily rag in his face. *Not today*, he pleaded silently. He may not always know what's best for her, but today he did. He prayed she didn't intend to argue with him. "Go ahead."

"I don't want to stay in the cabin by myself. And I don't want to sleep while you and the rest of the guys try to figure out what to do. But I know you're worried about me and the baby, and I haven't forgotten the promise I made the night you broke up the fight at Digger's. This is a dangerous situa-tion, and I'll listen and do whatever you tell me. The last thing I want is to give you anything else to worry about."

Relieved she didn't plan to put up a fight, he relaxed. "I'll be outside. And don't worry, you're safe."

He turned to go, but the quiet sound of her voice saying, "Promise me something first," stopped him. When he swung back around, every bit of defiance she'd shown the moment before was gone. She was now looking at him with sweet, trusting eyes that made him want to promise her the world. "Anything."

"Promise that whatever plan you come up with, I'll be included."

"Gypsy…"

"Rebel, please," she begged. "This is my problem more than it is any of yours. Cooper's my…father. I'm the one he's trying to hurt—"

"Kill," Reb interrupted.

"Kill," she repeated. "So I should be involved in whatever you guys are going to do, and…"

"And what?"

She bowed her head to hide the tears in her eyes. "And I don't want to be away from you. I'm afraid you're going to sneak me back into town and make me stay with Rose while you take care of everything."

The thought had crossed his mind numerous times.

Gypsy pleaded with her husband again. "Please don't send me away. Spending the night chained to the bed in that cabin away from you was torture. I was terrified we'd never see each other again, and I don't want to be separated from you even for a minute. Promise we'll stay together, Reb, please."

Even though he wanted to, he just couldn't say no. There was a huge fight coming their way, and the last thing Rebel wanted was his wife and their unborn baby smack in the middle of it. But he could see how scared she was, and he wanted to do everything he could to make her feel safe. "I promise."

She thanked him and lay back down.

"Get some rest," he told her. "I'll look in on you in a little while."

Gypsy closed her eyes and fell asleep before Rebel opened the front door.

* * * *

"Here he comes," Judd announced when Rebel exited the cabin. He tossed a pack of cigarettes to his younger brother as he joined the rest of the family under a lush maple tree.

When the rest of the men heard Judd ask Rebel if he had a plan yet, they all turned to him expectantly.

Taking a seat in the grass, Rebel leaned against the trunk of the tree and took a long drag on his Marlboro. "I'm working on it." He exhaled and surveyed the faces staring back at him. "Where's Flynn?"

"At the garage with Jimmy," Frank told him. "We thought it'd look better if it was open for business as usual."

Rebel nodded in agreement. "Good thinking." He took another long drag and extinguished the butt on the bottom of his boot. "Anyone heard anything?"

"Nah. Blackie told us to meet you here today, but we all came up last night, just in case," Kane explained. "If there's any information floating around, Flynn'll know about it. He and Jimmy should be up in a few hours. They're closing the garage at noon."

Rebel nodded and let his gaze drift to Blackie. Eyes closed, his older brother was sitting on the ground leaning his back against an oak tree a few feet away. The flask of moonshine, which Rebel hoped Blackie had the good sense not to finish, was resting between his outstretched legs. Leaning forward, he kicked his brother's boot. "You awake?"

"Do that again, little brother, and you and I are gonna have problems," he halfheartedly warned, not bothering to open his eyes. "How's your wife?"

"Okay. She's inside sleeping. Your leg all right?"

"I'll live."

"Good. I'm going to need you."

"No worries, Rebel," he said, finally opening his eyes. "That's what I'm here for."

Rebel nodded, knowing no thanks were necessary. He'd literally put his life on the line for his older brother more times than he cared to remember, and knew without a doubt that Blackie would do the same for him or Gypsy. Hell, he already had…and gotten shot for his trouble.

The six men sat outside for the better part of the morning rehashing the events of the past two days. Off to the side by himself, Rebel said little, taking advantage of the time to form what he hoped was a rock solid plan to end Gypsy's nightmare, once and for all. By the time the rest of his family showed up just after noon, he had almost every detail worked out.

Jimmy jumped from the cab of Flynn's truck carrying a large thermos. He pulled Rebel to the side and handed it to him. "How's Gypsy?"

"Beat up a little, but she'll be fine. What's this?"

"Rose's homemade chicken soup. She made me promise to watch Gypsy drink every last drop."

"Thanks."

"No problem." He hesitated before asking, "What about the baby?"

Trying not to think of the possibility that harm had come to the child his wife was carrying, Rebel shrugged. "It's okay,

I think. Gypsy didn't say anything otherwise."

"Where is she?"

"Inside. She's been sleeping all morning."

"You come up with any kind of plan yet?"

"Yeah. Let's go talk to the others. I only want to have to say this once."

Rebel and Jimmy joined the six other McCassey men.

They approached Flynn first. "You hear anything?" Rebel asked.

"Plenty. Cooper's looking for the key to a safe deposit box. But you probably already know that."

"Yeah. You know what's in that box?"

"Jewelry."

Rebel made a face. "What kind of jewelry?"

"The kind that was stolen from Rockland's Jewelry Store down in Baltimore during a robbery back in 1963. Mostly diamonds. The thieves took about a million dollars worth of stuff; cleaned the place out."

"Jesus, that was twenty years ago. Was Cooper involved?" Rebel asked.

"Him and someone who apparently worked there. The cops thought it was an inside job from the beginning but were never able prove it. They also never found any of the stolen diamonds. Not one single carat."

Rebel nodded. "Because Cooper had them safely stored in a safe deposit box."

"You got it."

"So who was this partner of his?"

Flynn shrugged. "The way Cooper talks, there is no partner anymore."

"You think Cooper killed him?"

"Sure do. Taking out the partner meant he didn't have to share the loot. His only problem then was getting Gypsy away from us. But that was solved by hiring whoever it was that snatched Gypsy from the garage, and probably a couple of flunkies looking for beer money to get her to that old cabin."

Rebel didn't always know where Flynn got his information, and most of the time, didn't want to. But it had always been one hundred percent reliable. Still, this was a life and death situation and he had to make sure it was from a good source. "You're sure about all this?"

"As sure as I'm standing here, cousin."

"Shit."

"Yeah," Flynn said reluctantly, "they probably know where we are, too."

"I know that, Flynn," Rebel spat.

"So what do you want to do?"

Rebel lowered the tailgate of Flynn's pickup truck and sat down. Through clenched teeth, he said, "What I'd really like to do is walk into town and beat Cooper to death; torture him the way he threatened to do to Gypsy."

Always taking his brother's threats seriously, Judd cleared his throat. "That's not a good idea, bro."

"No shit."

"So what do we do then?"

"There's not much we can do, Judd. They're coming after Gypsy. And they're not going to wait a hell of a long time to do it. One million dollars is a lot of money. Cooper isn't going to give up as long as he thinks she's got that key."

"Maybe you could just take Gypsy away," Kane suggested. "Once he knows she's gone, they'll have to give up."

The mere suggestion that they run and hide sent bolts of

white hot anger through Rebel's body. He slid off the tailgate, covered the distance between himself and his cousin in three long strides, and wrapped his hand around Kane's throat. "You know better than to suggest I run from trouble."

At the sudden violent turn of Rebel's temper, Blackie and Judd each took a tentative step closer, ready to step in when Kane began to gasp for air as Rebel squeezed harder.

"Unless you've forgotten, the number of times I've bailed your ass out of trouble is probably higher than you can count, all because you couldn't think quick enough to do it yourself." Rebel loosened his grip, and Kane fell to the ground. "I don't run from anything, boy. You'd be wise to remember that."

Rebel reclaimed his seat on the tailgate while his seven family members, obviously afraid to upset the temporary reign he had on his temper, watched and waited. It was Frank who finally broke the silence. "Why don't you tell us what you have in mind, Rebel?"

"We're going to let Cooper and whoever's helping him come to us," Rebel explained confidently.

"Why don't we just go out after them?" Brady wanted to know.

"Because we'd never know exactly how many of them there are or if we got them all. Letting them come here is our best chance to end this thing once and for all. Let's just hope they all come at once."

"How can you be so sure we can take them all?" Brady questioned. "Cooper could've scraped together two dozen men by now."

"He won't have many more men now than he did yesterday. Cooper's greedy. The less people he has to share his money with, the better."

Brady nodded in agreement.

"This isn't going to be easy, boys. But it will be plenty bloody. You can count on that."

A wide grin crossed Blackie's face and he clapped his hands together. "Hoo-wee, little brother, count me in!"

Rebel lit another cigarette. "This isn't a game, goddammit! My wife's life is at stake here. All our lives are. And what the hell are you getting so excited about, anyway? You get caught with a firearm and your ass goes straight back to prison."

"Yup," he said with a wink. Then he turned away and yelled, "*If* I get caught," as he disappeared behind the cabin.

Rebel rolled his eyes and closed the tailgate of Flynn's truck. "I need to load my guns. Something tells me we're not going to be alone up here much longer." Then he, too, disappeared, leaving Frank, Jimmy, Judd, Brady, Kane, and Flynn sitting in the grass without instruction.

* * * *

"So what do we do now?" Flynn voiced the question that was on everyone's mind.

"I know what I'm doing," Kane said, rubbing his throat, "staying the hell out of Rebel's way. I forgot how dangerous he is when he's angry."

Judd jumped to his brother's defense. "Well, you should've known better than to suggest he run, you moron. What the hell were you thinking?"

"I was thinking of a way to keep Gypsy safe. And don't call me a moron. Rebel's come to your rescue just as much as he's come to mine."

"Which should tell you that he doesn't back down from a fight," Judd yelled, "with anyone!" Then he stepped forward until he and Kane were standing nose to nose.

At the moment when Judd would've punched Kane, Frank stepped between his nephews. "Cut it out you two," Frank hissed. "We've got enough trouble without you boys causing more. And speaking of trouble, all hell's going to break loose up here once Cooper rallies his troops. I don't know about you, but I'd rather not be taken by surprise. Let's go inside and help Rebel get ready."

Frank's statement was met with murmurs of agreement. One by one, the rest of the McCassey's followed him to the cabin. Just before he opened the door, Flynn pulled his uncle aside. "I'm going to slip back into town and see what else I can find out. I'll be back before nightfall."

"Be careful, son."

Flynn saluted his uncle and took off, hoping he'd get back before the war started. He didn't want to miss all the excitement.

* * * *

Rebel heard the cabin's front door slam but didn't look up from cleaning his rifle, even when Blackie sat in the chair across from him.

"That was some show you put on out there, little brother."

"Kane's an idiot."

Blackie gave a slight nod. "Maybe. But don't you think you were a little hard on him?"

"He knows better."

"He's also on our side, Rebel. Don't chase away your allies."

"I don't need him."

"You're damn intimidatin' when you're angry, Rebel,"

Blackie admitted, "and as worked up as you are right now, I believe you could take on an army and win." When he got no response, he added, "Those boys out there were hangin' on your every word, you know. And until I saw that, I'd never understood the effect you have on people. You're a born leader. Hell, even I was waitin' to hear what you was gonna say next."

It wasn't like Blackie to offer compliments, and Rebel felt uncomfortable accepting one for doing nothing more than trying to protect the woman he loved. "I don't need your praise, Blackie, just your support."

Blackie chuckled and shook his head. "You really ain't afraid of a fuckin' thing, are you?"

Rebel's head snapped up. "Yes, goddammit," he was trying to come across angry, but was grinning by the time he said, "I'm afraid you'll never shut up."

Blackie grinned in return and picked up a .30-06 hunting rifle. He managed to stay quiet for a full minute while cleaning it, before opening his mouth again. "You know, there were guys in prison who woulda broke down and cried like babies if you'd done to them what you did to Kane. What happened out there?"

"He pissed me off."

"No kiddin'. Why?"

"He always takes the easy way out."

"He may have a point this time."

Rebel finally brought his head up again, flashing Blackie a lethal look.

Blackie gave his head a slight shake. "Uh-uh, little brother. Touch *my* neck and I'll put you through a wall."

"Shut the hell up, I'm not going to touch you."

"Then what's your fuckin' problem? Why not hide her somewhere safe until this is all over?"

"Gypsy stays with me."

"Why, Rebel?" Blackie pressed him for an answer. "You know what kinda trouble's headed this way. Why's it so damn important she stays with you?"

Rebel backed his chair away from the table. He picked up a box of ammo and tossed it to his brother. "Because I said so. Now, make yourself useful and load that gun."

As Rebel spun away from Blackie, he looked in Gypsy's direction and noticed she was awake. Hoping it was the clicking and clacking of parts as he assembled and loaded his guns that caused Gypsy to stir, and not the discussion he'd had with Blackie, he went and sat on the edge of her cot. "Sorry I woke you, darlin'."

The front door opened and the rest of the guys walked in, but Rebel ignored them and gathered Gypsy into his arms.

"How long was I asleep?" she asked.

"A few hours. You feel all right?"

"I'm okay. What went on outside?"

"It's nothing you need to worry about. Kane and I just got into it a little."

"I heard. What happened?"

He hadn't planned on telling her, but hadn't known she was awake when he was talking to Blackie. He didn't want to tell her that part of the reason he got so angry was that he agreed with his cousin. Gypsy would be much safer far away from the cabin. But he made her a promise and wouldn't break it, so he kept his explanation simple. "Kane suggested I stash you someplace safe, I got angry, end of story."

"From what I heard, that's far from the end of the story,

Rebel McCassey. What did you do to him that would have made men in prison cry like babies?"

He winced. It hadn't sounded so bad coming from Blackie, but hearing Gypsy say it made him feel like a tyrant. "You heard that?"

"Uh-huh."

Rebel reluctantly told her the rest of the story. "I just overreacted, that's all."

She backed out of his embrace and looked up at him. "I don't want you fighting with your cousin because of me."

"We're not fighting, darlin'." He smiled and brushed back her curly hair, which was now dry and very full. "Everything's fine."

As she momentarily forgot Kane, Gypsy's hand flew to her hair. "It's bad, isn't it?"

The smile that hadn't left his face, widened. "Let's just say it has a lot of body. I'll see if I can find something so you can tie it back in a ponytail."

Gypsy let go of Reb's hand and tilted her head to peek at Kane. He was sitting at the table scowling in Reb's direction, but when he spotted Gypsy staring at him, his expression softened and he winked at her.

"See," Rebel said, handing Gypsy a rubber band, "I told you everything was fine. Go ahead and fix your hair. When you're done, you're getting a shooting lesson."

Gypsy's eyes widened, and so did her smile. "All right, a shooting lesson!"

He should've known she'd react that way. "Don't get too excited, it's just a precaution."

"But I could help you," she insisted, excitedly. "You can use as many guns as you can get, right?"

Rebel eyed his wife carefully. If she'd been anyone else, he would've thought she was kidding. But Gypsy had proven that she would do or try just about anything, and he knew she was serious. "Don't even think you're going to be invited to participate in a gun battle, you little vixen. But I do want you to know how to shoot...just in case."

Chapter 16

Sheriff Ben Johnson finished giving instructions to the last of his deputies and turned off the CB radio. Pleased with himself, he sat in the chair behind his desk with a contented smile. It hadn't been easy, but all eight of his deputies were now otherwise occupied; each one of them off on their own personal wild goose chase that would keep them tied up for hours.

"You promised me this would be easy, Johnson," Johnny Cooper yelled at the sheriff. "And so far it's been anything but. I should've been in and out of this deadbeat town in less than a day. Instead, I'm sitting on my ass in your office while you play hide-and-go-seek with your deputies."

"Take it easy, Cooper," Johnson tried to reassure the overly excitable man. "It's all part of the plan."

"What plan?" Cooper stood and began pacing. "I had a plan, you idiot. A plan that was working fine until those two drunken, shriveled up prunes you said would make good guards got themselves killed. You also said the McCassey's would never find Gypsy. But they did. Now she's gone, and so is any chance I had to get that key."

Johnson had been just as surprised as Cooper when they showed up at the cabin and found the bodies of the two men guarding Gypsy, as well as the three of their other men suffering from gunshot wounds. Johnson didn't need to hear the descriptions of who stormed into the cabin and freed Gypsy to know it was Rebel and Blackie McCassey.

They were the only two men on Earth with enough balls to attempt breaking into a building without knowing what they were up against, kill two people, and not worry about disposing of the bodies. Not only that, the bullets from the four perfect shots that blasted Gypsy's chains free of the bedrail were from a .38 Special; the same caliber gun that everyone in town knew Rebel kept in his tow truck.

He didn't mind that the brothers were packing guns. Although Rebel had every right to arm himself, Blackie was on parole, which made it illegal for him to touch a firearm. That, along with the fact that the McCassey's had no idea he was the one helping Cooper, was going to work to his advantage.

Just the thought of finally getting a chance to stick it to the McCassey's made Johnson smile.

Cooper stopped pacing and slammed his hands on Johnson's desk. "This is your fault, Johnson."

"The hell it is," Johnson remarked. "I didn't have anything to do with Rebel and Blackie busting Gypsy out of the cabin. I don't even know how they found out she was there. Now, do you want to hear my plan or not?"

"Goddammit!" Johnny Cooper swore. "My plan had been working perfectly until now! First, after reading the newspaper in prison everyday for almost eleven miserable years hoping by chance my stupid bitch of a daughter would someday be newsworthy, she practically fell into my lap. Then I struck gold by discovering you're the sheriff of the town she lives in. Now, in less than half a day, my whole plan has been shot to hell by a bunch of damn rednecks; and I blame you, Johnson. You better have a quick and easy way to fix this. You owe me.

"You had quite a reaction when I called you last month, thirty-six years after the last time we saw each other. Do I need to refresh your memory of how important it is to both of us that this mess gets worked out?"

Despite his act of bravado, a chill ran up Ben Johnson's spine as he recalled the phone call he'd gotten from Johnny Cooper the month before.

* * * *

"Hello, Ben. This is the voice of your conscience. Remember me?"

"Who the hell is this?"

"I'll give you a hint," Cooper said. "It was dusk on a hot summer night in 1946. You and your girlfriend were visiting your grandparents. Ring a bell?"

It rang a bell all right.

Ben Johnson remembered the night like it was yesterday. He was sixteen. He and his girlfriend had gone to his grandparent's cabin for dinner. They went down to sit on the dock at the pond afterward, where his girlfriend announced she didn't want to see him anymore.

He'd been furious and only meant to scare her. But he couldn't control his rage and pushed her into the water. Before he could stop himself, his hands grabbed her shoulders, dunked her under water and held her there until she stopped struggling.

She was dead in less than a minute, and he was in a state of panic.

With a murder conviction he'd never be able to become a lawman. What was he going to do? Taking deep breaths, he was trying to get a hold of himself when his grandparent's fourteen-year-old neighbor, Johnny Cooper, walked out from behind a tree.

"Why'd you kill her, Ben?"

Johnson didn't answer.

"Come on," Cooper said with an evil grin. "I heard the two of you arguing about something, and I saw you hold her head under the water. What'd she do, dump you?"

No answer.

"Aw, don't worry about it, Johnson. All you have to do is tell the police that the two of you changed into your swimsuits after dinner and decided to go for a swim. She got a cramp, you couldn't find her right away because it was too dark, and by the time you did, she had drown"

It made sense to Johnson. But he'd known Johnny Cooper since he started visiting his grandparents at their cabin on the outskirts of Frederick when he was a kid. In Johnson's opinion, the boy had a few screws loose. And Johnson wasn't at all happy about him witnessing the crime. "Okay, Cooper, what do you want from me?" Johnson asked, anxiously.

Johnny Cooper was quiet for a minute, making Ben Johnson very nervous. "Nothing...now. But I know you're going to be a lawman someday. And a friend on a police force is good to have. Just remember you owe me one, Johnson," he said, as he turned to walk away. "When it's time to pay up, I'll be in touch."

Ben Johnson got away with murder by telling everyone the story Cooper had come up with. The police investigated and wound up ruling his girlfriend's death a simple drowning. Because the incident didn't even make the newspaper, not many people found out about it and Johnson was left free to go on with his life.

That night was also the last time he'd seen Johnny Cooper. But for years after he became sheriff, Ben Johnson kept track of his grandparent's former neighbor. And when the man went to prison for murder in 1972, Johnson was terrified he'd get a call from Cooper asking for help.

But it never came.

As more and more time passed without word from Cooper, Johnson became more confident, assuming he'd never again hear from the only witness to his crime.

"What do you want, Cooper?" Johnson asked the man on the other end of the phone.

"It's time to pay up, Johnson. I've got a business proposition for you. Meet me in the woods at that old cabin in two hours."

Before Johnson could protest, the line went dead.

The meeting between the two childhood acquaintances was brief. Cooper told Johnson that his daughter, Gypsy Lance, had a key that belonged to him. All Johnson had to do was let Cooper use his grandparent's cabin, help get Gypsy away from the McCassey's, and tell him where he could hire some men to help guard his daughter.

"I'll pay you two hundred thousand dollars, Johnson."

"Do you really expect me to believe that? Where would you get that kind of money?" Johnson asked skeptically.

"I was the one who robbed Rockland's Jewelry Store, you small town fool. I've got a million dollars in diamonds stashed in a safe deposit box at the Federal Savings and Loan on Fayette Street in Baltimore City. Gypsy's got the key. We'll nab her, bring her here to the cabin, and hold her while I go get the key. Then you can look the other way when I drown her in the pond."

A chill ran down Johnson's spine as he considered Cooper's offer. If he refused to help, Cooper would undoubtedly start making noise about the drowning all those years ago. Even if no one believed him, the rumors alone would probably keep Johnson from being elected sheriff again. He couldn't afford to let that happen.

Then Johnson thought about the upside to the situation. He knew the perfect way to distract the McCassey's and take Gypsy from the garage, so that would be a breeze. He also knew plenty of drunks who'd work for Cooper for beer money, so that part would be easy, too. Johnson didn't give a shit what Cooper did with Gypsy. In fact, getting to be the one to tell Rebel McCassey that his girl had been murdered was going to be worth risking his career to help Cooper.

After working everything out in his head, Ben Johnson was a very happy man. He'd finally be rid of the burden of owing Cooper a favor, was going to get to ruin Rebel McCassey's life, and would be two hundred thousand dollars richer to boot.

* * * *

Ben Johnson cleared his throat to get Johnny Cooper's attention. "I asked if you wanted to hear my plan, or not."

"I don't have much of a choice, do I? What is it, Johnson? And it better be worth hearing."

Johnson leaned back in his chair, put his feet on the desk, and crossed his legs. "Oh, it's worth it all right. And there's nothing to it, really. They're all up at that cabin in the woods. The one they call Ten Acres. All we have to do is take those men you hired, go up, and get your daughter."

"Just like that? You think they're gonna just let us stroll

onto their private property, no questions asked?"

"Of course not. They're probably going to shoot at us on sight. In fact, I'm counting on it."

"What the hell kind of a plan is that?"

"The kind that's going to get you your daughter and me, three, maybe four McCassey's violating probation to toss in my jail."

"And how are we supposed to do this with them shooting at us?"

"We shoot back, Cooper. You're a criminal. I assume you know how to handle a gun."

"Not only are you stupid, Johnson, you're crazy.

"I can't believe your plan is nothing more than walking onto private property owned by a bunch of rednecks and shooting as many of them as we can until they give up my daughter."

Actually, Johnson thought to himself, his plan was for Cooper and his men to fight it out with the McCassey's. He intended to hang back until the thick of the battle was over and seek out Blackie, Judd, Kane, and Brady; the boys he knew for a fact that weren't supposed to be handling firearms. If any of them were still standing, he'd arrest them for violation of probation. He'd been waiting a long time to ruin the lives of the McCassey's. Finally he was going to get the chance.

His plan was perfect.

Still patting himself on the back for being so brilliant, he shrugged. "That's the plan, Cooper. Take it or leave it."

"I don't like it," Cooper shouted, snarling. "But if there's an easier way to do what we have to without taking the chance of being pumped full of buckshot by some backwoods rednecks, I don't know what it is. So I'll take it. When do we leave?"

Johnson looked at the clock. It was just after four in the afternoon. "How many men do you have?"

"Eight. They're over at that local bar, Digger's, waiting for orders."

"Fine," Johnson said. "Go get them. Meet me under the big oak tree at the edge of town in two hours. That'll give us the advantage of sneaking up on them at dusk, as well as the cover of darkness for escape."

"The big oak tree at the edge of town," Cooper muttered. "I can't wait to get the hell out of this damn hick town. A few hours, in just a few more hours, I'll have the key to my future and the pleasure of silencing my past."

* * * *

Flynn McCassey had been roaming around town all afternoon hoping to gather information on what Johnny Cooper was up to, but so far, he'd come up empty-handed. The last place he decided to try, which normally would've been the first, except that it wasn't somewhere McCassey's went without someone to watch their back, was Digger's Bar. It was getting late, so Flynn decided to hang around for an hour, and if he didn't come up with anything, head back to Ten Acres.

For fifteen minutes, Flynn sat on a barstool nursing a beer that the bartender, Digger's sister, Angel, had served him. He watched the night shift of barmaids, as well as a handful of men, all of whom he recognized, come and go. But what interested him most was the group of eight men that walked in and sat in two booths across from the bar. Strangers weren't too common in Hagerstown. And although one or two may go unnoticed, a group that size stuck out like a sore thumb.

Flynn took a chance that the men were part of the bunch helping Cooper and figured that if he was going to get any information to help Rebel, they'd be the ones to watch.

When a dirty, disheveled man with red hair walked into the bar half an hour later and headed directly to the men in the booths, Flynn knew he'd found what he was looking for. Still nursing his beer, he pivoted on the stool. Pretending to be interested in the television on the other side of the room, he took in every word they said.

"Where the hell you been, Cooper?" one of the men in the group asked. "We been waitin' here almost an hour."

"I had a meeting," Cooper snapped, then suddenly lowered his voice. "I've got orders for you so you better listen good. Any of you screw this up for me, you're dead."

Flynn listened as Johnny Cooper told the men to meet him at the large oak on the edge of town at four o'clock.

"We're going to head up to a place those McCasseys call Ten Acres. Any of you know where that is?"

Every man shook his head. Obviously, none of them were from the area.

"Well, that doesn't matter. We've got someone to show us. So meet up at four and bring plenty of ammo. From what I understand about the McCassey family, they'll be well armed, and this could be a long night."

The men murmured among themselves a moment before Cooper added, "Kill any man you have to. And don't forget, I'm giving an extra thousand dollars to the person that brings my daughter to me *alive*."

Flynn waited until a few minutes after Cooper left the bar then raced back to Ten Acres.

Chapter 17

Flynn entered the cabin on Ten Acres just in time to witness Gypsy being given a lesson on how to use a pistol.

When Rebel noticed his cousin had returned, he took the gun from his wife and handed it to Judd. "Show her how to load it. I'll be right back."

Flynn was grinning when Rebel approached him. "Boy, does she have bad aim," he said, stifling a laugh. "I hope you're gonna think twice before putting a loaded gun back in her hand."

"I'm only giving her the .22," Rebel whispered to Flynn, "so even if she winds up shooting one of us by mistake, it won't do much damage."

Flynn got an are-you-sure-you-want-to-do-that look on his face, but Rebel ignored it and got to the point. "What'd you find out?"

Flynn talked slowly and repeated everything he'd heard. "You were right about someone from town helping him. None of his men know how to get up here, but Cooper said he had someone to show them. He didn't mention who it was, but I do know they had a meeting together right before Cooper showed up at Digger's."

Flynn also added that Kane's earlier suggestion of hiding Gypsy might not be a bad idea. "I know you don't want to make it seem like you're running away, but you didn't hear Cooper talking. He's crazy, Rebel. He gave his men orders to kill as many of us they had to. He even offered an extra thousand bucks to the man who brings Gypsy to him alive. He's gonna kill her if he gets his hands on her, man. Especially when he finds out she doesn't have that key."

His eyes fixed on Rebel; Flynn took a cautious step back. Rebel knew he was waiting for some kind of reaction, even if it was only for the expression on his face to change, but Flynn should've known from experience that it wouldn't. Very rarely did Rebel give away his emotions.

"Let's tell the others what you found out. We have some planning to do."

Silence had filled the cabin by the time Flynn finished his story, and all eyes were on Rebel, waiting for orders.

"We're going to spread out," he began. "Jimmy, you and Flynn take the south side of the cabin. Kane, you and Brady guard the north. Take the M16's and climb up the oak tree where our fort was when we were kids. You'll be able to pick off anybody you can see coming, but the trees are full of leaves so the chances of anyone seeing you from the ground are slim.

"Judd, I want you and Frank on the west side. Since the sun will be setting in the eyes of whoever approaches from that direction, you two will have the biggest advantage. Keep your eyes open. We can't afford to have anyone get past you. Blackie and I will stay on the east side, and I'm going to position Gypsy behind the boulder that sits in the brush at the edge of the woods. It's large enough to hide her, but narrow enough to let her see and get a shot off if she needs to."

Brady and Kane were too late trying to hide their sudden chuckles. Upon hearing them, Gypsy's temper flared. "I know I'm a bad shot, but I haven't had an entire lifetime to practice like you two." Grabbing the loaded pistol from Judd, she kept it pointed toward the floor as she glared at the guys. "You wouldn't think it was so damn funny if I shot you."

Brady and Kane shut up immediately, and Rebel figured it was because they were more stunned that Gypsy had almost cussed at them, than the fact that she'd threatened to shoot them. Wordlessly, he took a step toward his wife and loosened the pistol from her grip. Before handing it back to Judd, he stared at Gypsy, silently telling her this was not a good time to get Brady and Kane riled up.

"Anyway," Rebel continued, "Flynn said Cooper's got eight men not including himself. Plus whoever it is that's been helping him. That makes the odds pretty much even, because we know the area and they don't. And don't be afraid to take the first shot. If one of Cooper's men is in front of you, take him out.

"This is just like hunting," he reminded them. "Wait until you have a clear shot before firing, so you don't waste your ammo. A misfire won't do anything but give your prey a chance to get away, so make every shot count."

Rebel scanned the room. Any questions?"

"How will we know when it's over?" Flynn asked.

"Meet down at the mouth of the creek thirty minutes after the last shot is fired," Rebel told them. "Keep track of how many men you take down, and we'll add them up when we're all together. If we miss any, we can leave from the creek and hunt them down together. It should be dark by then, so any stragglers won't be hard to find; they'll probably be lost and walking in circles at that point."

When there were no more questions, Rebel took a deep, cleansing breath. "All right then, does everyone know what to do?"

They all nodded and he added one last thing. "Remember, this is private property and they're trespassing, so don't aim to wound, shoot to kill. It'll stand up in court, and I'll take the blame since it's my wife they're trying to hurt, and most of you aren't supposed to be handling guns. Watch each other's backs, too. Am I clear?"

More nods.

"Pick up your weapons and let's move out. And," he said before everyone left the room, "thanks."

Rebel's uncharacteristic show of emotion seemed to make his uncles and cousins uncomfortable, so each one just touched his shoulder as they armed themselves and left the cabin. Before Rebel could stop her, Gypsy followed.

Alone with his brothers, Rebel sat quietly on a cot and lit a cigarette.

"Second thoughts?" Judd asked.

Rebel took a long drag on his cigarette and released the smoke in rings. "Nope."

"We're doing the right thing, bro. Gypsy doesn't have a chance if we don't take out Cooper."

"I know, Judd. That bastard deserves to die. And I hope I'm the one that gets the chance to take him out. But I sure as hell don't want to waste him in front of Gypsy. She's strong, but I'm afraid seeing something like that would put her over the edge."

"You leave him to me, little brother," Blackie said, as he,

too, lit a cigarette. "I'll take care of it."

"I'm not going to let you do something that's my responsibility. I should be the one to—" Rebel stopped because Blackie raised his hand to cut him off.

"What I do ain't up to you, Rebel," Blackie told him. "Gypsy's your wife and it's your job to protect her, but if I get a clean shot at Cooper, I'll be damned if I ain't takin' it. That son of a bitch messed with the wrong fuckin' family."

Blackie took a drag on his cigarette while Rebel and Judd exchanged worried glances.

"Fine," Rebel said, rising from the cot. He didn't have time to argue. They had a job to do. "Let's do it."

All three brothers made fists with their right hands and held them out to each other, murmuring, "no worries". After staring at each other in silence for a moment, they dropped their fists when there was a light knock at the door.

Gypsy poked her head in the room. "Sorry to interrupt, but Frank's getting a little restless."

Rebel took her hand and led her into the cabin. Then he turned to Judd. "You better get going."

Judd picked up a .38 Special, shoved it into his waistband and covered it with his T-shirt. He walked to the door and stopped with his hand on the knob. "We'll take care of everything," he told Gypsy. "But be careful anyway."

She nodded. "You too, Judd."

"We should go too, Rebel," Blackie suggested. "We need time to make sure Gypsy's well hidden."

"Are you sure you want to do this?" Rebel asked, lightly caressing Gypsy's face. "It's not too late to change your mind."

Gypsy grabbed onto his forearm with both hands. "You

promised I could stay," she said, frantically. "I'm not leaving you, Rebel. I'm not!"

Without warning, Blackie butted into their conversation. "Are you tellin' me that you refused to hide your wife just because you gave her your word she could stay?"

"I'm not telling you anything," Rebel snapped. "Butt out, Blackie."

Blackie gave his head a slight shake. "You must be kickin' yourself right about now for makin' such a stupid promise." Turning to Gypsy, he said, "You got a lot to learn, girl. Now, not only does Rebel have to worry about Cooper, he has to worry about you, too."

Gypsy opened her mouth to say something, but Rebel silenced her by pulling her close and kissing her hard on the mouth. Then he handed her his old .22, and in a deep monotone voice, said, "Let's go."

The trio walked outside and headed to the rock at the edge of the woods. Still barefoot because of her bruised and swollen ankles, Gypsy carefully climbed behind it and sat still while the guys covered her with brush. When she was well hidden, Rebel knelt in front of her. "Stay put, darlin', this'll all be over soon. Are you sure you're okay?"

"I'm fine."

Rebel didn't believe for a second that she was okay, but admired the front she was trying to put up. "Keep that gun handy," he reminded her. "It won't do much damage, but it'll keep anyone who doesn't want to get shot from touching you. And stay put until someone comes to take you to the creek. If it isn't me, it'll be one of my brothers. I love you."

Before she could tell him she loved him too, he was gone.

Chapter 18

The sun had just begun to set when the first sounds of footsteps and muffled voices came from the direction of the main road. It sounded as though Cooper and his men were all bunched together in a group, which was good for the McCassey's. The unsuspecting men were heading right into Rebel and Blackie's line of fire.

"Here they come," Reb mouthed to his oldest brother. The dusk did nothing to hide Blackie's reckless grin. He looked like he was planning on enjoying himself.

The crack of the first shot nearly caused Gypsy to jump out of her skin. It had been so quiet that she'd almost convinced herself there wouldn't be a gunfight. Then a shot echoed through the woods, someone yelped in pain, and all hell broke loose.

* * * *

Johnny Cooper ran through the thick woods dodging bullets and cursing the sheriff with every step. He should've known this plan was too good to be true. According to Sheriff Johnson, the McCassey's were supposed to be holed up in their cabin trying to think of a way to hide Gypsy. Instead, they were hiding outside waiting to ambush Cooper and his men. The firestorm of bullets flying through the trees had been completely unexpected.

Narrowly avoiding another shot, Cooper watched the man next to him go down then took a quick look around. That damn sheriff had been right behind him when he and his men entered the woods. Now, of course, the double-crossing coward was nowhere to be seen.

Cooper wasn't about to fool himself into thinking he'd be able to avoid the McCassey's for long. He was already lost and running in circles. This was their home turf, and they knew it like the backs of their hands. He needed to find somewhere to take cover. Fast. And he had to find Gypsy.

He had to get that key.

* * * *

The deafening booms from the .357 Magnums Rebel and Blackie were firing together sounded like dueling cannons. Rebel watched as Blackie peeked around the trunk of a tree, caught sight of the man Flynn described as Johnny Cooper, who was scrambling for cover, and fired. Cooper managed to avoid the shot, but the man next to him wasn't so lucky.

Rebel had positioned himself far enough from the cabin that he'd be able to spot anyone long before they got to it, but close enough that he could see the rock where Gypsy was hiding. He'd cussed himself up one side and down the other a thousand times in the past hour for allowing her to be a part of this. The reaction Blackie had when he found out what was going on only confirmed that Rebel had been thinking with his heart instead of his head.

He and Blackie were the closest ones to the front of the cabin, and so far, no one had gotten past them. Gypsy was safe…for the moment. Keeping one eye in the general direction of his wife, Rebel turned his attention to the north side of the cabin. There was heavy firing coming from the direction of the oak tree where Brady and Kane were perched twenty feet in the air. That tree was lush and full of leaves this time of year, and he almost laughed at the thought of the confusion among Cooper's men when the gunfire had come from above.

Rebel dove for cover behind the nearest tree when he heard rustling in the brush behind him. He landed on the ground as a bullet split the bark just above his head. Catching sight of someone running, Rebel aimed his gun in the direction of the retreating man and fired. The moment the guy went down, Rebel turned and crawled on his belly over to Blackie.

"How many did you get?"

"Three," Blackie whispered. "You?"

"Two. Any more signs of Cooper?"

"Not since I fired at him a few minutes ago."

"Shit. Where the hell is he?"

"I don't know. But you and I got five, and I saw Judd a minute ago. He held up two fingers. So that's seven. Brady and Kane had to have gotten someone with all that firin' they were doin'."

"What about Jimmy and Flynn?" Rebel asked.

"I don't know. I ain't heard much from the south side."

Rebel swore. "Me either. I'm going around to check on them. Keep an eye on Gypsy for me."

Blackie nodded and turned to give his brother cover as he made his way around to the south side of the cabin.

Rebel found Jimmy crouched behind a tree holding onto Flynn, who was unconscious. Alarm raced through Rebel as he lowered himself to his knees and touched his cousin's forehead. "Is he alive?"

"Yeah. A bullet just grazed his head. He's out of it because he knocked himself out when he fell against a rock. He'll be fine."

Had the situation not been so serious, Rebel would've laughed. Leave it to Flynn to survive a gunshot wound to the head then knock himself unconscious.

"You see who shot him?" Rebel asked his uncle.

"I saw him but didn't recognize him."

"You sure?"

"Yeah, I'm sure."

"Damn! Who in the hell could be the one helping Cooper?"

"I don't know, Rebel, I haven't seen anyone I recognize."

"What about Flynn? Did he see anyone you didn't?"

"I don't even think he saw who shot him. I yelled to warn him, but with all the noise coming from those pieces you and Blackie were firing, he didn't hear me."

Gunfire from the west side of the cabin had Rebel scrambling to his feet. "I have to get back. Will you two be okay here for a while?"

"We'll be fine," Jimmy assured him. "Go."

Rebel wasted no time racing back to where he'd left his brother. "Who'd you see?"

"It was Cooper again. He was pretty far away, but I took a shot anyway. I know he's hit because he went down, but it ain't bad. He got up again."

"Gypsy?"

"She's fine."

Rebel breathed a sigh of relief. "Flynn's hit. Jimmy has him behind a tree."

Blackie cursed under his breath just as Brady and Kane stepped out from behind the cabin. "We only got one," Kane reported.

"Well that's eight," Rebel announced. "Cooper's still out

there. Blackie just hit him, but he took off running. Whoever's helping him is out there, too."

"What do we do now?" Brady asked.

Rebel looked to the west. Dusk was upon them. "It'll be completely dark in another thirty minutes. If Cooper was hit by Blackie's .357, he can't be moving very fast. I'd like to get him before we lose the rest of this light."

"You take the boys and go after him," Blackie ordered. "I'm gonna take a look around and see if I can't find the bastard feedin' Cooper his information. He led them here, so he's bound to be hidin' close by."

Rebel knew his brother had a tendency to carry things too far, and didn't like the idea of Blackie taking off without someone there to calm him down. But this might be his only chance to get to Gypsy's father, and he had to take it. "All right, but take it easy. You're going to be an uncle, you know."

"That's why I'm doin' this, little brother. Ain't no niece or nephew of mine gonna have to live in fear of nothin'; not if I can help it. I'll catch up to you all later."

Rebel watched Blackie disappear into the darkening woods and hoped that wouldn't be the last time he'd see his brother alive.

"What now, Rebel?" Frank asked.

"Now, we find Cooper."

"What about Gypsy? Are we taking her with us?"

"Well, I'm not leaving her here alone!"

"You want me to run her over to Jimmy and Flynn?" Judd offered. "They're well hidden. She should be fine with them."

Rebel took a deep breath and brushed back his long, dark, sweat-soaked hair. His brother was a damn good shot and Reb needed him close by. "No, Judd, I need you here. Kane?"

"Yeah?"

"Climb behind that rock and keep an eye on Gypsy. I don't want either one of you to move until I get back. Understand?"

* * * *

Kane liked to think that when push came to shove, he was just as tough and fearless as Rebel. But the minute he was ordered to watch out for Gypsy, Kane knew he was kidding himself. Being responsible for taking care of her scared the shit out of him.

But he owed Rebel. Not just for all the times Rebel had bailed him out of trouble, but for feeling like he was one of the reasons Gypsy had been kidnapped. He still felt so guilty that he'd stand alone in the clearing for Cooper to use as a target if his cousin asked him to.

"Kane?" Rebel said, impatiently.

He gave a thumb's up. "Yeah, yeah, I understand."

Rebel reached over and gave his cousin a slight shove. "Well, get going then. We're losing daylight."

Once Kane had reached the rock, Rebel, Judd, Brady, and Frank took off into the woods after Johnny Cooper.

Gypsy acted more than a little surprised when Kane snuck up on her from behind the rock. "Sorry I scared you," he said, then grinned at her. "And thanks for not shooting me. Rebel wants me to stay here until he gets back."

"Where is he?"

Kane took a few minutes to explain what was going on, where Blackie went, and what happened to Flynn. "He wants to find Cooper before it gets dark. Don't worry, it shouldn't take too long."

The words had no sooner left his mouth when the first of a barrage of gunshots came from the woods. "See?"

As the gunfire continued, it began to sound as though it was getting closer to the cabin. "That's getting awfully loud, Kane. It sounds like they're coming this way."

That's exactly what it sounded like.

Why would Rebel lead the battle in the direction of the person he was trying to keep safe? Unless it wasn't him. Maybe it was Cooper. Or maybe Cooper had reinforcements waiting by the main road, and it was their gunfire he and Gypsy were hearing. Why hadn't he just told Rebel he didn't want to take care of Gypsy? Because he owed him, that's why. If Kane was a cat, he'd owe at least seven of his nine lives to Rebel.

The gunfire was once again deafening.

When the sound of a bullet ricocheting off their rock made them both jump, Kane made a drastic decision. He grabbed Gypsy's hand. "Let's go."

Gypsy's eyes grew wide. "Go where?"

"We can't stay here! Another shot as close as that one and we're in big trouble."

She quickly reminded Kane of their instructions. "I promised I'd listen when Rebel told me what to do in situations like this, and we're supposed to stay here."

Kane pulled Gypsy to her feet. "He also told me to take care of you. And to me, that means keeping you out of the line of fire."

Kane rose from behind the rock and took a quick look around. The coast was clear. "When I say so, we're going to make a break for the cluster of oak trees where Brady and I were hiding. It's about fifty yards from here. Can you make it?"

Gypsy grasped Kane's hand tighter. "I don't even want to think about what's going to happen if I can't. Let's just do it."

She had true grit. He admired that.

The sound of another bullet striking their rock cut off what Kane was about to say, and he muffled Gypsy's scream by putting his right arm around her neck and pulling her to his chest. The next bullet tore into his left shoulder, but he managed to hold on to Gypsy as they both fell to the ground. "Ahh! Son of a bitch!" he yelled.

"Kane! Are you okay?"

"I'm fine, goddammit!" Ignoring the burning pain in his shoulder, Kane put his hand on the back of her head and forced it to the ground. "Get the hell down!"

"Oh, Kane..."

Kane was pretty sure she was crying, but he was too worried about making sure they didn't get killed to care. He let go of her and touched his wound. It was small, probably from a .22, but the bullet was lodged in his shoulder. "Calm down, Gypsy, I'm fine," he said, trying to be cheerful. "Rebel shot me in the ass once with a BB gun when we were kids and that hurt worse."

She wiped her eyes and looked at him skeptically.

"It's a true story, honest. Remind me to tell it to you sometime when we're not being used as target practice. Right now, we need to get to those oak trees. Ready?"

She took a deep breath. "Ready."

Kane took hold of her hand again, and she held on as if her life depended on it. "I don't see anyone around," he told her, "but that doesn't mean there isn't someone ten feet away waiting to shoot at anything that moves. So when we go, run like your ass is on fire."

Gypsy nodded.

"Now!" Kane yelled, and they dashed across the clearing toward the cluster of oaks. A few feet from their destination, someone began firing at them. Kane sped up, pulling Gypsy behind him. When they reached the trees and dove to the ground, the firing ceased.

"Whoever's out there is definitely aiming for us."

"How many are there?"

"There are two weapons being fired, but it's probably only one person with two guns."

"It's Cooper, isn't it?" Gypsy asked.

Kane knew it was probably Cooper. He was one of the only two men he and his cousins hadn't taken out yet. "I'm sorry, Gypsy. It's probably him."

Kane gave her shoulder a squeeze. "Keep it together, girl. Rebel will be back soon." He knew she didn't want to confront Cooper without Rebel by her side, and that was the best reassurance he could've given her at that moment.

More gunfire erupted in their direction, and Kane pushed Gypsy's head onto the ground again and covered it with his arms. "Goddammit!"

"What?"

"What do you mean what? He's getting closer, Gypsy. We have to get out of here."

"Where to now?"

Kane had no idea where to go. If they moved farther into the woods, Rebel and the others might mistake them for Cooper and shoot them. If they stayed where they were, Cooper would be upon them in a matter of minutes.

Kane sighed. "All right, I have an idea."

"I have a feeling I'm not going to like whatever it is you're about to suggest."

"You're not, Gypsy. But listen, I think the reason we're only hearing one gunman now is because Rebel and the others know Cooper's close to us. They're probably not firing because they don't want to hit us. I figure our best bet is to let Cooper know exactly where we are by having you yell at him. That way Rebel can follow the sound of your voice and get in here to help us. What do you think?"

With tears flowing, Gypsy said, "I think I'd do anything to have Rebel here now. I need him, Kane. I'm scared."

In an effort to comfort her, Kane pulled her against his chest again. Every girl he knew would have fallen apart long before now, but not Gypsy. She'd been brave through this whole mess, which is why he didn't really mind the tears. He just wished she'd waited until Rebel was back to start crying. "Hang in there, Gypsy girl," he crooned, stroking her hair. "It'll all be over soon."

She pulled away from him and tried to get control of herself. "I'm sorry, Kane. I just wish he was here."

"No more than I do, girl," Kane bent his head to the right and used the sleeve of his T-shirt to wipe the sweat from his brow. "No more than I do." He gave her a few seconds to collect herself before asking if she was ready.

"I'm ready. What should I do?"

"Just start yelling at him. But try not to say anything that'll really piss him off. We don't want him getting too excited with those guns. Just do what you can to keep him talking."

Gypsy crouched next to Kane behind the trunk of a tree and began yelling loudly to get Cooper's attention.

Chapter 19

Johnny Cooper was bleeding badly from his left side by the time he reached the tree where he was attempting to take cover. He had no idea what kind of gun the bullet that grazed him came from, but had a feeling if it had been a direct hit, he would've been dead where he stood ten minutes ago.

While leaning against the tree, he saw one of the McCasseys crawl behind a rock. Cooper fired a few shots at it then saw two people run across the clearing toward a tree. He could tell that one of them was Gypsy, and was about to call out to her when she began calling him.

"Are you out there?" she asked.

What a stroke of luck! That stupid girl was actually trying to get his attention. "I'm here!" he yelled back.

"What do you want from me?"

"I want my goddamn key!"

"I don't have it!"

"Well, I don't believe you. And you'll be sorry if you don't hand it over!"

"I'm already sorry!" she spat.

Cooper cursed. Damn! Nothing ever worked out the way he planned. "All right, girl. You want to play that way? Fine. I know you're hiding behind that big oak tree. And I know I shot the guy you're hiding with. Neither one of you can move too fast, so you can't get away from me. Tell me where that key is, and I might think about letting you go."

* * * *

Rebel, Judd, Brady, and Frank stopped short when they heard Gypsy's voice.

"Who's she talking to?" Judd asked.

Rebel turned and grabbed a handful of his brother's T-shirt. "Shut the hell up, so I can hear!"

The four men stood in silence.

"It sounds like she's talking to Cooper," Rebel announced.

The look of surprise on Judd's face mirrored the ones on Frank and Brady's. "What the hell for?"

"Probably to keep him from killing her!" Rebel snapped.

"Well, where the hell's Kane? Isn't he supposed to be watching her?"

Rebel reached out and shoved his brother. "Shut up and stop asking stupid questions. I heard her mention the key so she must be trying to stall him. It sounds like she's over toward the north side of the cabin, probably by the big oaks. We have to get over there *fast*."

Following Gypsy's voice, they raced through the woods as quickly and quietly as possible. Twenty yards from the cluster of oak trees, they saw her standing up, pressed tightly against the trunk of a tree. They arrived just in time to hear Cooper tell Gypsy he might let them live if she handed over the safe deposit box key. The men dropped to their knees and crawled the rest of the way to Gypsy to avoid being spotted. Only when they were within a few feet of her, did they notice Kane crouched at her feet.

The second Gypsy saw Rebel moving toward her, she crouched down and dove into his arms with a force that sent them tumbling backward.

He broke her fall with his body. "It's okay darlin'," he said when he realized she was crying, "it's okay. I'm here now."

"Oh, Reb," she cried, clinging to him. "The gunfire came so close, and Kane got shot, and he said we couldn't stay there, that's why we're here. Then we realized it was Cooper shooting at us, so I had to talk to him so you'd find us…"

She was talking so fast that Rebel was afraid she was going to hyperventilate. "Easy, darlin'," he said in a low, soothing voice. "Calm down."

When Kane crawled over and offered his cousin an apology, Rebel noticed the crimson stain of blood covering Kane's upper arm. "I'm sorry, Rebel. I kept her as safe as I could. But we got caught in your crossfire, and I had to get her out of there."

"You did the right thing, Kane. Where exactly are you hit?"

"There's a .22 slug in my shoulder, but it won't kill me."

"That was smart of you to have her talk to Cooper. We never would've found the two of you if it weren't for the sound of her voice."

It wasn't often that Rebel offered praise, and he could tell by Kane's slight smile that he appreciated it.

"Hey Gypsy, you little bitch, you still there?"

At the sound of Cooper's voice, Gypsy whimpered and did her best to curl into a ball in Rebel's lap.

"Tell him you're here, darlin'."

Gypsy grabbed onto Rebel's shirt and looked into his eyes.

"Answer me, dammit!" Cooper yelled.

"You have to tell him you're still here, Gypsy."

She shook her head. "I c-c-can't. I can't talk to him anymore. Please."

Her plea tore at his heart, but he needed her to distract Cooper. He could tell the man was getting nervous, and nervous men with loaded guns tended to get trigger happy. If Cooper started firing into the open, Rebel and his cousins would never be able to get to him.

"You have to," he ordered. The soft, soothing voice he'd used to calm her down was gone. In its place was a stern, authoritative one. "Just one more time. Tell him you're still here. We need to stall him until Judd and I can get close enough to bring him down. Do it now."

Fighting to keep her voice steady, Gypsy yelled to Cooper that she heard him and she was still there.

"Good girl," Rebel told her.

Before Gypsy could dissolve into tears again, Rebel was issuing orders.

"I want you to stay here with the guys. Judd and I are going to circle around the cabin and see if we can sneak up on Cooper from behind."

"You're leaving me again?"

"I have to, but I'll be back. I promise." He kissed her forehead and slid her off his lap. "Stay low," he whispered to Judd as they crawled away toward the cabin.

Frank moved over and put his arm around Gypsy, and she rested her head on the older man's shoulder. "I don't think I could've gotten through the past two days without the love of all of you."

"We love you, too, Gypsy. Hang in there."

Several silent minutes passed before Gypsy and the others heard the scuffle. She knew it was her husband and his brother attacking Cooper and prayed it would be over soon.

Gypsy covered her ears at the sound of a gunshot, but jumped to her feet when she heard Judd yell, "Rebel!"

Frank and Brady grabbed at her, but she brushed them off. Peeking around the tree trunk, she saw nothing but shadows. Why had Judd yelled Rebel's name? Was her husband hurt? Did he need help?

Apparently having figured out what Gypsy was thinking, Kane whispered, "Gypsy, don't..." and reached out to grab her. But it was too late. The words were barely out of his mouth when she took off running.

Kane, Frank, and Brady chased Gypsy to the other side of the cabin where she skidded to a halt when the only person she saw standing in the clearing was Cooper. Knowing they'd be no help to Gypsy if Cooper knew they were there, the three men stopped just short of where they could be seen.

* * * *

Johnny Cooper was in pain from his bullet wound and frustrated because nothing was going as planned. Then he heard rustling in the bushes to his left. Damn! The McCassey's had snuck up on him.

Cooper knew any hope he had of getting that key from Gypsy was gone. He'd never get the diamonds now, but neither would anyone else. He knew he was going to die here and planned to take as many people with him as he could. Pointing his gun into the bushes, he fired until the chamber was empty. No one fired in return, so he assumed he'd hit whoever was back there. Then he heard one of the McCassey's yell for Rebel, and seconds later, Gypsy ran into the clearing.

"I knew all I had to do was wait and you'd eventually show up." Cooper, only ten feet from Gypsy, tossed his empty gun to the ground and pulled a second one from behind his back. He took a step closer to his daughter. "This isn't exactly how I planned on killing you, but it'll do."

Gypsy tried to take a step back, but Cooper reached out and caught hold of her arm. "No way, girl, you're not going anywhere."

In a motion so fast it took Cooper by surprise, Gypsy reached around and pulled her own gun. Aiming for any part of his body, she shook herself free and pulled the trigger at the same time. Unfortunately, she only hit him in the leg.

"Ahh! You goddamm bitch!" He backhanded her, causing her to drop the gun and fall, then kicked her in her side and grabbed a handful of her hair, yanking her to her feet. He wrapped his left arm around her neck and pulled her body against his. With his right hand, he fired his gun into the air then placed it against Gypsy's temple. "If you're not dead in that brush, McCassey, then you'd better get over here. I've got your wife. Come on out and take a good long look because this is the last time you'll see her alive."

* * * *

Rebel couldn't believe his eyes when he saw Gypsy run into the clearing, and again when she pulled the gun and tried to shoot Cooper. Rebel was actually glad she hadn't killed her father. He wasn't sure she'd be able to deal with taking someone's life, even if it was the man who had killed her mother. Too bad for Cooper that killing a man wasn't something Rebel had a problem with.

But first thing's first.

It took every ounce of restraint Rebel possessed not to charge Cooper when he struck Gypsy. He was too far away to be of any immediate help to her, and his sudden action would've most likely caused Cooper to panic and shoot her. The problem he had now was that Cooper was holding Gypsy so close to his body that Rebel wasn't sure he could shoot him without hurting Gypsy, too.

Rebel motioned to Brady, who quietly made his way over. "I have to get them separated long enough to get off a shot," he said. "Cover me."

"Wait!" Brady said, grabbing his arm. "You can't just run out there."

Rebel yanked his arm loose from his cousin's grasp. "Well, I don't have time to come up with a plan this time."

"You hear me, McCassey?" Cooper shouted, "Come on out here and say goodbye to your wife."

Brady blinked and Rebel was gone. He'd jumped up and burst into the clearing with his hands up. "Let her go, Cooper."

"You got a lot of nerve stepping in front of me unarmed, McCassey. You want to die with your wife?"

Remaining calm, as calm as he'd ever been, Rebel kept his voice at an even, non-threatening level. "I said…let her go."

"Not a chance. This little bitch ruined my life, so now I'm ending hers. And there's nothing an unarmed man can do about it."

It happened so fast, that Rebel didn't think Johnny Cooper ever knew what hit him. As he went to pull the trigger of his .22, Rebel's hand flew behind his back and drew the .357 from his waistband. With the smell of sweat and anticipation burning his nostrils, Rebel focused on the right side of Cooper's head, squinted, and fired into the fading moments of dusk. The bullet hit its mark, causing both Cooper and Gypsy to drop to the ground.

Rebel threw down his gun and ran to his wife, who was

pinned under the weight of her father's body. By the time he got there, Frank, Brady, Kane, and Judd were beside him. "Roll him off of her," Rebel instructed. "Easy, now." He placed his hands on Gypsy's upper body and pulled her free.

She was unconscious.

Rebel knew he hadn't shot her, but he wanted to make sure she hadn't cracked her head when she fell. The first thing he did was check Gypsy for injuries. Relieved to find nothing other than a small cut where Cooper had backhanded her, he cradled her in his lap and gently tapped the side of her face. "Gypsy? Gypsy, darlin' wake up."

The five men holding their breath let out a collective sigh of relief when she finally opened her eyes. After blinking a few times, Gypsy turned her head to the side. When she caught sight of Cooper's body and the giant, bloody hole in his head, she jumped from Rebel's lap, ran to the edge of the woods, and threw up.

Brady and Kane turned away.

Frank and Judd each ran and grabbed onto one of her arms to keep her from falling; Rebel reached her just in time to gather the hair that had escaped her ponytail and hold it away from her face.

"I'm sorry," she said, when she finished and wiped her face on the shirt Rebel had taken off and handed her.

"You've just been through hell, Gypsy. You've got a right to be sick about it."

"Thanks, Judd." She turned to her husband. "Is it over?"

He pulled her close and kissed the top of her head. "Almost. There's one man left, the one who was helping Cooper. But none of us know who it is. Blackie went to look for him a while ago. I have to go help him."

Gypsy closed her eyes and took a deep breath. "I know, and even though I don't want you to go, I would never ask you to turn your back on your brother. So go find him, and come back safe."

Rebel nodded, marveling at her strength and the love she had for his family. "Frank's going to take you up the hill next to my granddaddy's house and leave you with Rose. They have a small cabin on the outskirts of his property. You'll be safe there." He cupped Gypsy's face and caressed her cheek with his rough and calloused thumb. "I'll come for you as soon as I can."

Gypsy glanced at Cooper's body one more time. "What about...?"

"Let the turkey vultures have him."

"It's better than he deserves," Gypsy commented, and wrapped her arms around Rebel. "Be careful," she said, and looked at each one of his relatives. "All of you."

* * * *

Ben Johnson watched the scene in the clearing from high atop his perch in the oak tree. He'd been hiding up there for close to an hour, discovering the secret spot when he stumbled upon Brady and Kane vacating it.

Johnson knew Blackie was after the person who'd been helping Johnny Cooper, but that's not why he decided to stay hidden. His original plan had been to catch those McCassey's who were on probation with firearms in their hands and haul them off to jail for violations.

It'd been his dream to ruin as many of their lives as possible for as long as he could remember. But up until now, he'd been miserably unsuccessful. Busting three or four of them today would've been the highlight of his career.

That was before Rebel killed Johnny Cooper.

Now, Johnson was the only person alive who knew where to find the safe deposit box that Gypsy held the key to. And one million dollars was a hell of a lot more appealing than risking his hide to haul in a few McCassey's for probation violations.

He'd been wondering how he was going to get his hands on that key, and now he knew. Since the McCassey men assumed the man they were hunting was headed back to town, Johnson decided to stay right where he was until they were long gone. When he felt it was safe, he'd head up to the remote cabin, snatch Gypsy, and force her to give him the key. He'd heard her tell Cooper she didn't have it, but she had to be lying. Johnson was sure she just wanted the loot for herself. They'd probably have to go back to the garage to get the key, but that was okay. Since the McCassey's knew it wasn't one of their own that had betrayed them, they'd never think to stake out their own garage.

When Gypsy finally handed the key over, he'd take her with him to the bank in Baltimore as a little insurance policy. Once the diamonds were safely in his possession, he'd abandon her and catch the first flight out of Friendship Airport for Mexico.

The plan was perfect.

All he had to do now was wait.

Chapter 20

It felt good to be clean.

The first thing Gypsy did when Frank dropped her off at the cabin was take a long, hot shower. The first thing, that is, after helping him drag Flynn out of the truck and into the living room.

Before they left Ten Acres, Frank had taken a look at the younger McCassey's head wound and decided he was bleeding too badly to go running around in the dark hunting bad guys. Amid Flynn's rumbles of protest, Rebel finally convinced him to stay with Gypsy and Rose...as protection. From the passenger seat of his own pickup truck, Flynn stuck his tongue out at Kane and told his cousin he'd do a much better job of guarding Rebel's wife. Less than a mile down the road, he rested his head on Gypsy's shoulder and passed out.

Gypsy lingered in the bathroom until a knock on the door had her scrambling to wrap herself in the fluffy white body towel Rose had left on the vanity. "It's Rose, honey, may I come in?"

Gypsy unlocked and opened the door.

She loved Rose. Strong, supportive, and nurturing, the older woman was everything Gypsy liked to imagine her mother would've been, had she lived.

"How's Flynn?"

Rose smiled. "Out like a light. Frank got the bleeding on his head to stop before he left. I think poor Flynn's just plain worn out."

Gypsy smiled back. "Well, I hope nothing happens here before morning. He'll be mad that he slept through it."

"That's the truth. How are you feeling?"

Sore, tired, scared. "I'm okay. I just need to rest. It's been a long two days."

"Well, why don't you come into the kitchen and let me fix you a bowl of chicken soup."

"Thanks, Rose, but I can't impose on you anymore. I'm not that hungry, anyway. I think I'll just go to bed."

Rose reached out to Gypsy. "You might be tired, but you've got to think about that baby you're carrying. He needs nourishment."

"He?"

Rose smiled again and gave Gypsy a wink. "I've got a feeling."

Gypsy relented. "Give me a minute to get dressed," she said, gathering the fresh nightgown Rose gave her. "I'll meet you at the table."

After polishing off two bowls of soup and three slices of fresh bread, Gypsy finished the glass of milk Rose had given her. "I guess I was hungrier than I thought."

"Well, you go on to bed now. Rebel will come in and wake you when he gets here."

"If he gets here." Gypsy was terrified something was going to happen to her husband. And as tired as she was, she didn't think she'd be able to sleep a wink until he was lying beside her.

Rose wrapped her arms around the younger woman and led her to the bedroom. "Oh, honey, if there's one thing I know about Rebel Raider McCassey, it's that he always does what he sets out to do. That boy's tough and smart. He can do anything, Gypsy. He'll make everything all right."

* * * *

Exhausted yet restless, it was thoughts of her husband's strong arms wrapped around her that finally helped Gypsy fall asleep.

Just before dawn, Gypsy woke with a start; the eerie feeling that someone was watching her made the hair on the back of her neck stand straight up. When she reached across the nightstand to turn on the light, a deep voice cut into her thoughts, "Touch that lamp and you're dead where you lay."

Gypsy froze. The voice was familiar, but she couldn't quite place who it belonged to.

"Now," the man whispered, "I want you to get out of that bed slowly, no sudden moves. And be quiet. You wake those two sleeping in the other room and I'll be forced to kill all three of you."

As soon as he said the last few words, Gypsy knew who had invaded into her room. She broke out into a sweat and her heart began racing as she tried to think. What was Sheriff Johnson doing here? What should she do? Panic threatened to take over, but thoughts of her husband and unborn baby forced her to stay calm.

Gypsy let go of the .22 she was holding and slid her right hand out from underneath the pillow. In order to protect Rose and Flynn, she wouldn't take a shot at the sheriff. It was too dark and her aim was terrible, anyway. So in all likelihood, the only thing she'd wind up doing is angering the sheriff and putting two other people's lives at risk.

She threw back the covers, got out of bed and stood still, waiting for him to tell her what to do.

"Put some more clothes on," he ordered. "I'm not looking to draw any unwanted attention."

She knew he had a gun on her, she could see its slight shadow against the wall. Quickly but quietly, she removed the nightgown and put on her filthy jeans and T-shirt.

"The window," he directed with a wave of his gun. "Climb through the window."

Thoughts of ways to escape cluttered Gypsy's mind as she climbed through the open window and waited for the sheriff on the other side. Now wasn't the time to run, though. It was too risky to flee in the dark when she was barefoot and didn't know the area, and too dangerous to defy the sheriff so close to the cabin where he could easily shoot Rose and Flynn.

When Johnson emerged, he waved his gun wordlessly again, motioning for her to start walking. A few hundred yards down the dirt road was a beat up old sedan.

"Get in," he commanded.

She opened the door and slid into the passenger seat. He holstered his gun and turned to her. "I want the key."

A light went on in Gypsy's head.

So, the sheriff had been the one helping Cooper. It all made sense now. Ben Johnson hated the McCassey's and Johnny Cooper wanted Gypsy dead. The sheriff had probably been more than happy to feed Cooper all the information he wanted to know. And she was sure he was looking forward to seeing the look on Rebel's face when he found out Gypsy was dead.

Gypsy's first instinct was to tell Johnson she didn't have the key. But it was, after all, one million dollars in diamonds, and he'd only think she was lying in order to claim the jewelry herself. Instead, she came up with an idea that would at least get her into town; a place she might be spotted by someone she could trust. "It's with my stuff at the garage," she told him, hoping maybe one of the guys might be staking out the building.

* * * *

Damn. He knew it. Going to the garage wouldn't have been a problem if he'd been able to get to Gypsy five hours ago. But he had a more difficult time avoiding the McCassey's than he thought he would, almost being spotted by Blackie and Rebel twice.

He was the sheriff, after all. So in reality, he could've approached them and pretended he was just out patrolling the town. But he'd been Hagerstown's sheriff for almost twenty years, and everyone knew that not once in all that time had he worked a graveyard shift. Rebel and Blackie would have known immediately that he was lying.

Now, it was almost dawn and the town would be stirring before too long. Not only that, three of his deputies would be coming on duty in another hour. He had to get that key and get out of town before anyone saw him.

Johnson parked on the side of the garage and cut the engine. "You got a key to get in?" he asked.

* * * *

Gypsy mentally patted herself on the back for being able to think on her feet. "There's one under the rain barrel," she lied. The barrel was full of water and he was going to have to try and knock it over. That would take time and make a lot of noise.

Lucky for Gypsy the barrel wasn't just full, it was overflowing.

"Damn!" Johnson cursed. "How the hell are we going to empty this thing?"

"You could try and tip it over," she innocently suggested.

"Get over here and help me."

To stall him, she said she could get a better grip if she had something to cover her hands with. "There's usually a pile of rags on the other side of the soda machine by the middle bay door," she told him. "I'm just going to grab a couple."

Johnson didn't even look at her when he mumbled, "Hurry up."

Gypsy knew what she had to do, and knew she had less then a few seconds to do it. Rebel never locked the middle bay door, so all she had to do was get a good grip on the handle and lift it enough for Outlaw to crawl under. The only problem with her plan was whether or not the dog could get out before the sheriff reacted to the noise.

She took a deep breath, and with trembling hands, grabbed the door handle and pulled with every ounce of strength she had. The first creak of the door, which occurred at the exact moment the barrel crashed to the ground, had Outlaw barking.

Cold rainwater rushed over Gypsy's bare feet as she gave one final pull, forcing the oversized door to fly open. The momentum knocked her down and she narrowly escaped being run down by Outlaw. The dog had burst from the garage and was growling ferociously at the sheriff, who was on his knees and desperately trying to remove his gun from its holster.

Finally getting a good grip on the nine millimeter, he aimed it at Outlaw. "I'm going to kill this mangy mutt once and for all."

"No!" Gypsy screamed. Unwilling to see harm come to her husband's beloved dog, she threw herself at the sheriff causing him to lose his balance. The gun flew from his hand and slid across the wet parking lot as he and Gypsy toppled over.

* * * *

Rebel and Blackie watched closely from across the street as the old sedan pulled up next to the garage. "You expectin' a delivery today, Rebel?"

"I get deliveries everyday," he said, taking what details he could see on the car in the darkness, "but never before dawn, and not from guys driving beat up sedans."

"You think it's a break-in?"

Rebel shrugged with interest. "We'll know in a minute."

The brothers watched the car closely. It was a good thirty seconds before anyone attempted to get out, but when the passenger door opened, they were shocked by what they saw.

"That looks like Gypsy."

Rebel blinked. It sure as hell did look like Gypsy. What was she doing there? And who was she with? He started to walk out from behind the pile of rubble where they were hiding, but Blackie reached out to stop him. "Hold on, little brother. Let's see who she's with."

Rebel shrugged his brother off, but did as he suggested. A few seconds later, the driver's side door opened, and the sheriff stepped out. "Jesus," he said, in a ragged breath, "its Johnson. Goddammit! I should've known!"

Rebel quickly filled Blackie in on what happened five days

before with the Jenkins family at Digger's Bar. He told him that Gypsy had protected Judd by hiding the gun, and that when the sheriff wanted to search her, she put him in his place by requesting a female officer.

"Then, after spitting the law in his face, she turned her back on him and walked away. That's when he warned me to keep an eye on her. I should've known then that he was up to something!"

Trying to calm his brother's rage, Blackie spoke as if he was talking to a child. "Take it easy, Rebel. Let's watch a minute."

"What the hell for? That bastard was obviously the one Cooper was getting his information from, Blackie. And now he's got my wife. I'm going to get her."

Blackie's hands shot out and closed tightly around Rebel's shoulders. "Calm down and use your fuckin' head a minute," he roughly ordered his younger brother. "If Johnson knew where to find Gypsy, then he was probably lurkin' around up at Ten Acres and overheard you talkin'. That means he also knows we're out lookin' for someone. He don't usually go out at night, Rebel. Everyone knows that. So why would he kidnap your wife and take a chance showin' up at the garage?"

When he didn't answer, Blackie tightened his grip. "Why, Rebel?"

He knew why. "Because he thinks Gypsy has the key to the safe deposit box holding the diamonds."

"Right. Now, what does him showin' up in town, even though he knows he's bein' hunted, tell you?"

Rebel knew Blackie was trying to make him think rationally; something he hadn't been doing since he saw Gypsy get out of that car. Still, he was getting tired of his brother's game. "It tells me he's desperate."

"And we both know that desperate men don't think clearly or rationally."

"So?"

"So, if we storm over there with our guns blazin', Johnson's gonna panic and probably shoot your wife. You know that, you told me yourself it's what you sensed when Cooper was holdin' that gun to Gypsy's head. Right now, Johnson's bein' careless. He's so intent on gettin' the key that it ain't even occurred to him he's standin' out in the open for everyone to see.

"We all know Outlaw's bark is loud enough to wake the whole damn town. And Gypsy's smart. You can bet your ass that the only thing on her mind right now is makin' enough noise to get him goin'. The good citizens of Hagerstown are nosey, and they'll be out in force once they hear all the commotion. I guarantee there'll be plenty of witnesses to testify to what the sheriff was doin' here tonight. Kidnappin' and attempted murder should get him put away for a good long time, and keep him far away from law enforcement when he gets out."

Rebel knew everything his brother said was true, and was grateful to Blackie for stopping him before he went off half-cocked and did something to get Gypsy hurt. "Thanks."

Blackie didn't get a chance to respond because the sound of the metal bay door at the garage being opened, along with Outlaw's barking, split the air. The brothers watched in horror at the unfolding scene; the sheriff pulling a gun on Outlaw, Gypsy trying to protect the dog by throwing herself into Johnson, and the two of them falling backward onto the wet parking lot.

"Now!" Rebel yelled to Blackie.

The brothers drew their guns and charged across the street.

* * * *

Shit! Ben Johnson wondered how he could've been so stupid. He got so wrapped up in those diamonds that not only did he forget about the McCassey's, he also gave Gypsy an opportunity to draw attention to them. Rebel's damn dog was making so much noise the entire town would be at the garage within minutes.

How could his plan have gone wrong? It had been so perfect. For two hundred thousand dollars, all he had to do was help Cooper get to his daughter. As a bonus, he'd be able to send a handful of McCassey's to jail.

Or so he thought.

He knew what went wrong...he'd gotten greedy.

And he was about to pay for it.

They're here, Johnson thought. He couldn't see them yet, but he knew there were McCassey's lurking in the shadows, waiting for the perfect opportunity to take a shot at him. This was a hell of a mess he'd gotten himself into. "As long as I'm going down, McCassey's, I'm taking as many of you bastards with me as possible!" Drawing his gun, he pushed Gypsy to the side and came up firing.

The few curious onlookers that had gathered in front of the garage scrambled for cover. Gypsy grabbed Outlaw's collar and crawled toward the side of the building, dragging the dog with her.

* * * *

The first shots from the sheriff's gun had Rebel and Blackie diving for cover behind a few of the cars in the garage parking lot. "Where's Gypsy?" Blackie asked.

"I saw her crawling away from the sheriff," Rebel whispered, aiming his .357 at Johnson. "Hopefully, she's hiding in the woods."

"Can you get a clean shot?"

"I'm trying, but that damn son of a bitch is moving around too much."

Footsteps behind them had Blackie turning and pointing his gun. Jimmy, Brady, Kane, and Frank skidded to a halt and put their hands up. "Whoa, Blackie. It's us."

"Sorry, Jimmy...guys."

"What the hell's going on?" Judd asked. "We heard Outlaw barking all the way down by the convenience store."

Blackie filled the rest of his family in on what was going on while Rebel kept an eye on Johnson, who was now yelling obscenities and challenging every McCassey in town to face him.

"I can't get a shot off from over here," Rebel announced. "I'm going in."

Judd stepped forward. "That's crazy."

"You got a better idea?"

"I'll go."

Angry, Rebel turned to look at him. "Forget it. You hear those sirens? Two dozen people have probably already called the cops, and you can bet those aren't Hagerstown's finest on the way. That's the Maryland State Police, boys. So you, you, you, and you," he said, pointing to Blackie, Judd, Brady, and Kane. "Ditch your guns and get the hell out of here. Go!"

None of them moved.

"Jesus Christ." Rebel swore in exasperation. Blackie's defiance, he could understand. But why now, after years of hanging on his every word, did Judd, Brady, and Kane decide to ignore him? He didn't have time for explanations, so he was honest. "Look, I can't afford to lose the four of you. Business wise...or otherwise. So please," he begged, "get the hell out of here. Go home, hide in the woods, check in with your parole or probation officers, whatever. Just be gone when those troopers get here."

The sirens were getting louder, and Kane's fidgeting gave away just how nervous he really was. "But what are you going to do about Johnson?"

"I'll handle him," Rebel said, "Jimmy and Frank can cover me," he turned back around and focused once again on the sheriff. "Beat it.".

When Rebel turned around again, they were gone.

"What do you want us to do?" Frank asked.

"I'm going to sneak up on Johnson from behind." Rebel handed Jimmy his gun and unhooked the sheath on his belt that held his Bowie knife. "It'll look better when the law gets here if I'm unarmed."

Before they could protest, he was gone.

It wasn't hard to get the jump on Johnson. He was so pre-occupied with sending bullets flying through the air that he obviously didn't hear Rebel come up behind him.

"Johnson!"

The sheriff stopped firing immediately and turned to Rebel. "Well, if it isn't the fearless leader of the McCassey clan. Where're all your loyal subjects?"

"I don't need any help handling you."

Johnson laughed and lowered his gun. "Is that right?"

"That's right."

"Well, come on then, Rebel," he said, mockingly. "Let's

see what you got."

Rebel's right hook struck hard and fast. It sent the sheriff's head whipping back, blood flying from his nose. The second punch was an uppercut to the jaw that caused him to stagger backward and come to a stop against one of the garage's bay doors. Rebel finished Johnson by grabbing his shoulders, bending him forward and kneeing him in the gut.

Johnson fell to the ground just as five police cruisers skidded to a halt in front of the garage. "Maryland State Police!" one of the officers yelled through his megaphone, "get down on the ground and put your hands behind your head!"

Rebel did as he was told. Lying flat on his bare stomach in the wet parking lot, he was handcuffed and helped to his feet. After being searched, he was led into Rose's office and isolated from the others for questioning.

Jimmy, Frank, and Gypsy were all questioned separately. They each told exactly the same story, starting with what they knew about Johnny Cooper and ending with Rebel's fight with the sheriff. As far as the Maryland State Police was concerned, Blackie, Judd, Brady, and Kane McCassey hadn't been seen by their family for two days, and didn't know a thing about what had taken place.

Chapter 21

Because Rebel was detained much longer than the other three, he and Gypsy weren't reunited until later that morning at Frank and Rose's cabin. Still shirtless, he pulled into the yard and stepped out of the tow truck at the same time Gypsy burst through the front door. She flew into his arms, and he caught her in a bear hug as she buried her face in the crook of his neck, taking in his scent and kissing his dirty, sweat-streaked skin.

Nothing in the world felt better than being close to Gypsy, and Rebel tightened his hold. "It's over now darlin'. It's finally over."

She unwrapped her arms from around his neck and looked into the royal blue eyes she'd come to love so much. "Thanks to you," she said, "and to Blackie and the rest of your family."

"Our family," he corrected. "You're a full-fledged member of the McCassey clan now."

Gypsy smiled. "Our family."

Still holding her, Rebel climbed the steps and walked onto the porch. Stopping just short of walking in the house, he set Gypsy on her feet and kissed her forehead.

"Let's go inside," he said, reaching for her slender hand. "I'm a mess and I need a shower. Bad."

The State Police had kept him at the garage so long that he'd flown out of there the minute they finished questioning him. He hadn't even bothered to put on another shirt.

The first thing Rebel did when he entered Frank and Rose's living room was approach Kane and Flynn. They each had a body part bandaged and were sitting on the couch drinking beer; at ten o'clock in the morning. "I appreciate everything you two did for Gypsy and me. You really came through."

They both blushed. "Jesus, Rebel, you don't have to get so sticky sweet on us," Kane told him. "You've done the same thing for us a hundred times."

Blackie strode over and pulled his younger brother aside. "So."

"Sooo?" Rebel drawled.

For a split second, Blackie looked uncomfortable. Then he broke into a grin and extended his hand. "Your wife's aces, little brother, I like her. You know I ain't never been a very big fan of women. Most of the ones I've come across have all been sneaky, vindictive, and untrustworthy. Rose is the only woman I ever met who was an exception to that rule. But after spendin' so much time with Gypsy, I realized she's a good woman, too. She really loves you, man. I'm proud to call her sister."

Rebel stared at Blackie in surprise as he shook his brother's hand. "Thanks. That means a lot coming from you."

Both men grinned, and Rebel held out his arm to Gypsy, who was making her way over to him from across the room.

"What are you two so happy about?" she asked.

The brothers exchanged knowing looks over Gypsy's head.

Blackie wrapped his arm around Gypsy's shoulders and attempted to pull her away from Rebel. Happy to see his older brother genuinely interested in something other than causing trouble, he released her and watched happily as Blackie gave her a tender kiss on the cheek. Gypsy's green eyes lit up at the display of affection, showing just how much she loved her new family.

"So tell me, girl, when am I gonna be an uncle?"

* * * *

Gypsy smiled at her oversized brother-in-law. He'd risked going back to prison to help save her, and she knew that underneath his tough exterior, just like Judd, Blackie was also a good man. "Early spring. Are you going to be around?"

"That depends."

"On what?"

"On whether McCassey's Garage is doin' any hirin'. I've been thinkin' about goin' straight for a while," he said grinning, "just until I get bored."

Rebel laughed. "You can have your job back, man. You earned it."

"Yeah, well, a guy's got to protect his sister." He winked at Gypsy. "Ain't that right, girl?"

Hearing Blackie refer to her as his sister made her feel just as loved and accepted as it had when Judd said it. "Thanks again, Blackie. For helping Rebel save me, for watching out for me, and for wanting to be around when the baby comes. If it wasn't for you, this whole thing could've turned out very differently."

"Oh yeah? Well, in that case, remember me when your

kid's born. Blackie's a good, honest name, you know."

Rebel chuckled. "Uh-huh. It's done real well by you."

"Behave yourself, little brother," Blackie said with a grin, "or I'll teach your kid everything I know."

"Then someone should warn the good people of Hagers-town to get out while they can."

Blackie laughed good-naturedly and let go of Gypsy. "I'm goin' outside for a smoke. I'll catch you two later."

When he was gone, Rebel draped his arm around Gypsy's shoulder and pulled her close again. "Are you happy?"

She tilted her head up and smiled at her husband. "I've never been this happy, Reb. The new life you've given me is so wonderful it almost feels like my old life never existed. I got lucky when I found you."

"As I recall, darlin', it was me who found you…lost in my woods."

"You took good care of me that day, just like you have everyday since. I don't know what I'd do without you."

"You could always hook up with one of my brothers. They'd just pick up where I left off."

She playfully punched his shoulder. "That isn't very funny."

He cupped her face and stared into her eyes. "I'm here, Gypsy, and I'm not going anywhere for a long, long time. I'll always love and take care of you, this baby, and any other chil-dren we're lucky enough to have. You'll always be safe and protected." He leaned down and brushed her lips with his. "No worries."

Epilogue

Four years later

Gypsy leaned against the side of the barn and laughed as Outlaw barked at her son, Chase, keeping the two-year-old from getting too close to the campfire. He was a handful, that one, just like his older brother. And according to all the pictures she'd seen, they were both the spitting image of Rebel at that age, right down to the royal blue eyes and jet black hair; which they refused to let her cut because they wanted to look just like their daddy.

Upon hearing his dog bark, Rebel bent down and scooped up his youngest son, bringing a protest from both Chase and six-month-old Jade, who'd been happily sleeping in the crook of her father's left arm. "Where's your brother?"

"I dunno, Daddy," Chace responded.

"Here I am." Rebel turned and found his three-year-old son, Raider, sitting in Blackie's lap eating a candy bar. "Uncle Blackie gave me chocolate, see?" The little boy held two candy-coated hands out to his father.

Rebel looked at his brother and laughed. "Uncle Blackie has a lot of cleaning up to do. You be good, now. I'll be back."

"Bye, Daddy."

Spotting his wife by the barn, Rebel made his way over to her with their two younger children.

"Looks like you've got your hands full." She reached out to take Jade, who was now happily playing with a fistful of her father's long hair, but he handed her Chase instead.

The boy wiggled to free himself from his mother's grasp, but Rebel reached out and swatted his behind softly. "Behave yourself."

Chase immediately stopped squirming and wrapped his arms around Gypsy. "Love you, Mommy."

Gypsy kissed the top of the boy's dark head and set him on his feet. "I love you, too. Go on and play," she told him, "and stay away from the fire."

"Okay!" He ran off with Outlaw following closely behind.

Rebel laughed and shook his head as he watched his youngest son. "We should've named him after Judd," he commented. "Their personalities are carbon copies of each other."

Gypsy rolled her eyes. "I guess we're in for big trouble, then."

Judd snuck up behind Gypsy and kissed her left cheek, then handed his brother a cold can of Budweiser. "Who's in trouble?"

"Us," Rebel said. "Chase is just like you."

The grin that broke out on Judd's face went from ear to ear. "And here you two thought all the hard times were behind you. Boy, were you wrong."

Blackie joined them, wiping what was left of Raider's chocolate disaster onto his jeans, and lifted Jade from her father's arms. Cuddling the baby girl against his broad chest, he smiled when she grabbed a fistful of his long dark brown locks and pulled. "Who's wrong?" he wanted to know.

"Rebel and Gypsy. They're in for it with Raider and Chase. Those two are McCassey's through and through."

Laughing, Blackie began planting kisses on top of Jade's tiny head. He loved everything about his niece. Her baby smell, the thin, curly, strawberry blonde hair that was just starting to come in, and her royal blue eyes that always looked at him with so much trust and love. "I don't know, little brother. Somethin' tells me those two are gonna be the least of your problems. This one's a heartbreaker already. You and your boys are gonna be beatin' the men off her with sticks."

"Man, that sure is gonna be a sight," Judd said, trying not to laugh, "Rebel trying to deal with boys being interested in his daughter." Judd unrolled a pack of Marlboro's from his shirt sleeve. He offered a cigarette to each of his brothers, who declined; Rebel because he was trying to quit, and Blackie because he was holding the baby.

When Judd spotted Dawn, a girl he'd had his eye on for the past few weeks, he kissed Gypsy and Jade's cheeks and walked off.

Blackie sighed and shook his head. "Lovesick fool."

"What about you?" Gypsy asked. "Don't you think it's time you picked out a woman for yourself?"

"Are you kiddin'?" He held Jade in the air over his head then brought her down and encircled her in his arms again. "I got my one and only woman right here." Blackie took the baby's bottle from Gypsy. "Come on, little darlin'," he put the nipple in Jade's mouth and turned away from her parents. "Let's get the hell outta here before your daddy tries to beat *me* off with a stick."

Gypsy rolled her eyes at Blackie's language.

"Hey," Rebel said, defending his brother, "he's trying. At least he didn't say any obscene four letter words this time."

Thinking about what a hard time Blackie had keeping his vocabulary clean around the kids, Gypsy laughed out loud as Rebel wrapped his arm around her waist and pulled her to him.

"I know he's trying. But the first time Raider's preschool calls complaining that he told some kid not to touch his fucking toy, Blackie's going down there to explain why."

It was Rebel's turn to laugh. "Yeah, you're right. Maybe I should go over there and take Jade from him. He might be teaching her to spit."

"Oh stop it, Reb. Blackie couldn't love Jade more if she were his own daughter. He doesn't even mind emotional females anymore. And besides," Gypsy said wiping at a spot on her shirt, "she already knows how to spit."

He smiled. "You know, I never thought I'd see the day either one of my brothers would take an interest in anything that didn't have to do with trouble. Especially kids. Although Judd started changing when he met you, I never really expected Blackie to live past thirty-five. He was on the fast track to hell when he got out of prison three years ago. I like to think you had something to do with mellowing them."

That surprised her. "Why me?"

"Because you showed them up close and personal what it was like to be adored and loved. Sure, we were loved by our relatives growing up. But it wasn't the same as being in a house full of love. And that's exactly what you showed us all when the four of us lived together in my parent's old house the first year we were married. It was the first time there'd ever been any love in that house."

"But we all cared about each other, Reb. I didn't do anything special."

"Of course you did; going to Judd for help when you needed something, curling up and falling asleep on Blackie's shoulder waiting for me to get home at night, asking the two of them to be in the delivery room with us when Raider was born. You needed them. You wanted them around—and not just when it was convenient, but all the time. They'd never experienced anything like that and it made them feel loved.

"You're more to Blackie and Judd than just my wife, you're their sister. And you know how the men in my family feel about sisters. They'd go through hell for you. You're the one that made us a real family for the first time. Maybe that's what made them see that there are actually things in life to enjoy, and that they could only be enjoyed from outside a prison cell."

Gypsy sniffed, which caught Rebel off guard. He turned her around and looked into her eyes. "What's wrong?"

"That was so nice of you to say."

He smiled and wiped at her tears with his thumbs. "Every word is true. We may have saved your life, Gypsy, but you made all of ours better."

"Oh Reb." She jumped into his arms and he held her tight. "I never knew I could be so happy."

"Me either, darlin'. Me either."

ABOUT THE AUTHOR

Lauren Sharman has been creating characters and writing short stories since she was a little girl, but it was her love of reading, as well as encouragement from her husband, Joey, that finally inspired her to write novels. At home in Maryland, she and Joey have two amazing kids who constantly keep them smiling, an incredibly cool John Deere tractor, and share a passion for muscle cars, music, and steamed crabs.

In addition to romantic suspense, Lauren is also published in mainstream fiction; her novel, *Growing Up Little* was released by Whiskey Creek Press in May 2006. Her other releases from Whiskey Creek Press include "Her Shadow", a short story in the *HATE Anthology* (August 2006), and the upcoming sequel to *No Worries*, titled, *The Devil's Candy* (May 2007).

Lauren is an active member of both the Maryland Romance Writers, Romance Writer's of America, and is an RWA PRO. She loves talking about her books, so feel free to e-mail her at LaurenSharman@adelphia.net, or check out her website at www.LaurenSharman.com!

*For your reading pleasure, we invite
you to visit our web bookstore*

WHISKEY CREEK PRESS

www.whiskeycreekpress.com